"You're different…

"I know you say that things don't change, but you certainly have," Melanie said with a smile.

"Yeah?" A smile turned up one side of Logan's lips. "How so?"

"You're so mannerly. You're downright civilized," she said with a low laugh. "I've heard marriage will do that to a guy when he isn't looking."

Logan lifted his wineglass. "To being house-trained."

"To being house-trained." She laughed and lifted her glass in response.

Twenty-three years had changed more than Logan thought. In both of them.

Because she wasn't the same girl she'd been all those years ago, either. Marriage might have civilized Logan, but it had opened Melanie's eyes to just how vulnerable a woman's heart could be. She'd lost more than a husband in her divorce.

She'd lost her family…and her ability to blithely trust a man to do right by her just because it was the right thing to do.

Dear Reader,

So many books are focused on young love, and while that stage of life is certainly exciting, there are other stages that are equally exciting, dramatic and deeply romantic. For this miniseries, I wanted to write books about women who had depth and experience and men who were old enough to know what they wanted...and exactly how to get it.

I remember my twenties like they were yesterday, but I'm a different woman in my forties. I'm not so easy to fool, and I know what I have to offer. It's a whole different playing field now!

So I hope you'll enjoy the women who dine with the Second Chance Club. Meet us at the lodge with that gorgeous lake view, and we'll settle in for an evening of good food, laughter, encouragement and a hearty reminder that life is just as magical now as it ever was before.

Lift your glasses. Here's to one more chance at happiness.

Patricia Johns

HEARTWARMING

Their Mountain Reunion

Patricia Johns

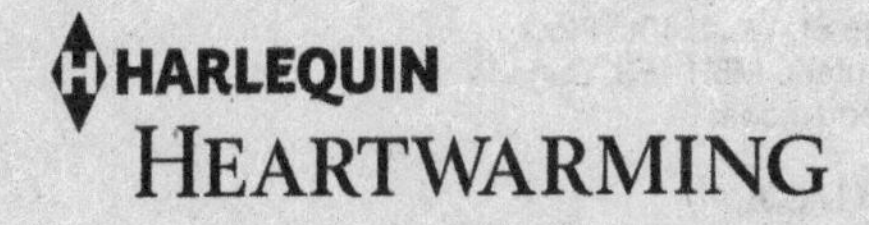

HARLEQUIN®
HEARTWARMING™

Recycling programs for this product may not exist in your area.

ISBN-13: 978-1-335-88970-6

Their Mountain Reunion

This edition published by arrangement with Harlequin Books S.A.

For questions and comments about the quality of this book, please contact us at CustomerService@Harlequin.com.

Harlequin Enterprises ULC
22 Adelaide St. West, 40th Floor
Toronto, Ontario M5H 4E3, Canada
www.Harlequin.com

Printed in U.S.A.

Patricia Johns writes from Alberta, Canada. She has her Hon. BA in English literature and currently writes for Harlequin's Heartwarming and Love Inspired lines. You can find her at patriciajohnsromance.com.

Books by Patricia Johns

Harlequin Heartwarming

Home to Eagle's Rest

Her Lawman Protector
Falling for the Cowboy Dad
The Lawman's Baby

A Baxter's Redemption
The Runaway Bride
A Boy's Christmas Wish

Love Inspired

Montana Twins

Her Cowboy's Twin Blessings
Her Twins' Cowboy Dad
A Rancher to Remember

Comfort Creek Lawmen

Deputy Daddy
The Lawman's Runaway Bride
The Deputy's Unexpected Family

His Unexpected Family
The Rancher's City Girl
A Firefighter's Promise
The Lawman's Surprise Family

Visit the Author Profile page
at Harlequin.com for more titles.

To my husband, who I love more every day.
You're the best choice I ever made!

CHAPTER ONE

"Come for dinner," Angelina had said. "We do this once a month, and it's a select group. So...invitation only, if you understand. You'll love these women. They're interesting and strong and resilient. Come once, and see what you think—and dress for it."

Dress for it. Melanie Isaacs had been tempted to feel offended at those words, but she was too tired these days to bother. She'd attended countless events and charity dinners during her marriage, so it wasn't like she didn't have the wardrobe to cover a simple dinner.

Angelina Cunningham was an old friend. They'd gone in different directions after high school and lost touch until Melanie got a friend request on Facebook and they politely started updating each other on their lives. Melanie's divorce was much fresher than Angelina's. Melanie and Angelina had both gotten Mountain Springs property out of their divorces, but Angelina's was far more spectacular. Angelina was the sole proprietor of Mountain Springs Lodge, which dominated one side of the glacier-fed Blue Lake up in the Colorado Rockies. On the other side of the turquoise lake, hunched next to a rickety wharf, was the lake house Adam had magnanimously given Melanie in the divorce because he felt she "deserved it." It was meant to assuage his guilt.

Now, Melanie smoothed on some plum lipstick and dropped the tube into her purse. Her little black dress—a satin knee-length number—still fit like a glove, scooping down to reveal just a hint of cleavage. This was dressier than she wanted to feel tonight. She didn't want to stand out. It still felt weird not to be Adam's wife and the busy stepmom to his kids. She'd grown used to sensible clothing that said *married* instead of *available*. This postdivorce transition was exhausting, and all she wanted was to curl up in the overstuffed chair by the window overlooking the lake with a glass of wine and her journal. But she'd already agreed to this dinner, and Angelina had seemed so excited about it. Melanie would go, make nice and leave early. A cozy evening could still be hers.

Besides, she'd gotten an email from an old boyfriend recently, wanting to come see the lake house—something about tracking down his father, who used to own it. She should have known that would come back to complicate her life sooner or later… Maybe she was naive to assume that Logan McTavish would melt into the background of her life and stay there. So getting out for at least part of the evening couldn't hurt.

Mountain Springs Lodge was nestled behind a rocky outcropping for privacy. The large log cabin–styled lodge sported wide windows that sparkled with the light of the sinking sun as Melanie drove up. Gable windows peered from the tall peaked roof, and she paused to admire the building before she parked.

Angelina had spruced the place up since Melanie had been here last. Inside, sparkling bevel-edged mirrors were hung on the glossy wooden walls, catching the warm light and scattering it in every direction. Angelina had decorated with higher-end furniture, defying the rustic surroundings with elegant hall tables and crystal vases overflowing with fresh lilac bouquets.

There was a broad staircase leading up

to what Melanie assumed were the suites. Melanie ambled past the reception desk and peeked into a sitting room with leather couches and a wide stone fireplace that had no fire in it on this hot night. The view of the lake out the floor-to-ceiling windows was stunning.

"You landed on your feet, Ange," she muttered to herself. As a decorator, herself, she had to admire what Angelina had done to the place. The last time Melanie was here for a graduation dinner, it was a seventies-themed hunting lodge.

To the right, dark wood French doors opened as Angelina strode through, smiling. Angelina was dressed in a chic wine-colored dress that clung to her to curvy figure. Her blond hair fell in glossy waves over her shoulders. Her makeup was impeccable, and the minute Angelina entered the room, the girl at the desk dropped her book and looked alert. It was clear that Angelina was the boss around here.

"Melanie!"

Melanie couldn't help but laugh as Angelina wrapped her in a perfume-scented hug, then released her. Angelina nodded toward the French doors. "The ladies are waiting."

Melanie put a hand on Angelina's arm. "Which ladies, exactly?"

"The Second Chance Dining Club."

Melanie blinked. "The what now?"

"We keep our little group quiet, but when we find someone who we think will benefit from what we offer, we invite her to dinner."

"What do you offer?" Melanie asked, hesitating. If this was going to be some sort of sales pitch, she was leaving now.

"A shoulder to cry on. Some sympathy. Some hard-won wisdom. We're a group of women who understand," Angelina said. "We've all been married before and we know how hard it is to put your life back together after a divorce."

"Oh..." Melanie breathed. So much for distraction from her own heartbreak. "Look, if this is a multilevel marketing thing—"

"Hardly!" Angelina laughed. "This isn't business, Melanie. This is personal. No one is selling anything. And I invited you because... I care."

Melanie looked past Angelina's shoulder, but couldn't make out much.

"You look amazing, by the way," Angelina said. "It's just dinner. On me. Be my guest."

"Thank you." Did Melanie want to do this?

A bit of moral support might be nice, but she probably didn't know these women, and while a divorce was soul-crushing, it was also incredibly private. Or at least a woman tried to keep it that way with all the nosiness. But she was here, dressed to impress and already at the resort, so she might as well follow.

Angelina led the way into the dining room. There were guests at tables throughout the room. The murmur of conversation, the tinkle of cutlery and the laughter of a family group mingled together in a pleasant ambience. Over by a window overlooking the water was a table of women, all of whom had looked up when Angelina and Melanie walked in.

Angelina beelined over to that table, and she gestured to a free chair right beside the window. It was the best view—and also the hardest escape. Was that the plan?

Melanie took her seat and looked around the table, feeling suddenly shy.

"Hello," she said.

"This is Melanie Banks," Angelina said, taking the seat next to Melanie. "At this table, we go by our maiden names. It's just our thing. It reminds us of who we were before the wedding. It helps."

Yes...before the wedding. Except Melanie didn't want to go back to those inexperienced days. Was she the only one?

"Let's do a few introductions," Angelina said. "This is Gayle Steel—" She gestured to the older woman with her hair twisted up in a smooth silvery updo. Melanie thought it was prematurely white. "She's retired, but she used to run the Mountain Springs Bank. She has five grown children and...how many grandkids now, Gayle?"

"Eleven," Gayle said.

"Her husband left her after thirty-five years of marriage," Angelina added.

"For his golfing buddy," Gayle said with a small smile.

"Oh, wow..." Melanie murmured, trying to cover her surprise.

"It was ten years ago. Yes, I should have noticed he was gay, but somehow didn't. I'm over it. Mostly," Gayle said with low laugh. "This group of ladies is a great help."

Yes, well, Melanie had a few things she should have noticed, too—namely a rather serious affair that had been going on for about two years before she found the incriminating text messages. So, who was she to judge?

"And this is Renata Spivovitch, and she's an activities director and nurse for the Spruce Ridge Retirement Home, and she has three kids, all in school now," Angelina went on, gesturing to the woman with short cropped brown hair, a round figure and an interesting face. She looked to be about Melanie's age and met her inquiring gaze with an easy smile.

"I was the one who left my husband," Renata said. "He wanted to move his mistress into our family home with me and the kids, and figured we should all live together quite comfortably."

Melanie stared at her in shock. "He…he actually tried to do that?"

Renata shrugged in reply.

"That was…a year ago now?" Angelina asked.

"About that," Renata confirmed. "I'm less over it than Gayle is."

Gayle chuckled, and the women exchanged a smile.

Angelina gestured to the stunningly beautiful woman with rare looks and a frank expression on her face. She couldn't be more than thirty. "And this here is Belle Villeneuve. She's was a model for about ten years, and married her talent agent."

A model. Yes, that explained those perfectly aligned looks, but there was something open and friendly about her, too. Melanie couldn't help but like her.

"He dumped me when I quit modeling and put on some healthy weight," Belle said. "He called me obese and replaced me with an eighteen-year-old."

"I'm so sorry—" Melanie said.

"Oh, it was good riddance. I was a wreck when I was with him, and as it turned out, I had the better lawyer."

"A much better lawyer," Angelina said with a small smile. "Their divorce was finalized last year, and she made out with a full half of his business."

The women around the table chuckled. It seemed that Belle had bounced back rather well, and the women here enjoyed little details like that.

"And that brings us to you," Angelina said. "Did you want to introduce yourself?"

"I'm Melanie," she said. "I'm newly divorced, and I'm in town for a few weeks. Angelina asked me to come to dinner tonight, so… Hi, everyone."

"Do you mind if I fill them in on a few details?" Angelina asked.

"Uh…sure." She'd told Angelina the broad strokes when they chatted earlier. Though she hadn't really wanted to blab to everyone at large, there was something about the energy around this table that made sharing seem natural.

"I know a little bit about her situation," Angelina said. "Correct me if I get it wrong, Melanie. But she married her husband quite young—midtwenties?"

"I was twenty-four," Melanie confirmed. "We were married for fifteen years."

"He had children from his first marriage whom Melanie selflessly raised, until one day he traded her in for a younger model."

That summed it up rather succinctly. Except, Melanie had been the one to ask for the divorce. There was no trusting him again after that—the betrayal was too deep.

"Is the divorce final?" Renata asked.

"Yes. As of two months ago," Melanie confirmed.

"And did you…do all right?" Belle asked hesitantly.

"I got the lake house and some cash," Melanie replied. "There will be spousal support for three years. I wanted to start an interior design company, but I'll need to take a few classes online to get myself current again. So the money will help in the transition."

"Good, good." This from Gayle. "So, you don't have to panic about making enough to pay your bills."

"Not immediately," Melanie said with a wan smile. That was something. Maybe she should be grateful that she hadn't been left in a worse position.

"Property on Blue Lake is worth a small fortune. That was smart to ask for it," Renata said.

"I didn't ask," Melanie said. "I haven't decided how nice he was being to hand it over, actually. We bought it when the kids were school-aged. I told him about my hometown and how gorgeous our lake was, and he found it all very quaint and inspiring. So, he surprised me with the deed one summer, and he sent me and the kids off to the lake."

"While he...worked?" Belle asked, raising a delicate eyebrow.

"Presumably," Melanie replied with a faint shrug. "I found out later that he was cheating on me for much of our marriage. The irony is, his kids hated coming here. They didn't want to be cooped up in some lake house or wandering around a little town where they didn't know anyone. Besides, they didn't like me. I wasn't their mother. I was just some substitute their father foisted upon them."

"So you don't have fond memories there," Angelina said softly.

"Not exactly." Melanie shrugged. "It's okay. It's a beautiful property and I'll make it my own. Or sell it. I haven't decided which yet."

"What happened to their mother?" Renata asked.

"She died rather tragically from cancer. When I married Adam, he had three grieving kids, the youngest of which was a toddler, and I decided to devote myself to them. They needed love, and I thought I could make a difference with them."

"So you didn't have any kids of your own?" Belle asked.

"No. Three were enough to keep me busy." Melanie wasn't sure if she regretted that now. A baby wouldn't have saved their marriage, but it might have been nice to have one child who didn't resent her for not being mom enough.

A waiter came by with a bottle of wine for the table. The other women seemed to know the menu by heart and gave their orders immediately. Melanie took a moment, then ordered the mountain trout with herbed potatoes. When the waiter left again, Melanie looked at the women around the table.

"What about you, Angelina?" Melanie asked. "What happened to your marriage? You never did tell me."

The table fell silent, and Angelina's expression saddened. "We met and married on a cruise. I had no idea who his family was, and I thought that the man he was on vacation was the same man he'd be in the rest of his life. I was wrong about that. His family was incredibly wealthy, and I wasn't good enough for them, it turned out. They tore us apart. We only lasted a year."

"And you got the resort in the divorce," Melanie said.

"I did," Angelina agreed. "I poured my heartbreak into fixing it up. I've done rather well for myself in the last ten years. He might have given me the resort, but I made it what it is today."

"Was there another woman?" Melanie asked.

"No, he didn't leave me for anyone else. I know you'll think I'm crazy for saying this, but you're actually lucky that there was another woman," Angelina said. "Your husband might have preferred another woman to you, but mine just preferred being without me. Period."

Melanie felt her eyes mist. "Oh, Ange..."

"It's okay." Angelina reached for the bottle of wine. "Life marches on. And when you have a circle of loyal girlfriends, it's a whole lot easier."

Angelina poured a glass, and as Melanie accepted the glass from her, a figure standing in the open doorway of the dining room caught her eye—and her heart hammered to a stop. Logan. She'd known she'd see him one of these days, but she hadn't expected the last twenty-three years to just drop out beneath her like that. Logan stood there, and when their eyes met, his dark gaze blazed into hers, a breathless moment, and then he moved away from the door and disappeared out in the foyer.

"Logan McTavish," Angelina said softly. "He's a guest at the resort for a couple of weeks. Sorry, maybe I should have warned you about that."

Melanie pulled her attention back to the table and took a sip of wine, putting the glass down in front of her. "I didn't know he'd arrived yet. He's here looking for me."

"Oh?" Angelina raised her eyebrows, a smile tickling her lips. "Did you want to go talk to him?"

"No, no. We're here for dinner. I'm sure I'll see Logan soon," she replied, trying to sound more casual than she felt.

"So...he's heard you're divorced, then?" Angelina asked.

"No!" Melanie shook her head. "I mean, I mentioned it. But it isn't like that. He needs access to my lake house. He's got his own stuff he's dealing with. Besides, I'm already reeling from my divorce. The last thing I need is—" She didn't finish the statement. She wasn't sure what she was running from. The last thing she needed were the memories. To be reminded what that kind of love had felt like back when she was artless and young and thought that her youthful beauty would be enough to secure lifelong happiness.

"Although, for the record, there's no harm in moving on," Angelina said.

"I've been married once," Melanie replied. "I'm in no rush to jump back into it. It was harder than I thought. Besides, two months postdivorce is rebound time. I'm not interested in mangling my heart for kicks."

"That's where I'm at," Belle said, holding out her glass for Angelina to fill. "Here's to being single. I only want to worry about myself right now."

"I think I'd like to meet someone else," Gayle said quietly, and they all turned to look at her. "I would. A nice man…but a man who was actually attracted to me. I've never had that. I thought it was normal that he spent more time with his golfing buddy than he did with me. I'd like a chance to be with a man who'd rather cuddle up with me than golf. It might be nice to be thought of as more than Mother."

That was something Melanie could sympathize with. Maybe she wanted to be more than Stepmom, too. When color tinted Gayle's cheeks, Melanie leaned forward.

"You can have that," Melanie said earnestly.

"I think so. I'm not exactly dead yet," Gayle agreed.

"Yeah, me neither," Melanie said, meeting Gayle's eye with a smile.

"Here's to being more than Mother," Renata said, raising her glass. "And I think we should order another bottle. What do you say?"

Melanie chuckled. Forty was a far cry from dead, too, but that didn't mean she wanted another romance. Right now, all she wanted was some semblance of control. Leaving her cheating ex had given her some of that, but she had less control than she liked over the healing process after a divorce, and a few girlfriends in the mix might be just what she needed to get back on her feet.

LOGAN MCTAVISH SANK into a chair on the balcony of his room. His room didn't have a lake view—those had all been filled, so his room overlooked the parking lot and the mountains, a full moon hanging low over the peaks. The cool evening breeze felt good after the heat of the day. He leaned back and took a sip of ice tea.

He'd arrived in Mountain Springs that evening. He'd tried finding his father, Harry Wilde, from Denver, but the man's phone numbers had changed, and so had his address, apparently. So he had moved on to the next option—tracking him down through mutual acquaintances. That was where Melanie had come into the picture. He knew she owned the old lake house now, and he figured she might have heard some gossip, at the very least. And he wanted to see her—was that stupid of him? Probably.

The thing was, he'd been hanging on to this box his late mother had left his biological father for the better part of a year. Logan had been struggling with some personal issues since his mother passed away, and he was finally willing to face a few of them. To try to do the right thing by some of the women in his life. Mom had wanted his father to have this box—and it was his duty to deliver it.

Logan's phone blipped, and he picked it up. He had a new text from his son, Graham, who was traveling with some friends in England for the next two weeks. It was another photo of food. It looked like a melted cheese sandwich to him. Another text came.

Welsh Rarebit.

Rabbit? he texted back.

Rarebit. It's like grilled cheese—but with beer.

Beer? Logan shook his head. He had no idea what that was supposed to mean, but

Graham was obviously alive and well if he was texting pictures of food, and as a dad, he liked the reassurance. His son might be old enough to vote and drink, but Logan worried all the same. He should probably be worrying about locating his own father so he could deliver that albatross of a box.

Instead, he was sitting up here in the relative darkness, thinking about Melanie Banks…right downstairs.

He'd seen Melanie in the dining room. It might have been twenty-odd years, but there was no doubt about her identity. She had the same bright eyes, the same playful lift to her lips. She sparkled. How did she do that? Whatever youthful sex appeal he used to ooze had dried up, he was pretty sure, but she still had it… He hadn't been able to hear her voice from where he'd stood just outside the dining room, and he'd been transfixed until she spotted him. But she obviously wasn't there to see him, so he hadn't interrupted her evening.

How does it taste? he texted his son. There was a lengthy pause, and he almost put his phone down and gave up on an immediate reply when his phone blipped again.

Amazing. Who do I have to fight around here for the recipe?

Logan grunted an amused laugh. Graham had hopes of opening his own restaurant one day. Logan had taken his own risks in starting up his construction business, but he knew the odds for restaurants, and they weren't good. But he wouldn't kick Graham's dream out from under him.

He found his mind turning back to Melanie with her dark brown hair that fell just past her slim shoulders. And he hated that thinking of Melanie still felt like a betrayal to his late wife, Caroline—to be noticing another woman's allure. And yet he was angry with Caroline, too. Was that allowed—to be generally pissed off with the dead? Because he had grievances with both his late mother and his late wife. And apparently, they had a few grievances with him.

He heard the click of a woman's heels on asphalt, and he glanced up from his phone to see Melanie. He froze. She wasn't far from him, and she stopped at a car. She'd parked right under his balcony! There was a soft glow coming from the vehicle.

Melanie went around to the driver's side, looked inside and heaved a sigh.

"Did I really do that?" Her voice carried up to him, as she unlocked her car. It chirped, and she opened the door and got inside. He leaned forward, taking a better look at her car. It was expensive—a Mercedes. The engine growled a couple of times, but it didn't turn over.

Melanie got back out. He heard her say something that sounded unladylike, and he couldn't help but grin at that.

"What's wrong?" he called down to her, and Melanie startled, then looked up. She smiled hesitantly.

"I thought I saw you earlier tonight."

"That was me," he said. "It's been a few years."

"A few," she said wryly. "I wasn't sure when you'd arrive in town. How are you doing?"

And it was like those twenty-three years just slid away again...and she was the beautiful girl he couldn't get enough of. His gaze dropped down to her left hand, bare of rings.

He cleared his throat. "I'm...good."

A lie. He was grappling with flawed relationships with the women he'd loved who were already gone, and he was tasked with finding the last man he wanted to see on this planet. But that wasn't the kind of thing a guy started with.

"I'm not. My car won't start," she said. "I left a light on inside."

"You need a boost?" he asked.

She paused, looked back toward her vehicle, then said, "Yeah, I do. Is it a wild inconvenience?"

"Nah." He pushed himself to his feet and pocketed his phone. "I'll come down."

Logan slipped on his shoes and headed downstairs. The sitting room with the view of the lake was occupied by several couples having drinks, standing in front of the wide windows.

Logan headed out the front doors and angled his steps around to where Melanie was parked. She stood by her car waiting, the warm wind ruffling her dress around her knees.

"My truck is parked over there." He nodded across the lot. "I'll bring it over."

"Thank you." Her voice was soft, and instead of walking away, he met her clear gaze.

"You haven't changed a bit," he said.

She barked out a laugh. "I'm forty."

"So?" He shot her a grin. "I'm telling you. You look great."

"Thanks." Her gaze moved over him in a quick up and down. "You, too."

She was being nice. Life had beaten him up and he knew it. But whatever—let her be the nice one tonight.

"Look, I've always felt bad about—" He cleared his throat. "Uh—you know, how we parted ways."

"You mean how you completely ghosted me?" she asked dryly.

"Yeah… I'm sorry. I was immature. I have no excuse."

She didn't answer that. She'd been young, too, and she'd been a whole lot more mature than him. But she wasn't the only one he'd treated badly through the years, and he was only now facing up to that.

"We're both grown up now," she said with a faint shrug. "You mentioned having a son when we talked—how old is he?"

"Graham is twenty-one now—he's taking a degree in art history," he said, and wasn't sure why he was suddenly so talkative with her. "He wanted to be a chef. I told him to be more practical. So he chose art history."

A smile crinkled the fine lines around

Melanie's eyes and she chuckled. Having her relax a bit felt better.

"He took after his mom, then?" she asked. "That's a wild guess, because you were no artist."

"Yeah, it would seem," he said with a rueful smile. Graham looked like his mom, too—the same fair hair, the same blue eyes. "I'm happy with some power tools, and he's lecturing me on food and art. What can you do?"

She nodded, then dropped her gaze. Right. He was supposed to be helping her out with her car.

"I'll just go get the truck," he said, and without waiting for a response, he headed across the parking lot and retrieved his truck. Once he'd parked next to her and fetched the cables from the back, he found Melanie watching him.

"So how was dinner?" he asked.

"Better than I anticipated," she said.

"Yeah?" What had she been anticipating? He nodded toward her car. "Pop your hood."

Melanie reached down and undid the clasp, then pushed her hood up.

"Is Angelina more fun than you remembered or something?" he asked. She had a mysterious look about her, too, these days. Everyone had grown up, moved on. Become more.

"Logan, we're all more fun than I remembered. We're old enough to be interesting at long last."

Logan chuckled as he attached the cables to her battery. Melanie hadn't fully forgiven him, he could tell. Not that he blamed her. He'd been a jerk. He'd left for college, had a whole new life, realized that a long-distance relationship with his high school girlfriend was going to be harder to maintain than he'd realized, and instead of talking to her about it, confessing his own feelings of inadequacy and heartbreak, he'd just cut her off. The few times she'd called him, he'd told her that talking on his cell phone was too expensive. It had been mean, and he'd thought about it numerous times over the years and felt like a complete jerk.

"You don't know if I'm improved at all," he said, shooting her a teasing look as he connected the cables to his own battery.

She shrugged. "I don't know, you're reconnecting with your dad."

"Well..." He sucked in a breath. "I'm trying to find him, at least."

"Why now?" she asked.

Why indeed. Because he felt like a failure in all the ways that mattered most and he needed to change something.

"My mom passed away a year ago, and she made me executor of her will. She left this locked wooden box to my father, and requested that I hand deliver it."

"So one year later, here you are," she observed.

He'd recently come across some old diaries his late wife had written, and that explained his added sense of urgency here. His wife hadn't remembered the same cozy marriage that he did. Apparently, he'd been pretty selfish over the years.

"Better late than never," he said. "I was hoping you might know where he's at."

"Me?"

"You live here now," he said.

"For a few weeks. I'm not up on local gossip yet. When did you last talk to him?"

"About twenty years ago."

"Wow."

He nodded toward the car. "Turn the key."

Melanie got into her car and this time the engine turned over. She hit the gas a couple of times, revving the engine, then got out again.

"Thank you, Logan. I didn't want to be stuck here tonight."

"Not a problem." He unclipped the cables from his vehicle, and when he came over to her car, he paused. She stood next to the car, her arms crossed as if she were cold.

"So how are you going to find your father?" she asked.

"I'll start by nosing around a bit, I guess," he replied. He didn't actually want to be here—back in the town where he'd been raised and where he was always on the outside of his father's family. The memories here were too bitter…all but the memories with Melanie, at least.

"Logan, I'm going to level with you," Melanie said. "This divorce has put me through the wringer, and that lake house isn't exactly the gift my ex seems to think. I don't want to just sit by the lake and rehash painful memories. I'd like have some kind of control over my situation."

"I know the feeling," he said. "You have a better idea?"

"You want help tracking down Harry?" she asked.

He was surprised she'd even offer. She must really want to avoid those memories.

"I wouldn't turn it down," he replied. "You sure that's a good idea? I mean, I might not be a great source of happy memories, either."

"You aren't, but you were a lifetime ago," she replied. "Adam is more recent. Besides, it might give me something more immediate to focus on… I mean, if you want the help."

He smiled ruefully. "All right. Fair enough."

"I don't know how to start over, Logan." The joking had evaporated from her tone. "Obviously, I have to, but… How did you do it after your wife died?"

"I'm not sure I have," he admitted. "I guess we just keep moving forward. See what happens."

She nodded. "Well, it's different for you. Your wife didn't cheat on you for years because you weren't enough. I'm not trying to belittle your grief, I just mean that maybe you don't need the fresh start that I do."

Maybe his wife hadn't cheated, but there had been a different kind of betrayal that had lasted for years. He needed that fresh start as much as she did, but he wasn't sure he deserved it. Things with Caroline hadn't been so simple…

"You'll figure this out," he said. Look at her. She was gorgeous. If she wanted a new husband, a new start, she'd have no trouble doing that. "Seeing you in the dining room—" He cleared his throat. "I mean, you look good. You look comfortable. I think you'll land on your feet, is what I'm trying to say."

"I hope so." Melanie paused. "Because right now, I really miss the kids. Adam's kids, I mean. I feel like I've got an empty nest. For the last fifteen years, I was their stepmom. It was my full-time job. Not that they miss me, I'm sure. I was just a stand-in. Tilly made sure I knew that."

"Tilly?"

"She's the youngest. She was about two when I married Adam."

"Maybe you don't have to start over, exactly," Logan said quietly. "Even if you wanted to, you couldn't erase your history. You couldn't erase *them*."

Any more than he could erase Graham, or Caroline, or the truth of their marriage.

"I'm not a part of their family anymore, though," Melanie said with a shake of her head.

"You aren't married to their father anymore, but you might still be part of the family for the kids. It's too soon to tell," he replied. "How long have you been divorced?"

"Two months."

"That's fresh."

She was silent for a moment. "It's late. I need to get home."

"Right." He nodded. There was a lot there she wasn't saying, but he wasn't the one she'd open up to, anyway.

"So you want some help tracking down Harry, then?" she asked. "Give me something to do besides think?"

He glanced up at her and smiled. "Yeah. I'd take the help."

"I'm my own worst enemy if I just sit and brood," she said.

"Aren't we all?" he said.

Logan backed his vehicle up to give her space to drive out of her spot. Melanie slid into the driver's seat and undid the window. "Come by the lake house tomorrow, then." She raised her voice over the engines. "He's got to be somewhere, right?"

He shrugged. "I could always look up his kids. I'm sure they'd be thrilled to know my mom remembered him in her will."

Melanie grimaced. She knew enough of his family history to appreciate the awkwardness there.

"I'll come by in the morning," he said. "Late morning. I'm not a monster."

"Much appreciated. Thanks for the boost," Melanie said, and with a flutter of her fingers in farewell, she pulled out.

Melanie had said they were all old enough to be interesting now, and maybe he was, but that came with a price. He was also more jaded, a little broken. He wasn't a guy who could hand his heart over anymore, either.

Maybe it was good that he was self-aware enough to know that about himself. Because Melanie still had a way of tugging at him without even trying. And he couldn't let himself be tempted to take those risks he used to launch himself into without a second thought.

He now knew what it felt like to fail.

CHAPTER TWO

LOGAN HAD ONE of those deep sleeps where he woke up uncertain of where he was or what year he was in. But he felt better for it.

Breakfast in the resort dining room was hearty—bacon, eggs, waffles, hash browns... It was meant to fuel the people going out in canoes or hiking up the mountain to the falls. Logan wasn't doing either of those, but he was glad for some food that would stick with him. As he ate, his mind was on the lake house that his father had owned.

Had it been weird for Melanie to vacation in his dad's old haunt? He'd wanted to ask her more about that last night, but it hadn't felt right. They'd hardly become reacquainted again. Besides, his behavior when they broke up didn't leave him with any right to curiosity.

Logan pulled up in front of Melanie's lake house, and he turned off the engine. He'd been here a few times as a kid. Dad seldom took him to his family home where his wife and other kids were. Mom would drop Logan off here at the lake house, and Logan and Dad would have an awkward day together where they didn't talk too much—and whenever they did talk, Dad would tell him something about his other children.

Junior is really into trains right now. Do you like trains?

I'm not five.

Yeah, I know. I just... Yeah...

The day was warm already, and as he got out of the truck, a dragonfly buzzed past his head. He paused and looked around the front yard. The grass had been cut recently, but the flower beds were fallow. Those weeping willows on either side of the house trembled in the breeze. This was the kind of place that was timeless... That front door could open and he could see his dad standing in the doorway, hands pushed into chino pockets. Funny how, when he was young, he could be both excited to see the guy and filled with anger at the same time. He'd always been hoping for something that he never got—some level of acceptance that never happened.

Logan headed up the front path, knocked

on the door and waited. There was no answer at first, but he could hear some rattling around inside. He knocked again, harder this time. The rattling stopped, and he heard footsteps, then the door was flung open and Melanie shot him a grin, nudging her hair out of her face with the back of her wrist. She was breathing fast. She wore a pair of gardening gloves, a skirt and a loose floral top that scooped down low enough to expose a diamond solitaire necklace.

"Hi," he said, looking her over. "What's going on?"

"There's something up in the attic. It was scratching last night, and I want to see what I'm dealing with."

"Like…raccoon scratching, or mouse scratching?"

"I'm thinking squirrel, but that's just a guess."

"Squirrels can be vicious if you corner them, you know," he said.

"Hence the gloves," she said, giving him a wry smile and holding her hands up.

"You want help with that?" he asked.

"If you're offering," she said. "I was just about to go up there and see if I could scare it out."

"You'll probably need to hire a pest control guy," he said.

"Probably. But I want to know what I'm dealing with first," she replied.

"All right. Do you have a broom or something?"

Melanie pulled one from behind the door. "Great minds think alike."

Logan swung the door shut behind him and stole a look around. The old house smelled different now—sweeter, airier. There'd been some major renovations inside, too, from what he could see. New floors, a new kitchen. He followed her down the hallway that led to some bedrooms, where she stopped and looked up at the trapdoor in the ceiling. It had a piece of twine hanging down, and she reached up, not quite able to reach it. Logan stepped up behind her and grabbed the twine, but as he did, he was suddenly aware of how close she was—the soft fragrance of her hair, the warmth of her back. He gave the twine a pull and the door dropped down, then he stepped back.

He'd never been up in the attic—never even noticed the trapdoor, truth be told. He'd spent more time out on that rickety wharf listening to the lap of the water against the pilings and pretending to fish. It was something that let him turn his back on his dad for a couple of hours and neither of them felt guilty.

Melanie shot Logan a smile, vaulting him out of his memories, then she pulled down the folding stairs. She flicked a switch on the wall and the light came on upstairs.

"I'm glad that still works," she murmured, and she took the first step.

"What am I here for?" he asked with a laugh. "I thought I was supposed to go up first and take the worst of the rabies."

"Do you want to?" She turned to him with a deadpan expression.

"I'm the man here. I'll never be able to live with myself if I went up there behind a woman."

She laughed, then stepped back. "Feel free."

He paused on the steps, listening. All was quiet except for the soft sound of Melanie's breathing. The stairs squeaked under his feet as he climbed up, and when he got to the top, he looked around.

There was no sign of a critter that he could see—not immediately, at least. There was an old kayak along one wall, a deflated inner tube, a set of water skis. He went all the way up, ducking his head so he didn't catch a wooden beam. Melanie came up after him, and she peered around cautiously.

"I don't see anything," he said, and went over to the crack where the floor met the sloping roof. He ran the broom along it, looking for a hole or something. "You might want to put a few mouse traps out."

"I'll pick some up in town today," she said, but her voice was tight.

He looked over at her, and he found her looking at the kayak, mist in her eyes.

"You okay?" he asked.

"Memories." She shrugged, blinking it back.

Yeah, him, too.

"The kids used to love taking that thing out onto the lake," she said. "I was always scared they'd drown. I mean, this is a deep lake. Remember Tanya Harrington who drowned in senior year?"

"Yeah." It had been a blow to the community. Blue Lake was nothing to play with. It was strange watching someone else moved by old memories in this lake house. It seemed out of place, like only one person should be able to have that kind of experience here.

"I used to make the kids come back and put on life jackets," she went on. "And they'd pretend to be all sulky about it, but I could tell they liked that I made them do it. They could roll their eyes and save face."

"You were good for them," Logan said. "I remember that stage with my own son. All the attitude."

She met his gaze and smiled wanly. "When Adam came to see us here at the lake, the kids snuck out without their life jackets again. So Adam put the kayak up here and said they could find something else to do."

That sounded like a solid parenting choice to him. He would have done the same.

"So...you two spent a lot of time here with the kids?" Logan asked.

"Adam worked a lot." But there was something in her tone that had sharpened.

"Yeah?"

"No. That's a lie. Or I think it is. I found out he was carrying on some affairs. So when he said he was working and I took the kids out here to the lake house, who knows what he was doing."

Right. He sighed. "Sorry."

"Whatever. That's life."

"It shouldn't be."

Melanie moved over to a stack of cardboard boxes in a far corner and pulled open the lid of the top box. She looked down into the contents, then moved it aside and opened the next one.

"What did you find?" he asked.

"Just old junk." She pulled out a clock radio. "Whatever wasn't good enough to keep at the house we ended up bringing out here. And this is what I'm left with—the cast-off crap."

Logan chuckled. "You also have the most amazing view on the lake."

"There's that." She smiled. "Sorry, this house means something to you, too. I keep forgetting that."

"It's okay." Her grief seemed fresher, anyway.

"I guess I'm angrier than I thought. I thought the last year of separation would do more for me."

"Hey, I'm pissed still, and it's been five years since Caroline died. There's no real timeline there."

"Why are you mad?" she asked, looking up at him.

He'd said too much. He hadn't meant to,

but when she was opening up, it was hard not to answer in kind.

"It's nothing," he said.

"Your wife was faithful, wasn't she?" Melanie asked.

"Oh, yeah. Definitely." He nodded toward the next box down. It looked older than the others. "What's in that one?"

Mostly, he was trying to distract her from his issues. He'd thought he was dealing with his grief pretty well, but then he'd found those diaries, and it set him back to day one in a lot of ways. It was hard to lay his wife's memory to rest with a sense of betrayal lodged between them.

Melanie opened the next box and made a sound in the back of her throat. She reached inside, rummaged around.

"What is it?" he asked.

"It's not ours."

Ours. He noticed the language there. She meant her and Adam. Melanie pulled the box out between them, and Logan squatted down to look inside. If it didn't belong to the Isaacses, then maybe it had belonged to his dad.

There were a couple of fishing trophies, a box of lures that looked pretty dusty. There was a framed picture of some guys in a fishing boat, and in the bottom of the box was a little cloth bag next to some mouse droppings and a chewed corner of the box.

"A mouse—" Logan said.

"You think that's all it was?" Melanie asked.

"Might be. I'd put down those traps before I worried too much."

He was still trying to deflect. He looked closer at the picture, scanning the faces. His dad was in the center, smiling easily and holding a fish. He wasn't sure what he felt looking at his father's features. He didn't take after his dad—not like Junior did. Junior was Harry's spitting image.

Logan pulled the little cloth bag out of the box, shaking off shreds of cardboard. It tinkled softly. He pried open the drawstring and poured out a little chain bracelet. It was decorated with gold frogs covered in green crystals. His heart sped up in his chest, and he licked his lips. He knew this design.

"That's pretty," Melanie murmured.

"It's my mom's," he said.

Melanie looked at him, eyes widening.

"She wore a necklace with a frog on it just like these. I used to like it when I was a kid."

He could remember sitting on her lap, fiddling with the little green frog pendant. She wore it less as he got older. It hadn't been worth much, and maybe it went out of style, but she kept it in a box on her dresser, and he used to sort through it from time to time, looking at the chains and baubles that she didn't wear anymore but he remembered from when he was little.

"So your dad kept a memento," Melanie said.

"In a box in the attic," he said. "It's not like he took it with him to the family home. But maybe he'll care that she left him something, after all. I don't think he even knows she's dead."

"What's in the box she left him?" Melanie asked.

"I don't know. It's locked."

And that had felt a little like a betrayal, too. Who was Harry that he deserved this special treatment? There had been no locked box of wonders for Logan, even if his mother had left him everything else.

Melanie looked up and met his gaze. "You can take this box with you."

"Yeah, thanks." He tucked the box under his arm. He looked at Melanie for a moment. "Was it weird for you that Adam bought you my dad's place?"

Her cheeks pinked. "He isn't from here. He had no idea."

"I know. But for you—" Logan paused. "We walked past here that one time, remember? When we walked like five miles, and it was so hot?"

He'd been purposely bringing her here—sharing a memory with the girl he loved... But that was a long time ago.

"It felt a little weird. Yeah," she said. "But I wasn't part of choosing the place. Adam bought it as a surprise, so..."

"Did you tell him?" he asked.

"I did. I told him everything. If I held things back, I felt guilty, like I was being unfaithful somehow." She looked away. "Ironically."

"Huh." So whatever Logan had been to Melanie had been no threat to Adam. What, was he hoping he had been? Adam was some rich guy who bought lake houses as gifts. He'd had a loyal and honest wife. He'd had it all, and the likes of Logan probably hadn't even entered the guy's mind. Plus, he'd been married to Caroline by then.

He pushed back the memories. That was all long in the past.

"Let's go down," he said.

MELANIE LED THE way to the kitchen and turned back to look at Logan as he deposited the box on the counter. He'd clammed up, his face like granite.

Logan was good-looking in a different way now that he was older, and she found herself admiring that bit of gray around his temples, the strength in his shoulders—not quite the same as youthful muscle. It was honed from years of hard work, and there was a different kind of confidence in the way he held himself.

But she didn't want to be noticing these things exactly.

"I saw your dad when we took possession of the lake house," Melanie said. "He came to hand over an extra set of keys."

"Yeah?" Logan eyed her for a moment.

"I asked about you," she said, and the warmth came back to her cheeks. "He said you'd started up a company and were married with a son. He seemed really proud of you, for what that's worth."

"I don't know where he was getting his updates. I haven't spoken to him since Graham's birth."

"Why?" she asked with a frown.

"I called him to tell him I had a son, but

Caroline and I hadn't actually gotten married yet. That was a stickler for him, which I find really ironic, considering he and my mom weren't married. He said I was messing up like he had—and that just really got to me. *I* was a mistake. *I* was some foul-up in his eyes. But Graham was no mistake or accident. Sure, he was a surprise, but he was the center of my world."

"That's awful," she murmured.

"Caroline and I did get married when Graham was about a year old, but I didn't invite my dad. I wasn't doing it for him. It was for us. Although, there was a small part of me that figured I was putting him in his place by marrying her. I don't know..."

"And you never did talk after that?" she asked.

"I know it sounds petty—one nasty thing said—but it was one nasty thing that explained all the rest of my confusing relationship with him. And I'd had enough. I had my own family and I was tired of dancing for his approval. So I was done."

Logan had always been like this. He had an easily wounded heart under a gruff, reticent shell. It had always been hard to get through.

"You're a different kind of dad, yourself, though," she said.

"Yeah, you bet. I made a point of doing better than he did." His expression softened. "But then, my dad was great with his other kids. It was just me who got the shaft. So I guess you could say that he improved, too..."

"You're still his son," Melanie said.

Logan didn't answer, but he met her gaze with a resigned look. These were old wounds for him. She remembered him talking about it when they were teens. He'd been more like his father than he liked to admit—that shell of his was a whole lot like Harry's. She'd experienced it when he cut her off a few months after he left for college. He'd told her it was over, and then just shut down. There was no discussion. No closure, no reason. A whole lot like Logan had probably felt when his dad did the same thing to him. Except for a little boy, it was more damaging. She'd gotten over it. He never had.

"So how are we going to track him down?" Melanie asked.

"The address my mom left was this one—the lake house. I did go to the house in town he used to live in yesterday, but a different family lives there. I tried looking him up in the White Pages from Denver, but his number isn't listed."

"Is he..." she hesitated "...still alive?"

Logan shrugged. "Far as I know. Mom updated her will only a couple of years before she died, but if she gave this address to locate him, maybe she wasn't up-to-date on him, either."

"Where should we start?" she asked.

"I'm thinking we can check the newspaper office and look through some obituaries, just to be sure. And I could see if I can find my half brother. For all I know, they all moved away."

"It's a start," Melanie said. It felt good to have something else to focus on, someone else's heartbreak. She was tired of her own. Besides, soon she was going to have to enroll in some classes and restart her life in earnest, and she was avoiding it. The only real interior decor she'd done had been for her and Adam—was she even any good? Did she want to find out? Back when she'd willingly abandoned her job to be the stay-at-home mom for Adam's kids, she'd felt like a hero, but now it just felt stupid. She'd given up everything for Adam—her career, her ability to financially provide for herself… She wasn't making that mistake again.

As if on cue, Melanie heard the rumble of a car engine, and she looked out the kitchen window. A little red sports car pulled up and parked haphazardly behind her own car. The engine turned off, the door opened, and Melanie's heart stuttered.

"Tilly?" Melanie said aloud, and Logan came around the side of the counter and looked out the window beside her.

Tilly got out of the car, her sun-bleached hair pulled back in a messy bun, her makeup consisting of a bit of lip gloss. She'd grown up over the last few months. The last time Melanie had seen her stepdaughter was when Melanie came by the house to pick up some paperwork. It had been an awkward few minutes for Melanie while Tilly had virtually ignored her. *Dad left that envelope for you. I've got stuff to do, so...* That had stung, and she'd had to hide her emotions. But now, Tilly seemed older, more sure of herself. Tilly placed her sunglasses on her head and walked around to the back of her car where she popped the trunk. What was she doing here? She knew that Melanie had gotten the lake house in the divorce. In fact, Tilly had been rather vocal that she thought it was unfair, since it had been such an integral part of their childhood. Melanie, it seemed, had already been emotionally sliced out.

Tilly resented her stepmother. She hated this place, but she'd hated Melanie getting anything from their father more.

Melanie went to the door and pulled it open, watching as Tilly lifted out first one bag and then another. Then she struggled with a third—a large suitcase.

"Your stepdaughter?" Logan said from across the kitchen.

"That's her," she said grimly. Her heart sped up. She wasn't the one who was supposed to be intimidated, but this girl had a way of making Melanie feel small. She'd honed it over the last few years. There was something about Tilly's complete and unwavering belief in herself and her father.

"I'll let you two catch up, then," Logan said.

Melanie shot him an apologetic look. "I'm sorry about this."

"Don't be," he said. "It looks like she needs you."

Did she? Melanie felt a knot forming in her stomach. Tilly had been the toughest to raise, and the angriest during the divorce. The girl was beautiful and statuesque. She was confident, smart and, with the help of her father's money, she would go places. So why had she come *here*?

"I'll let you know what I find out in the newspaper office." Logan slipped past Melanie just as Tilly attempted to gather up her bags. She put one over her shoulder, and tried to stack the other on top of her suitcase, pulled the handle up. But the driveway was gravel, and those little airport wheels weren't going to go far.

"You want a hand with that?" Logan asked, raising his voice.

"Yeah. Okay." Tilly put down all of the bags, stepped back and pulled out her phone. Logan deposited the cardboard box onto the hood of his truck, then came back and picked up her bags, hoisting them easily enough. He carried them to the front door and put them down on the step. He shot Melanie a roguish smile.

"Have fun with her," he said softly.

"Thanks." Apparently, Tilly was planning to stay for a bit.

Logan turned and gave Tilly a nod, which

Tilly didn't seem to see since she was typing on her phone. He carried on past her.

"Tilly?" Melanie said, raising her voice.

"One sec."

Melanie stood there, waiting while Tilly walked ever so slowly up toward the house. Finally, she tucked the phone away and looked up.

"Hi," Melanie said.

Logan's truck rumbled to life and started backing out of the drive. Part of Melanie wished he'd stay. Being alone with Tilly was more than intimidating right now, but Tilly wasn't Logan's problem. She wasn't supposed to be Melanie's anymore, either.

"I'm going to be here for a few weeks," Tilly said.

"You do realize that this is my house," Melanie said. "Right?"

"This is the *family* lake house." Tilly didn't look up. "I grew up here."

Seven summers constituted a rather large part of a girl's childhood, but it was still a stretch.

"This is my home now," Melanie said.

"Dad always said he'd give it to me, you know," Tilly said.

Were they really going to stand here and

argue about the legality of the divorce agreement? Melanie tried to calm the rising anger. Tilly had a way about her—archly demanding that reality bend toward her wishes.

"Tilly, call your father," Melanie said with a sigh. Let Adam argue with his daughter.

"Dad said you wouldn't mind."

Did he now? Tilly picked up the two smaller bags and carried them past Melanie into the house. She put them down in the living room, then came back to muscle the large suitcase inside.

Melanie shut the door and looked across the room at her stepdaughter. Tilly wore a mask of indifference—the same one she'd been using the past several years. Logan's and Harry's defensive shells were as thin as bubbles compared to this girl. But she was here—and she wouldn't have come for nothing.

"Why are you here, Tilly?" Melanie asked.

"I needed somewhere to go," she retorted. "So, who's that guy? Your boyfriend?"

"Not that it's your business, but he's a friend of mine." Her father had had enough romantic partners—and a new steady girlfriend had materialized pretty quickly after the separation. Tilly should be up-to-date on how adults moved on.

"He seemed pretty comfortable here," Tilly countered.

"I'm just that good of a hostess." Melanie crossed her arms.

"Because it's tacky to start hooking up like a week after you're single," Tilly said tartly. "It makes you look slutty."

"Excuse me?"

"Just saying."

Melanie wouldn't be baited. Tilly wanted a fight, but Melanie was no longer legally obliged to provide her with one.

"He's just someone I used to know."

Tilly rolled her eyes. "Whatever. You're single and all."

"So how come you're here and not with your father?" Melanie asked.

"Because Dad's in Japan," Tilly said, rolling her eyes. "On business."

Melanie had always been the go-to childcare for the last fifteen years. She'd wondered how Adam would balance things on his own with his last child still at home.

"Doesn't he have a girlfriend now?" Melanie asked.

"Exactly."

That didn't explain a lot. "And he said I wouldn't mind you being here?"

"Yeah." Tilly huffed out a breath. "I need to just…unwind. I'm not some kid anymore, okay? I figure you owe me this much." She looked around the kitchen. "I'm hungry."

Apparently, she hadn't noticed the irony of both being terribly grown-up and expecting the adult in the room to feed her.

"What do you want to eat?" Melanie asked.

"I want, like, something sweet, but like, not."

Melanie suppressed an eye roll of her own. You could either fight with Tilly or give in. And until she could send the girl off to her father, she'd at least have to feed her. "I'll make you a BLT."

Tilly sank onto the couch, her focus on her phone. Who was she texting so fervently? Melanie eyed her for a moment.

"You know you can't stay here, Tilly," she said. "Just for the record. I'm not your crash pad while you party."

Tilly didn't answer, and Melanie dropped some bread into the toaster. It felt too much like old times. She'd raised Tilly since she was a toddler, but there had come a point when Tilly had just…disconnected from her. Whatever warm relationship they'd shared had been over, and they'd never gotten it back.

"God, he's such an idiot!" Tilly burst out, dropping her phone into her lap.

"Who?" Melanie asked.

"No one. I'll leave soon. I just have to figure a few things out."

So…not a few weeks, then?

"What do you need to sort out?" Melanie asked.

"Like where I'm going!" Tilly snapped back, but tears rose in her eyes. "Okay? I'm not just going to drive off into the sunset. I need somewhere to go."

There was something deeper going on here—very likely something to do with whomever she was texting. Tilly wasn't the type to be without a boyfriend for long, but she was only seventeen. If she was entangled with some older guy taking advantage, Melanie did have the adult responsibility to inform her father.

"Who's the idiot?" Melanie asked. "Humor me."

"Simon."

Her on-again, off-again boyfriend. At least that wasn't an alarming update.

"Tell you what," Melanie said, pulling out her cell phone. "I'm going to call your father for you."

She was no longer Tilly's stepmother, and if Tilly needed some advice, her father was the one to give her guidance. She dialed Adam's cell phone and it went directly to voice mail. Melanie sighed and opted for a text instead.

Tilly is here at the lake house. She needs her father.

Tilly had always needed her father, and Adam had always been too busy. Except now, after a painful divorce from Tilly's dad, that dysfunctional family dynamic was no longer Melanie's responsibility to try to balance out. Their marriage was over, and Adam was going to have to step up and be the dad his daughter needed.

CHAPTER THREE

LOGAN PARKED HIS truck out in front of the old brick building, his gaze drawn to the faded *Mountain Springs Journal* sign. It had been a long time since he'd been back in Mountain Springs, and somehow, he'd expected more to change around here, but the old newspaper office was exactly the same—just a little more worn.

When he was about twelve, Logan used to work as a delivery boy for the journal, and his mom, Elise, used to drive him down to this very office so he could pick up his papers at four thirty every Saturday morning.

Logan had asked his dad if he'd help with his newspaper delivery job, but Harry had said no.

"It's too early, Logan," Harry had said. "Why don't you sleep in on your weekend?"

As if Harry knew what his son did on a regular day. Later, Harry took his seven-year-old son, Junior, to early-morning soccer practices and drove him around to all sorts of out-of-town games. So it hadn't been about the hour. It was about which son had asked. That was a sting that never quite went away. He was a second-class kid for Harry Wilde—an inconvenience more than anything. Logan hadn't even gotten his father's last name—Harry hadn't fought for that. He was Elise's son.

So, Elise had gotten up early every Saturday morning, and she'd driven him to the newspaper office to pick up his stack of papers, and then she'd driven him out to his route. She'd sit in the car reading while he finished up, and then they'd head home together for a pancake breakfast. Even when she was sick with a cold or flu. She'd just fling a winter coat over her pajamas, and while he delivered his papers, she'd sleep in the car with her box of tissues, a hot water bottle and the emergency blanket they always kept in the car. Mom had been the one Logan could count on, and eventually he stopped asking Harry for anything. Harry didn't seem to notice.

The problem was, he never did thank his mom for the way she stepped up no matter how hard it was on her. Even as an adult, his mother used to chastise him. *You take a lot for granted, Logan. A thank-you wouldn't kill you.* He did try to pay his mother back by driving her around to her appointments and picking up some groceries for her every week or two. He might act like he had no feelings but he did have them.

Logan got out of the truck. Main Street in Mountain Springs was warm and smelled of the bakery down the road. This wasn't the tourist hub; it was the regular part of town where no business bothered pretending to be a chalet or a log cabin. Trees were planted along the sidewalk, offering some dappled shade, and in front of the journal's glass door were two large planters with an abundance of pink and white flowers flowing over the side.

Logan hadn't submitted an obituary to the *Mountain Springs Journal* when his mom had passed away, even though she'd lived in this town for thirty years. He'd figured the people who cared had kept up with her.

And there was a significant angry part of him that hadn't wanted to tell his father about Elise's death. Harry hadn't deserved to know. He used to think about his father's negligent parenting, but his mother had suffered from it, too. She never got a break. She seldom got financial help. He couldn't remember her buying herself new clothes, although she must have from time to time—for the most part, the money had all gone to other necessities. Harry had moved on with his marriage to Dot and the kids that resulted, and he hadn't looked back.

Thinking about his mother's passing now, it might have been wiser to just post the obituary, because now Logan had to break the news to his father himself…and maybe he could see what Caroline had been talking about in those diaries, after all. He was stubborn, jaded and difficult.

Would an obituary have killed him?

Logan pulled open the front door of the newspaper office, and a chime sounded as he came inside. There were some new faux leather visitor chairs, and it looked like the bullpen had been updated a bit. Two local journalists sat at desks facing the wall—one on the phone jotting down information, and the other glued to a game of solitaire on the computer screen. The receptionist was a middle-aged woman with ash-blond hair, and she smiled as he came in.

"Hello," she called cheerily. "Can I help you with anything?"

"Hi," Logan said as he came up to her desk. "I'm wondering how I might be able to get a look at your obituaries for the last few years. I checked online, and I couldn't find anything."

"If we posted everything online, there'd be no reason for the newspaper," she replied meaningfully.

"Right..." He squinted at her. "So, obituaries. How would I check the old ones?"

"We used to have most of them backed up on the computer," she replied. "But we had a virus and we lost a lot. But we do have the old microfiches. You can go back to the fifties on those. Old technology sometimes lasts longer, you know?"

"Yeah..." He smiled faintly. "It can be that way."

"But I do have some more recent obituaries on our new system that I can check, if you want. They go back three years."

"That would be great," he said.

"What's the name?" she asked.

"Harold Eugene Wilde. It might also be under Harry Wilde. That's Wilde with an *e*."

While the receptionist checked her system, Logan sucked in a deep breath. It felt wrong to be standing here, checking if his father was even alive. This seemed like information a son shouldn't have to sleuth out. His dad might not have been much of a father in his life, but he'd still *been* his father. If he were dead—

"Nothing under either of those names for the deceased, but his name does come up as a survivor to another person who passed," she said, glancing up. "His wife, it says. A Mrs. Dorothy Eleanor Wilde."

Dot—the stepmother with the distracted smile and limited patience. Logan hadn't known her well—but he'd resented her a whole lot as a kid. She always had new clothes, and she had a way of saying his father's name that sounded halfway between an exasperated sigh and a question.

"When was that?" Logan asked.

"November last year," she said. "I'm sorry."

"Thanks..." Logan licked his lips. "Can I see it?"

"Sure." She turned her screen so he could read the write up. It had the regular information—where she was born, where she went to school, who she left behind... Along with Harry, their children were listed as having survived her. Logan's half brother was listed as Dr. H. Eugene Wilde Jr. Apparently, he was doing pretty well for himself.

"So if Harry died after his wife did, you should have the obituary."

"If the family had one posted, yes," she confirmed.

He felt lighter, somehow. He was glad that Harry was still alive, he realized. He'd lost one parent already. Even if his dad wasn't much of a parental figure, he didn't want to lose them both.

He stepped outside into the June warmth and stood there for a moment, deciding what to do next. His father was alive, and it was just a matter of figuring out if he was still in Mountain Springs. He'd thought about what he'd say to his father when he found him, but somehow, all those imagined conversations seemed to fall flat.

Logan looked up the street toward Mountain Drive. He wondered if The Peaks, the café where he used to meet up with Melanie, was still there. They'd sit nursing coffees with too much cream and sugar for a couple of hours while they talked and he'd play with her fingers on the tabletop… He pushed back the memories. Whatever they'd felt all those years ago, they were adults now. He was a dad, and she had stepkids of her own who resented her like crazy. It was funny how life came around in a circle.

He hadn't been back in town for at least ten years. He'd taken Caroline to Mountain Springs one summer to see his mother before they helped her move to Denver to be closer to them, and that was the last time he'd stepped foot in this town.

And here he was, a widower in search of his elderly father, and somehow it felt like for as much as he'd changed and grown over the years, Mountain Springs tugged him back to the same old feelings and the same old problems. But he wasn't the same rebel on a motorbike who'd spent his formative years in this town. He'd grown more cautious with age, more wary.

As he headed up the sidewalk, he spotted The Peaks—it was still there. The sign still showed the same silhouetted mountains you could see when you looked west. That cluster of three jagged peaks were called God's Daughters, and they made it onto all the local postcards.

Inside, there was some welcome air-conditioning and the decor had been updated considerably. He spotted a menu on the wall—paninis, grilled focaccia sandwiches, wraps, pitas, gluten-free and paleo options… This place used to be strictly soup and sandwiches—the kind where you chose wheat or white, toasted or not.

He glanced around the tables, and he stopped short when he saw her. Melanie still came here? Somehow, he felt like it should have remained sacrosanct, but maybe their relationship hadn't left the mark on her that it had on him…

Melanie sat with her back to him, her hair pulled up into a messy bun, similar to the one her stepdaughter had sported. Maybe the kid had picked the trick up from her. She hadn't noticed him come in.

He approached the counter and placed his order—a BLT toasted on wheat and a black coffee—and when they handed him his food, he headed over to where Melanie sat.

"Hi," he said, and she startled and looked up.

"Logan! What are you doing here?" she said. "Have a seat, if you like."

"I got hungry," he said, lifting his tray an inch as proof and he slid into the seat opposite her. "So you come here still?"

"I used to bring the kids here." A hint of

color touched her cheeks. "It's changed management about four times since our days, so…"

"Yeah." He smiled faintly. "It's not the same."

"No, not at all."

They both fell silent for a moment, and Logan met Melanie's gaze across the table. She was still so pretty… And while it wasn't the same as years ago, sitting with her in this café still brought a strange sense of familiar warmth. She'd been his sweet spot here in Mountain Springs.

"I was just at the newspaper office." He said, lifting his sandwich. Then he frowned slightly. "How come you aren't at home with—" He searched for the name, taking a bite of the sandwich at the same time.

"Tilly," she provided.

"Tilly," he repeated past the food. "Did she leave?"

"No, I escaped." She smiled wanly. "She seems to have moved herself right in. I was the one to text her father."

"Did you hear back from him?" Logan asked.

"He's in Japan on business. That's all he

texted. I think the assumption is that I'll just take care of things, like I always did."

"Japan?" he said with a frown. "Where was Tilly staying before this?"

"At the house, by herself. Her brother's at Harvard, and his sister is in Denver—she has her own place now. Tilly's the last one left at home."

Right. It sounded like this kid had a little too much freedom. When Graham was that age, he had a curfew and had to ask to borrow the car. But now at twenty-one, Graham was traveling alone without adult supervision in Europe, so it all came down to the kid. But her ex's assumption that she'd take care of things irked him just a bit. It wasn't like he had any right to get jealous, but she *was* divorced. She wasn't Adam's wife anymore, and that detail mattered to Logan.

"So what are you going to do?" Logan asked, trying not to betray his deeper feelings.

"What can I do?" She shrugged. "I've got to be the responsible adult, whether I'm legally required to be or not."

IN FACT, MELANIE wished she had anywhere at all she could send Tilly to just to escape dealing with this girl. Tilly had never been an easy kid to raise, especially as the stepmom. Adam was overly indulgent, and every time Tilly batted her lashes and called him "Daddy," Adam would cave in. Tilly had learned pretty quickly who the "good guy" and who the "bad guy" were in the house, and by the time she was twelve, she'd stopped calling Melanie "Mom" and had started calling her by her first name.

"You aren't my real mom," Tilly had informed her with an icy glare. "You're just the one my dad married."

Where she'd gotten that little barb, Melanie had never found out. But someone had clued her in, and whenever Melanie told her *no* to something—a sleepover at a friend's place, a new pair of expensive jeans—she'd just roll her eyes and say, "Never mind, Melanie. I'll speak with my father."

And now this bundle of sunshine was sitting in Melanie's living room eating a bag of potato chips and texting.

Given the choice, Melanie was exactly where she wanted to be—as far from Tilly as possible. And she didn't even feel guilty. She was no longer just the one Adam had married. She was now his ex-wife, and the whole painful mess of his family life was no longer her responsibility.

Logan took a bite of his sandwich, wiped his lips with a napkin and regarded Melanie with a quizzical look.

“What?” she asked. She picked up her mug of coffee and took a sip.

“How long did you raise this kid for?” he asked.

“Since she was two,” Melanie replied. “There was a time that she loved me so much that she followed me into the bathroom and I couldn’t even shower alone.”

Logan smiled at that. “Yeah, I remember that stage with Graham.”

“I don’t know what changed, exactly. I think it might have been things her siblings talked about around her, or just the fact that her father would completely disregard anything I’d put in place for the kids—” She looked around herself. “You know what’s really crazy? I used to bring the kids to this café all the time when we’d come to the lake. And where do I go when I want some space? Right back here.”

“Yeah?” His expression softened. “Here?”

“It wasn’t like that…” she said. It wasn’t in memory of him or anything… Or maybe it had been a little bit. It was a reminder that she'd had a life before she married Adam and became stepmom to his kids, and given up everything that made her feel like herself. And her romance with Logan had been a part of that life. But she wouldn't be admitting that to him now.

"Do you miss the kids?" he asked.

Melanie felt tears mist her eyes. "Am I crazy if I say yes? For better or for worse, those kids were the center of my world for fifteen years. But I've got one of them in the lake house as we speak, and where am I? Hiding from her."

"Isn't that parenting, though?" Logan asked. "You get so frustrated you could strangle them during the day, and then you watch them sleep at night, and you're so flooded with love for the little monster..."

"I guess so." She met Logan's gaze and shrugged. "But I wasn't their real mom."

Logan nodded and dropped his gaze. "I had a stepmom. I know the complicated feelings there..."

What did that mean—was she as bad as Dot had been?

"But Dot couldn't stand you," she said.

"I felt that way as a kid. There was a lot of tension. I blamed her."

Just like Tilly blamed Melanie. She tried to push back the stab of recrimination. Kids shouldn't be held responsible for their parents' complicated relationships.

"Do you still resent her?" Melanie asked.

"She's dead now."

"Oh..."

"But yeah, I guess so. She was the adult. I was just a kid."

Had Melanie wasted the last fifteen years, trying to be a mom to those three kids when she'd always be the evil stepmother?

"So maybe if I peek in at Tilly when she sleeps tonight, I'll like her more," Melanie said with a small smile, hoping to deflect with a bit of humor. Logan chuckled.

"What about the other kids—how old are they?" he asked.

"Michael is twenty-two this year, and he's starting his master's degree in clinical biology in the fall at Harvard, like I mentioned, and Viv is twenty-five. She's a medical intern in Denver. She works day and night."

"Successful," Logan said, but she saw something in his eyes—she felt it, too. This was a step above how she'd been raised. If

Adam hadn't paid off her student loans, she'd still be paying them off.

"Adam's kids had the money behind them to make it happen," Melanie replied. "Not every kid gets the support that his kids got."

"Yeah." Logan let out a breath. "But you had a part in their success."

"I like to think so," she replied. But how much? Right now, with Michael and Viv focused on their own lives and Tilly's determination to make her feel about two inches tall, she felt more like a glorified nanny.

"Tell me about your son," she said, changing the subject.

"Graham," Logan said, and she noticed how he relaxed just by saying his son's name. "He's a good kid. He finished his second year of college in art history, but he wants to be a chef. I talked him out of it. I feel bad about it now, but I wanted him to be more practical—he's not a kid with that kind of money behind him, you know?"

"No, I get it," she said.

"But food is his passion. He's in England right now, exploring their cuisine."

"Are the British known for their food?" Melanie asked.

"Say that to Graham and he'll give you a

lengthy lecture on their beers, cheeses and comfort foods," Logan said with a chuckle. "But he's a good kid. He was in the tenth grade when his mom died of cancer, and—" Logan shrugged sadly "—he rallied better than I thought he would."

"That must have been hard for both of you," she said quietly.

"Yeah. I wasn't sure how I'd go on alone, but you just do. One day at a time, until your kid graduates high school and you realize he's just fine. He's more than fine, he's great."

"You're a proud dad," she said.

"Definitely." He took another bite and swallowed before he continued. "I'm picking him up from the airport Sunday, and I'm going to have to pretend I didn't miss him as much as I did."

"Why?" she asked. "It sounds like you have a wonderful relationship."

Logan smiled. "Maybe it lets us both pretend we're tougher than we are. We're guys. We don't feel stuff."

Logan still had that shell, and it seemed he'd passed it on to his son. But seeing him as the doting dad, missing his grown son and worrying about him all the same…

it was strange how much could change in twenty-odd years. She remembered him as the rebel with the motorcycle and the bad attitude. He'd been her first heartbreak, and getting over him hadn't been easy. But that was a long time ago, and her heart had gone through a whole lot more since.

"So did you take that degree in engineering?" Melanie asked.

"Sort of," he replied. "I majored in accounting, and I minored in structural engineering. I now own a construction company. I know enough to manage the company, but I work with experienced engineers."

Melanie raised her eyebrows. "Smart."

"That surprise you?" he asked with a small smile.

A little, actually, but it wasn't polite to say. "It's just different seeing the adult version of you."

"So what about you?" he asked. "Did you go in for nursing?"

"Interior decor," she replied.

He nodded slowly. "Okay… I guess I can see that. It seemed like you stayed home with the kids…did you work part-time, or—"

"I—" She hated being asked this. "I devoted my time to my husband's kids. So no, I didn't actually work with it."

"Right." His expression softened. "You regretting that now?"

She sucked in a breath. "I don't know. They needed me then, and I did love those kids, even when they were putting me through the wringer. Their mom had died. They needed love, even if they didn't want to admit it. I thought I was investing in my family for the long term. So looking back on it, maybe I should have focused a little more on myself, but…"

"Your heart was in the right place," he supplied.

"It was," she agreed. "But I'm starting up my own business now. I did some decorating for charity events during my marriage, and I decorated and redecorated our houses in Denver and Vermont… I have experience and taste. But I've never had a full-time position in decor, and I'm not exactly up-to-date anymore… It's something I started before I met Adam, and everything changed. So I guess I feel like I owe it to myself to try again."

And this time, she wasn't going to let her own ambitions get derailed by another guy.

Being a martyr for other people's needs was stupid in the long run—she wasn't doing that again.

"I'm sure you can do it."

"I'd better be able to," she replied. "Because I'm on my own now."

"With your ex-stepdaughter," he added with a teasing smile.

"With Tilly..." She rolled her eyes, her thoughts going back to the teenager who drove her crazy. "Tilly told me she wanted her father to give her the lake house."

"Why?"

"I don't know. What Tilly wants, Tilly gets. That's how it always went, at least. Then Adam gave me the lake house in the divorce—probably to avoid giving me the house in Vermont—and Tilly's furious."

"Did you want the house in Vermont?" Logan asked.

Did she? She might have been the one who'd left, but she'd been a heartbroken mess, and she hadn't actually been looking at how much she deserved to get out of their union. "I don't suppose it matters anymore. Adam had a whole team of better lawyers. Besides, I'd have to be able to maintain the house in Vermont. It was more than I could afford on my own."

Logan smiled. "I guess we both grew up."

"It happens to the best of us," she replied with a shrug. They were quiet for a moment, then she shot him a questioning look. "Did you find your dad yet?"

"I know he's not dead," Logan said bluntly.

She choked on a laugh. "Okay..."

"He was listed as having survived Dot in her obituary three years ago. And there was no obituary for him since. So it looks like he's still around."

"Your half brother would know where he is, wouldn't he?" Melanie remembered Junior. He'd been a few years younger—just starting middle school when they'd been in high school. "Or your half sister?"

Logan didn't answer, but he chewed the side of his cheek.

"If you want to find Harry..." she said, softening her tone "...Junior is a place to start."

"Yeah, I know. I'm just not real keen on meeting up with my dad's other kids."

"Even now?" She frowned.

"We've spent the last two decades studiously ignoring each other," he said. "Harry's family was happier pretending I didn't exist. That didn't change."

"Are you going to keep trying to find him?" she asked.

"Yep."

There he was—the rebel she remembered. It was the same grim smile from when the principal accused him of cheating on his math final. He hadn't cheated, but apparently a dusted-up kid from the wrong side of the tracks had no right getting a grade that high. Logan never had shied away from a fight until now.

"If you track down Junior, he can at least tell you where Harry is." Melanie put up her hands in mock surrender. "That's all I'm going to say on the matter."

He met her gaze, and for a moment, he stared into her face, his own expression granite. What was it about that dark stare that could still make her breath catch? But she was older now, and wiser. While a stony reserve used to be mysterious, she knew better. She didn't like not being able to read a man she was involved with. But after twenty-three years, Logan might count as a friend.

"I should probably get going," she said. "I need to get some groceries in the fridge."

"Sure." Logan nodded, and that granite expression finally cracked, revealing a deep well of sadness. Her heart gave a squeeze.

"What are you doing tonight?" she asked, before she could stop herself or think better of it.

"Not sure," he said. "Why?"

"Why don't you come for dinner?" she said.

"What about Tilly?" he asked.

"I don't know what to say. I'm not looking for privacy with her."

"Don't let her chase you off, either," he said.

"Easier said than done with this kid." But Melanie smiled. "Come for dinner, and you can update me on your search for Harry, and I'll at least have distraction from my ex-stepdaughter who can't stand me."

"How can a guy resist that kind of invitation?" Logan said with a low laugh.

"I know, right?" She laughed. "This is what I've come to."

"What time?"

"Say…six?"

"I'll be there."

Melanie pushed back her chair and rose. She was feeling more optimistic already.

She'd get some groceries, and then she'd go back and face Tilly…like she had any choice. But at least she could have an ally in Logan—he'd come back to Mountain Springs about as gracefully as she had, complete with unresolved personal issues.

There was comfort in that. She wasn't the only one.

CHAPTER FOUR

LOGAN LOOKED OVER his shoulder as Melanie disappeared out the door. Coming back to Mountain Springs, he hadn't anticipated talking to her this intimately. He'd figured he'd walk these streets, find his dad, pass over that box and leave again. And in the meantime, maybe he'd relive a few memories, but Melanie—in his head, at least—was going to be focused on her own life. He didn't think they'd hang out…or that he'd still find himself drawn to her. In another life, this might have been an opportunity, but not now.

The words from Caroline's journal were still swimming in his mind: *Logan just doesn't get it... He doesn't listen. He won't talk to me—not honestly. Unless he doesn't actually have any feelings under there. He won't open up. If I ask for something, I'm guaranteed not to get it. I can't help but wonder if other husbands are easier to be with. Are they all like this, or just him? I love him, don't get me wrong, but loving him is hard work, and every year it gets harder. Is it supposed to be like this?*

He'd thought his marriage was happy until he read her diaries. Standing by his wife, being faithful, coming home every night and providing for both her and their son…that had felt like success until he'd seen himself through Caroline's eyes. Maybe he was too much like his old man, after all.

Track down Junior—that was Melanie's solution. And she was right, of course. But he'd never liked his brother much. They shared a father, but not a family. Still, he'd be the one who'd be able to give Logan an address.

He pulled up the web browser and typed in his brother's name: *Dr. Howard Eugene Wilde Jr.* One of the first few entries to pop up was for an office in town. Mountain Springs Medical Center. And Dr. H.E. Wilde Jr. was listed under psychiatry.

"Huh," he muttered. He wasn't sure what he thought of that, but at least his brother was still local. It would make him easier to track down.

He could call the office, but he was mildly curious to see what Junior had become. The kid who'd had their father's attention, his priority and his help in paying for a college education. They were both adults now, and maybe it was time to let grievances go.

THE MEDICAL BUILDING was on the south side of Mountain Springs—a newer building with three stories and not enough parking.

Psychiatry was on the third floor, and Junior's office was at the far end. When Logan came inside, the waiting room was empty. The receptionist looked up with a distracted smile.

"Do you have an appointment?" she asked.

"No, I don't," he said. "I was hoping to see… Dr. Wilde." It felt awkward to use his brother's professional title.

"Dr. Wilde isn't available this afternoon," she replied. "But I can see if there are any spaces later next week—"

"I'm his brother," Logan added.

"Oh…" The receptionist took a closer look at him. "What's your name?"

"Logan McTavish."

She frowned slightly. "One moment. I'll see if he's available."

She disappeared down a hallway, and Logan glanced around the waiting room. It was calm, quiet, a faint puff of air-conditioned air stirring the pages of a magazine on a cherrywood coffee table.

He pulled his hand through his hair and looked up as a shorter portly man came into the room.

"Junior?" Logan said. He could see the younger man in this older version. Junior looked tired. He'd be in his midthirties, and his blond hair was receding. He wore a pair of gray dress pants, a buttoned shirt rolled up at the sleeves to his forearms and a loosened tie. There was a wedding ring on his left hand.

"Hi, Logan," Junior said with a bemused smile. "I go by Eugene now. Or Dr. Wilde."

"You aren't actually asking me to call you Doctor, are you?" Logan asked.

"No, of course not," he said quickly. "Eugene is fine."

"Right. Eugene."

"It's been a while," Eugene said with a smile.

"You were a kid when I saw you last," Logan agreed. "You were still Junior back then."

Junior nodded slowly, and he glanced down at his watch. "You'll have to excuse me, but I have plans with my family in a few minutes. My son has a Little League game, so I can't take long."

"This will be quick," Logan replied.

"Did you want to come into my office?" His brother gestured down the hallway.

"Sure," Logan replied. The receptionist stared after them with undisguised curiosity as he followed.

There was a dark wood desk on one end of the spacious office, a leather couch and a wingback leather chair on the other, and some framed pastoral paintings on the walls. It looked like his half brother was doing pretty well for himself.

"Do you need money?" Junior asked, shutting the door and turning to face him. "Because I don't give loans, I'll tell you now."

"What?" Logan eyed the younger man skeptically. "Maybe you haven't changed as much as I was hoping. No, I don't need money. I own my own business in Denver and it's thriving, thank you."

"Right. Sorry." Junior's expression softened slightly. "You wouldn't believe how many old acquaintances stop by to say hi and ask for a loan."

Acquaintances... Was that what Junior

thought of him—like some old friend of the family? But then, Logan had never really been more than that to Harry's kids.

Logan shrugged. "I don't have too many old acquaintances in Denver, so I don't have that problem."

"Lucky." Junior glanced around. "So what kind of business do you own?"

"Construction," Logan replied. "I build houses."

"That sounds great..." Junior nodded distractedly. "So, what can I do for you?"

"I need to find Dad," Logan said.

"Why?" he asked, and he stilled, his arms over his chest and his gaze locked on Logan's face quizzically. So this was the line for Junior—access to their father?

"Does it matter?" Logan asked. "He's my father, and I need to see him."

"The thing is, his health isn't great," he said. "He's had a few small strokes in the last year, and he's pretty fragile right now."

"How bad is it?" Logan asked.

"He's in an assisted-living facility right now, and he'll probably have to stay there. He's seventy-five this year."

"Yeah, I know..."

"So he can't handle too much," Junior went

on. “My mother passed away a year ago—I’m not sure if you heard—but it was really hard on Dad. He just kind of…caved in.”

“I only found out about your mom today,” Logan said. “I’m sorry for your loss.”

“It was hard on the whole family,” his brother said. “But especially on Dad.”

They fell silent for a moment, and Logan pressed his lips together. This was as awkward as he’d thought it would be.

“I heard about your wife’s passing,” Junior added. “Dad told me. I was sorry to hear that.”

“Thanks. My mom would have been the one to let him know about Caroline’s death. That wasn’t me.”

Junior’s eyebrows went up. “Well, all the same, I’m sorry to hear it. How is your son? You have one boy, right?”

It seemed that Junior… Eugene…had kept up on the details of his life better than Logan had done in return. He felt mildly bad about that.

“He’s doing pretty well,” Logan said. “He’s traveling in Europe right now.”

“Hey, that’s great! I did a Europe trip after high school.” Junior’s face lit up. “I did Germany, Austria and France.”

"Because you had a father to help pay for it," Logan said, but he bit back the rest of what he was going to say. His half-brother had done Europe? This was the first he'd heard of that particular inequality. Harry hadn't helped Logan out financially at all.

His brother's smile fell. "Right… Look, I know things weren't always fair that way, but I didn't have any control over that."

"I'm not blaming you," Logan replied.

"All the same, I'd really prefer it if you didn't bring that stuff up with Dad."

"That's your professional advice?" Logan asked bitterly. "As a psychiatrist, you figure burying all this family stuff is the healthier way to go?"

"As a son worried about his father's failing health," Junior replied tightly. "I'm sure you both have a few grievances, but this isn't the time."

So Harry had some grievances with *him*? Great. That sounded promising. He could step in line.

"Look, I'm not here to make waves," Logan said. "My mother passed away, and she left a locked box for our father in her will. She also left instructions that I was to deliver it personally."

"Your mom passed?" Junior froze, the fight seeming to go out of him.

"A year ago," Logan said. "It sounds like it was the same year your mom passed."

"What took you so long to deliver it?" he asked.

Logan shrugged. "I'm trying to do better with these things."

For whatever it counted for now.

"I'm sorry, all the same. How does all of this make you feel?" His brother asked quietly.

Logan eyed his brother with an icy look. "Shut up, Junior."

The younger man smiled wanly. "Sorry. It's part of the job."

"I'm not here for grief counseling. I'm abiding by my mother's last wishes. Period."

"I actually didn't think Dad and Elise were in contact anymore," Junior said.

"Hey—they were adults. I have no idea if they talked from time to time, but if they did, they didn't have to answer to us for it."

His brother didn't answer that.

"If you could just give me the address to the place where Dad is staying, I can be out of your way and you can carry on with your plans for the day," Logan said.

"Like I said, Dad is in a fragile state—"

"What do you think I'm going to do?" Logan asked testily. "Do you think I'm going to yell at him or something? I'm here to deliver something and let him know that my mother has passed away. That's it."

Junior rubbed his hand over his chin, then sighed. "Fine. There are nurses to make sure he doesn't get too agitated."

That sounded like a warning, but Junior went to his desk, opened a drawer and pulled out a business card. He passed it over. "You can ask for him at the front desk, and they'll see if he's interested in a visit."

Logan hadn't considered whether Harry would be interested in seeing *him* after all these years. Logan nodded and tapped the card against his palm. "Thanks. I appreciate the information."

"No problem."

Logan headed for the door, and he glanced back as he opened it. Junior stood there, his expression clouded, spinning his wedding ring on his left hand. It was an expression Logan had seen on his face before, back when Eugene was still called Junior and Logan was talking to their father about something.

Jealousy? Worry? Competition? What had that look been covering all these years?

"Say hi to your wife and kids for me," Logan said, and he realized that he didn't know any of their names.

His brother didn't answer.

Logan had an address now. He could visit his dad, and then get back out of town and put the last of these uncomfortable memories behind him.

MELANIE PUT THE plastic bags full of groceries on the floor next to the fridge, and looked into the sitting room. Tilly was on the couch, flipping through the few staticky local channels they got with just an antenna.

"What happened to the cable?" Tilly asked, sounding bored.

"I used to only set it up for the month that we were here."

"Why don't you have it now?"

"Because this is now my home, and I'm not catering to the tastes of kids anymore."

And she wasn't here for TV watching—she was putting her life back together.

"Other people watch TV," Tilly said, casting her an annoyed look. "What, are you too good for TV now?"

"You understand that this isn't your home anymore, right?" Melanie snapped. "I'm not responsible for your cable TV, or your cell-phone bill, or whatever else will make you comfortable. I've bought some groceries, and you'll just have to make do with what's here, unless you want to buy your own."

"So that's how you're going to play this?" Tilly retorted.

"Play what?" Melanie spread her hands. "Tilly, you've spent literally years of your life loathing me, and now your dad and I are divorced!"

Tilly's phone blipped and she looked down at it. For a moment, Melanie saw the girl's eyes mist, then she turned away and started typing. Melanie sighed. Was she being cruel here, pointing out the obvious? Melanie was the only mother Tilly had ever known, but the girl had also been raised with a solid understanding that she wasn't Tilly's "real mom." Her "real" mother was enclosed in photo albums and in framed pictures that still hung on some walls in that house—a gentle woman with a sweet smile.

Maybe it felt good to be free of it all. Melanie didn't have to swallow back her retorts and pretend she hadn't heard the icy words in other rooms. She didn't have to pretend it didn't embarrass her when her stepkids sassed back in public, and she didn't have to walk past pictures of her husband's late wife, pretending she didn't mind.

Tilly… Melanie's heart gave a squeeze. She used to be little and snuggly. She used to love Melanie, once upon a time. But those days were beyond reach.

It hadn't been all difficult times. There was the time that Tilly had made her a Mother's Day card at school, complete with glitter, hearts and flowers. Melanie had treasured that card. There were the field trips she'd volunteered on, the bake sales she helped the kids prepare for… And there were the times here at this very lake house when Melanie let the rules slide and bought a bunch of frozen pizzas, boxes of cookies, bags of frozen fries, and let the kids fend for themselves. They'd loved it. That was probably the best summer she'd ever had with them.

Melanie started unloading the grocery bags. She was going to make spaghetti tonight with her own specialty meatballs. An easy meal, but it always went over well.

Her cell phone rang. Melanie picked it up

off the counter and looked at the number. Was that Adam? She picked up the call.

"Hello?"

"Hi, Mel..." Adam's voice was warm, sweet... For just a moment, it was like the last couple of years had slipped away. Except they hadn't.

"Hi, Adam," she said. "Thanks for getting back to me."

"So how's Tilly?" he asked.

"Not great," Melanie replied. "She's having trouble with Simon again. And she's *here*."

"Simon." Adam's tone darkened. "I don't like that kid."

"Me neither," Melanie agreed. "And I told you this when she was fifteen!"

"You said she was too young to date," Adam countered.

"I also told you that Simon was emotionally manipulative and had a mean streak," she said. "Remember that part?"

"Yeah, yeah...but she really liked him."

"And what Tilly wants, Tilly gets. At least from you."

"She's my little girl." Adam's voice softened. "Come on. She used to play you, too."

"She did not!"

"Remember that Mother's Day card? And you let her go to that sleepover? You think she didn't play you?"

The card with the sparkles and the hearts… Melanie felt a lump rise in her throat. Did he have to take that memory from her, too?

"Mel?" Adam's voice softened. "Look, my point is, we both raised her. She played me, she played you and we both loved her, right? So maybe she came to find you because she misses you."

"I'm not getting that vibe," she countered.

"She's always been a complicated kid," Adam replied. "You know her. I think she's mad at me."

"Why?" Melanie asked.

"For our divorce. For messing up the family," he replied. "I know she acts like a little toughie, but you know her. Remember that time I forgot her piano recital?"

"This isn't the same thing," she replied.

"She called me Adam for a year after that!" Adam said. "I'm just saying, the kid can hold a grudge, and maybe this is—"

"All about you," Melanie supplied.

"So I'm a jerk for suggesting that I might have messed up a lot of things?" Adam asked with a short laugh. "I'm taking some responsibility here, Mel."

"Tilly needs her dad right now," Melanie said, lowering her voice. "Whatever it was that made her decide to come to me, I'm not her solution anymore. You and I are divorced, and your kids are now your sole responsibility."

"And fifteen years of being their mom—" Adam's voice was quiet, sad "—that doesn't mean anything to you anymore?"

"If it meant something to you, maybe you should have stayed faithful," she shot back.

"Hey, I'm not defending myself here. I messed up. I get that! I'm just saying, I'm not even in the country right now, and Tilly went to you. You know her...probably better than I do! You were the one who raised her—Girl Scouts, spelling bees, shopping trips, birthday parties... That was all you, Mel."

"Yeah..." It was a whole lot more complicated than he made it sound. "So who was Tilly supposed to be with while you were gone? Someone's going to be worried sick!"

"I let her stay on her own," he replied.

"What?" She frowned. "You think that was wise?"

"For two weeks. I was letting her take some responsibility."

So much so that Tilly had driven all the way to Mountain Springs. She might look like a grown woman, but she wasn't grown up yet. Her father, of all people, should recognize that.

"I don't know why she's on your doorstep," Adam went on, "but of anyone in this world, I trust you with my little girl. And maybe I shouldn't have left her on her own, but I didn't have you to tell me otherwise, did I?"

"Not anymore, Adam," she confirmed with a sigh.

"Can you just…look out for her for a bit until I get back?"

"How long is that?"

"I'm back on US soil in five days."

"And you'll come get her?" Melanie asked.

"Yes. Mel, you know this kid. She might be full of attitude, but she's the same Tilly."

The same girl who played her father like a violin… What was this, an attempt to get her father's attention? And suddenly, she realized, it didn't matter. She didn't owe Adam anything, but she still cared for this girl, and Tilly needed an adult who loved her right now. Whether she was acting lovable or not.

"Mel?" Adam said.

"Fine," Melanie replied.

"Thank you," Adam said, a smile in his voice. "I feel better already. Really, thank you."

"You're welcome. I expect you to come out here straight from the airport."

"As soon as I can," he said.

Not exactly a confirmation that he'd do as she asked. He'd always been like that—somewhat reassuring but never giving her quite what she needed, either. Melanie said goodbye and ended the call. Tilly wasn't the only one who played her—Adam always had, too.

Melanie didn't want to be buddies with her ex. She didn't want to be on the same team, creating some kind of fictional united front because that's what adults did. She was freshly divorced, and she had the right to take some time to herself while she figured out her life again. She had the right to a little bit of privacy!

And she couldn't even get that much.

Melanie looked up to see Tilly standing in the doorway, and her heart sank. Tilly dropped her gaze.

"That was my dad?" Tilly asked.

"Yeah. He says he'll be back in five days."

Tilly nodded. "Is he mad?"

"That you're here?" Melanie asked. "No, I think he's relieved. At least he knows where you are."

"But you're mad," Tilly said, her tone tinged with bitterness. "I'm not your problem, right?"

"I'm sorry you heard that," Melanie said. "You aren't anyone's problem. You're the girl I raised."

Tilly didn't answer, and Melanie sighed.

"Tilly, why are you here? I mean, really. Because if you had free run of the house for two weeks, I don't see why you'd come out here instead."

"It was Simon," Tilly said, and her chin trembled. "With Dad away, we were going to do a road trip together. And we started driving, and he said some mean and stupid things, and we started fighting, and..."

"But you have the car—"

"It's *my* car," Tilly retorted. "I dropped him off at a bus depot and drove off."

Melanie couldn't help the smile that tugged at her lips. "You kicked him out. I like that. So why come here?"

Maybe Adam was right and Tilly wanted

to feel safe. Was Melanie more of a mom to Tilly than she'd admitted?

Tilly rolled her eyes. "I wanted some time at the lake. My tan needs work."

Apparently, the sharing time was over. Melanie sighed and turned back to the groceries. Tilly's phone pinged again.

"Is that Simon?" Melanie asked.

"Yeah."

"Is he apologizing and begging for your forgiveness?" Melanie asked.

Tilly didn't answer. That meant no, and it didn't surprise her. Simon had never respected Tilly.

"You want some free advice?" Melanie asked. "Turn off your phone and work on your tan. As long as he's getting answers to his texts, he's still in control."

"You're divorced. I'm not sure you're the one to give relationship advice," Tilly said.

Melanie turned back to putting away the groceries. That girl's barbs always were rather well aimed.

Tilly's phone pinged again. She didn't start typing this time, though. From the corner of Melanie's eye, she saw Tilly turn her phone off and tuck it into her back pocket. Taking advice? That would be a first!

"You're worth more than him, you know, Tilly," Melanie said.

Tilly didn't answer, and she walked out of the room, peeling her shirt off as she went, revealing a bikini top underneath.

Five days.

CHAPTER FIVE

LATER THAT EVENING, Melanie dished the steaming marinara sauce into a bowl. It smelled great, if she did say so herself. She'd spent the better part of her adult years perfecting this recipe. Her spaghetti and meatballs were carbs swathed in comfort. And for too many years in her marriage to Adam, she'd needed some comfort of her own.

Outside the kitchen window, the wind ruffled the leaves on the apple tree. The apples were small, dense and green still. She'd never been at the lake house when the apples were ripe, she realized. Adam had paid for a landscape company to come and take care of the property on a regular basis… What had happened to all those apples? Did they just drop and get thrown out?

She'd pick them this year—make apple pies and sauce. That could add to making this place homier…more hers. Food mattered—good, wholesome, tasty food that could make her grateful for the moment she was in and stop thinking about the pain of the past.

There was the rumble of an engine, and Melanie leaned forward for a better view past the gnarled, twisted limbs of that apple tree. Logan's black truck came to a stop, the engine turned off, and she found herself smiling in spite of herself.

"Who's here?" Tilly asked from behind her.

"A friend of mine," Melanie said.

"Who?"

"Logan McTavish. You met him earlier."

"So that's who you were cooking for," Tilly said.

"You know what?" Melanie turned toward the teenager. "I'd have cooked this regardless. I'm worth a decent meal, too."

Maybe Tilly needed a few lessons in how to take care of herself, because Melanie hadn't done nearly enough in that regard over the last few years. It was too easy to get sucked into giving, giving, giving and feeling like a saint because of it. She wished she'd done less of that now. Tilly could have seen an example of a woman who didn't hand herself over for all the wishes and needs of others.

Melanie wiped her hands on a towel and headed for the front door. She pulled it open just as Logan came up the steps. He held a bottle of wine in one hand.

"Hey," he said with a smile. "Something smells good."

"Come in," she said. He handed her the wine and came inside.

Logan had changed his clothes since she'd seen him earlier. He was now in a pair of relaxed charcoal dress pants and a black ribbed T-shirt. They might both be twenty years older, but his physique hadn't lost anything over the years. He was well muscled and his stomach was flat. How had he maintained that? He caught her appraising glance, and she felt her cheeks heat.

Tilly had left the room again, leaving them in relative privacy.

"How did it go today?" she asked, turning back toward the kitchen.

"I found Junior," Logan said, following her. "He's a psychiatrist now."

"Really?" That was hard to picture—little Junior Wilde, the blond-haired kid who used to resent Logan so much.

"He's married with kids, has his own

practice—he's all grown up," Logan confirmed.

"Was it…nice to see him?" she asked hesitantly.

Logan sighed. "Not entirely. He doesn't trust me. He didn't want to part with Harry's address. I guess he figured I'd stress him out. Harry had some strokes, so… I guess he's fragile."

"It's good to see your dad now while you have the chance, though," she said.

"Tell Junior that."

Melanie led the way into the kitchen, and she grabbed a pair of tongs from a drawer and put them on top of the salad. She had the table set already—the same dishes and cutlery that they'd brought here a decade ago—the cast-offs from their regular home. They'd do for now.

"What was the problem between you and Junior?" Melanie asked. "I mean, looking back on it as an adult… What went wrong?"

Logan was silent for a moment. "I was jealous, and he was insecure. I think it's as simple as that. My father met my mom, had a short but passionate romance that resulted in me and they split up. Harry met Dot a couple of years later, got married and they started their own family. Dot and my mom—they never got along. Dot was motherly, sweet, kind, but my mom had the allure, you know? She was smart, feisty and drop-dead gorgeous. So there was always a bit of insecurity for Dot, I think. She had Harry's heart, but Mom…you remember her."

Melanie nodded. "She aged like a movie star."

Logan seemed to have taken after his mother in that respect—chiseled and fit.

"And Mom enjoyed it a bit," he said with a shrug. "Anyway, Harry had to make his wife happy, and after having been married, I understand that. But keeping Dot happy meant prioritizing her and their children over us."

Maybe Mel was more like Dot than she wanted to think, trying to do everything she could to hold her family together. At least Dot had seen the danger, because Melanie hadn't. She'd figured she could trust Adam and that checking up on him was vulgar. She still thought it was. If a man had to be chased down and supervised in order to stay faithful, then he wasn't worth having.

"Did Dot think he'd cheat on her?" Melanie asked, her voice low.

"I don't know…maybe." He met her gaze

and winced. "I'm sorry, Mel. I didn't mean to sound that casual about infidelity. I know you've been through hell with your marriage, and—"

"Maybe I identify with Dot," she said with a faint smile. "The motherly one."

"From where I'm standing, motherly isn't exactly what I'd call you," he said, a smile tickling his lips.

She blushed at that. "I wasn't fishing for compliments."

"You don't need to. You're stunning. I get that you probably need some time to get your feet under you again before you can see that, but you aren't exactly some matronly woman on the sidelines."

That was what Adam had used her for—taking care of his kids while he did whatever he wanted behind her back.

"We aren't supposed to be talking about me," she said. "Your dad wasn't fair to you. You were just as much his child—regardless of who your mom was."

"Yeah, I agree," he replied. "Which is why I was jealous. I got the crumbs off their table, and I knew it."

"Did Junior know it?" she asked.

"How could he not? But Junior was insecure, too. He had our father's love and support, but he always seemed to see me as a threat. I don't know why. He got a whole lot more from Harry than I ever did."

Melanie remembered that. When Logan had been in his senior year, he'd been trying to figure out how to afford college, applying for scholarships, looking for bursaries, anything, really. He'd been smart and he'd gotten a few different scholarships, and those combined with money he'd earned and his mom had saved had been enough to get him started. But she could still remember that forlorn look on his face when he got back from asking his dad if he'd pitch in.

The answer had been no. And she'd recognized then that this wasn't just about money—Harry's no had been to more than cash.

"But now you and Junior are both fathers," she said. "It should be different between you, shouldn't it?"

"Having a son of my own only shows me how little my dad cared for me from the start," Logan said. "You know my biggest fear? Losing my relationship with my son. It would crush me. My dad didn't care about that with me."

But he had cared about that relationship with Junior—that was between the lines.

"Maybe having kids of his own has given Junior a bit of perspective into what it must have been like for you," she said.

Logan shrugged. "I'm not going to hold my breath. Most people don't change that much."

Mel looked toward the table…she'd set three places. She had her own complicated relationship with her stepdaughter. Would Tilly be messed up by all of this? Would she end up being a forty-year-old telling someone the story of her disinterested father and the stepmom who failed her?

"I'll see if Tilly wants to eat with us," Melanie said. "I hope you don't mind."

"Of course," Logan said. "She needs to eat, too."

Melanie shot him a grateful smile. As she headed toward the bedrooms, she heard a sound coming from the bathroom—vomiting. Melanie winced, then came to the bathroom door. She tapped on it and leaned against the jamb.

"Tilly?" she repeated. "You okay in there?"

Tilly vomited again, then there was a flush. Was she sick, or was this the beginning of an eating disorder? Melanie was worrying like a mom again.

The door opened and Melanie stepped back. Tilly looked pale and haggard. The smell of sick lingered around her.

"Do you have the flu?" Melanie asked.

"I need to lie down," Tilly said. "My stomach is upset."

Melanie reached out and touched her forehead, checking for a fever. It was instinctive—the need to check the body temperature. Tilly pulled away.

"Leave me alone." Tilly teetered toward her bedroom.

There had been no fever. It was possible she had a stomach bug, but it was also possible that Tilly was exercising control over one thing she could—her weight. If Melanie were still married to Adam, she'd be the one handling this—asking questions, looking for signs of bulimia, encouraging Tilly to talk.

Tilly disappeared into her bedroom and the door shut with a decisive click. Music turned on—the message clear. She didn't want Melanie's help.

Mel headed back toward the kitchen. Logan sat at the table, the wine open and two glasses, half-filled, sitting on the table. He raised his eyebrows.

"She's not feeling well," Melanie said. "I guess it's just the two of us."

He didn't answer, but he did rise to his feet in a polite gesture until she'd sat down on the chair opposite him at the table.

"You're different," she said with a smile. "I know you say that things don't change, but you certainly have."

"Yeah?" A smile turned up one side of his lips. "How so?"

"You're so mannerly. You're downright civilized," she said with a low laugh. "I've heard marriage will do that to a guy when he isn't looking."

It was one of the things she'd liked about Adam. He knew how to live with a woman already—pick up his socks, remember important dates. But he knew how to hide things from a woman, too.

Logan lifted his wineglass. "To being house-trained."

"To being house-trained." She laughed and lifted her glass in response.

Twenty-three years had changed more than Logan thought. In both of them. Because she wasn't the same girl she'd been all those years ago, either. Marriage might have civilized Logan, but it had opened Melanie's eyes to just how vulnerable a woman's heart could be. She'd lost more than a husband in her divorce. She'd lost her family and her ability to blithely trust a man to do right by her.

LOGAN SERVED HIMSELF some pasta while Melanie dished up salad, and then they switched serving dishes, her fingers lingering under his while they got their grip.

He had missed Melanie, he realized. It wasn't like he'd spent twenty years missing her, because he'd been devoted to his own family. There had been no lingering longing there—he'd been true to Caroline in every sense. But seeing Melanie again reminded him of the way he used to feel around her—alive, vibrant, able to conquer the world. And maybe it had been a hearty dose of youthfulness that made him feel that way in high school, but seeing her again seemed to reawaken it. He felt like he could face things again. And looking her in the face, seeing that spattering of faint freckles over her nose, the way her brown eyes glowed with warmth when she smiled… She made him feel things—soft, gooey things that he probably had no right to feel anymore.

Logan took a sip of wine. It was oddly comfortable in her little kitchen. No pretenses, a ticked off teen in the other room… This was familiar territory for him, and he shot her a smile.

"Thanks for inviting me over," he said.

"I was afraid of facing an evening with her," Melanie said with a low laugh. "I mean, I could tell you something more appealing than that, but that girl intimidates me."

"She shouldn't," he said. "You're a successful woman. You've got to remember being her age—the power of youth."

"I do. But when I was seventeen, I was dating you," she countered with a small smile.

"That's true… And you were just as intimidating. She's got nothing on you."

Melanie smiled at that. "I wasn't quite so spoiled."

He took a bite of spaghetti. It was perfectly cooked—just a little al dente and the sauce had a bit of spice to it that was a surprise.

"Mmm…" he murmured past the food in his mouth. "This is really good."

"Thanks. It's my specialty."

"Do you know why Tilly's here yet?" he asked.

Melanie shrugged. "She dumped her boyfriend mid–road trip, and decided to come here."

"Like she kicked him out of the car?" he asked with a frown.

"You have to understand Simon." Melanie swirled noodles around her fork and took a bite. She swallowed before she continued. "She's been on and off with him for a couple of years. He's demanding, mean and emotionally manipulative." She started twirling the noodles around her fork again on her plate, and he ate in silence as he listened. "I've never liked him, but forbidding her from seeing him didn't work. I tried—trust me. It only drove them together. He made her feel like she was the lucky one to be with him, instead of the other way around. He talked down to her, ignored her until it was convenient, and was a generally terrible boyfriend. So if he crossed a line and she finally took a stand, I'm glad."

"Is there some forlorn teenaged boy wandering down a highway somewhere?" he asked, his own fork held aloft over his plate.

Melanie laughed at that. "She dropped him

off at a bus depot. He'll be okay. Besides, I know his parents. They'd come get him. I highly doubt he'd actually get onto a bus. Simon is a very self-entitled kid."

"She has style." Logan took a bite and chewed for a moment. "She shouldn't put up with that. Graham dated a girl I really didn't approve of when he was the same age. She was just…mean. She'd insult him and embarrass him in public. I didn't know why he put up with it."

"He's not still with her, is he?" she asked.

"No…" Logan shrugged. "He figured it out on his own and broke up with her. I was so relieved. I didn't want him going through life being treated like that. He's a good kid—a good young man. He's kind and smart and…deserves better."

"Exactly," she replied. "Tilly might be a handful, but she deserves more than Simon offers, I can tell you that."

"What does her dad think?" Logan asked.

Melanie shrugged. "He's never liked Simon much, but he and Simon's father are connected professionally, so…"

"So he's okay with it?" Logan asked.

"No." Melanie shook her head. "He gave her whatever she wanted, and that was

Simon. But on a deeper level, he wanted to let his daughter figure it out on her own. Like you did with Graham, I guess. I see the wisdom there."

"I get it," he agreed, and for a moment, they fell silent. "This is surreal, the two of us discussing raising teenagers."

"Isn't it?" Her smile slipped. "I'm not raising her anymore, though."

"So what happened there?" he asked. "What's the story with your ex?"

"Adam," she said. "I met him when I was twenty-three. I was working as an interior design assistant, and he was older, more mature, and wanted commitment pretty quickly. It was a real change from the guys my age I'd been casually dating. And I fell in love."

"I get that." He'd been one of the guys who hadn't wanted commitment. Caroline had had other plans for him, and the memory still made him smile.

"So I became a stepmom to a toddler, a first grader and a fifth grader, all at once," she said. "It was a huge leap, but I thought I was ready for it. Adam was like…a fairy tale, I guess. He was wealthy, smart, attentive. I thought I'd met my guy."

"So you raised his kids," he said. "You didn't have any of your own?"

"He had three children," she said with a faint lift of her shoulders. "And Tilly was still pretty small. She was this tiny little girl with pale blond hair. She was stick thin, and still in a diaper. And she needed so much love. For the first year, she clung to me constantly and could only fall asleep if I rocked her. I thought I'd have my own children later, but then Adam and I talked about it, and we really thought that three was enough. Besides, they'd lost their mother to cancer, and they needed me."

"So you raised Adam's kids, kept his home together and then got cheated on," he said.

"That sums it up." She sighed. "I thought he was my forever. And a good relationship requires some give and take, right?"

"It also requires fidelity," he said.

She smiled ruefully at that. "Thank you. I agree with you, there."

He remembered how Graham's birth had changed him. He'd gone from being someone's boyfriend, someone's son, someone's employee to becoming someone's father—he was the one responsible for giving this tiny person a good life, stability, love and guidance. Becoming a dad had turned his heart inside out.

"Do you regret it now—not having a child of your own?" he asked.

"I keep getting asked that, and I don't know..." Her voice was soft. "Maybe. But then, Adam and I would be battling over custody. It wouldn't make the divorce any easier. Though it might be nice to have a child who still loves me."

"You've got a teenager in your home, using up your space, your food, your emotional energy... I gotta say, Mel, you aren't quite so alone as you feel right now."

She smiled at that. "That girl hates me."

"Graham has hated me at times."

"Like when?" She looked up.

"Like when I took away the car keys for a month the time he came home three hours past curfew when he was sixteen," he replied. "And the time when he was fourteen, when I told his friends he wasn't a badass-mother-anything, and made him come home with me. I mean, every time he acted up and I put my foot down. That's parenting. We aren't their friends. We raise them. It's pretty thankless."

"It's feeling thankless," she agreed.

"She dumped her boyfriend, and she came to you. That says something."

Melanie looked over her shoulder toward the hallway, then smiled wanly. "She used to love me, you know. Back when she was little. She used to crawl into my lap and snuggle. And she used to insist that I tuck her into bed a particular way and read her the same story over and over again... Then she got older and figured out I was nothing more than a stepmom, and I didn't actually count."

"Nah, she found out she had some power," he said. "They discover that they're capable of hurting an adult, and they get drunk with it."

"You make it all sound so simple," she said.

There was movement in the doorway, and Logan looked up to see Tilly standing there. Her hair was pulled back into a ponytail, and she looked pale.

"That smells good," she said.

Melanie turned around. "You hungry? Come eat with us."

"I'll just take some to my room," Tilly replied, and she came to the table, picked up her plate, dished herself up a heaping pile of spaghetti. She dropped three meatballs on top and grabbed a fork.

Tilly didn't look at him, and Logan didn't say anything. When the girl had retreated again, Logan shrugged.

"See?" he said.

Melanie shook her head. "I get what you're saying, Logan, and I appreciate it, but this isn't going to last. Her dad is going to come get her, and I'll fade very quickly into the background. I'm not deluding myself here."

She knew her situation better than he did. He suddenly felt bad for making assumptions. Who was he, anyway—just a guy who happened to have raised a son. That didn't make him any expert on raising girls, or on marriage.

"Okay…" he said. "I'm sorry."

He just hated the thought of her being alone after all this time. After all she'd given. She deserved better, too.

"I made choices, and this is the fallout," Melanie replied. "That's life."

Melanie raised her gaze to meet his, then she reached for his empty plate.

"Let me help clean up," he said. He gathered up the plates and headed for the sink. He rinsed them off and stacked them on the counter. He felt her touch on his elbow and he turned. She was closer than he'd anticipated. She looked mildly surprised, too, looking up at him, her lips parted.

"Oh..." she breathed, but she didn't move.

"Sorry." Logan should have stepped back. But he couldn't bring himself to do it. A wave of longing swept over him. She was beautiful in a deeper way than she'd been before. Years only seemed to make people more of what they already were—and she only glowed more than ever before.

"You know how we're talking about what the kids deserve?" he said quietly. "You deserved a whole lot better than you got, too."

And so had Caroline. She'd deserved a guy who could have made her feel grateful to live with him. Instead, she'd been stuck with him. Some guys cheated and deserved what they got. Other guys, like him, messed things up in smaller ways—but the result was the same for the women who'd loved them.

"I left him, didn't I?" she said quietly.

"Yeah. You've got some style, too. I'm glad you did."

"Why?" There was a teasing gleam in her eye.

"Maybe I'm enjoying this. I couldn't flirt with a married woman."

She dropped her gaze and stepped back, her cheeks pinking slightly. "You left me, Logan."

Her words stabbed beneath whatever armor he still had up, and he winced. So maybe she saw it earlier than Caroline had.

"I'm really sorry about that," he said. "I was an idiot. I don't know what to say. Even if we weren't going to work, you deserved a proper discussion about it. You deserved to cry, or smack me, or whatever… I was too much of a coward to face it."

"I know, and life went on," she said with a shrug. "But I'm fragile right now, too. So maybe you could…not use your charms on me, if you wouldn't mind."

"I wasn't trying anything, Mel," he said quietly.

"Okay. I just thought I should say what I was thinking."

"You think I'm charming?" he asked, a smile tickling at his lips.

"Oh, shut up." She laughed, though, and the heaviness of the moment broke.

Fair enough. She'd made herself clear, and he wasn't really looking for a relationship, anyway. But there was something about being with her that made this whole visit back to Mountain Springs easier…and a whole lot sweeter.

"I do have one favor to ask, though," he said.

"Yeah?" Those warm eyes met his again, and he felt his pulse jump in response. She could still do that to him…

"I think we're friends again," he said. "Granted, I'm a charming friend, but… friends nonetheless, right?"

"I think so," she agreed.

"The thing is, I don't want to visit my dad for the first time alone. I just… It's going to be awkward, and I imagine we'll both be on better behavior with a witness present."

Melanie chuckled. "A witness, huh?"

"Will you come with me?" he asked. "As a friend. You even get to see me at my least charming. It might be helpful."

Melanie smiled, then rolled her eyes. "Sure."

"Thank you."

He'd meant to take a look at the lake, but he wanted a bit more time alone with Mel. And that wasn't safe right now. He looked down at Melanie with her soft brown hair and those warm eyes that asked for nothing but still seemed to tug him in.

"Why don't I come pick you up in the morning about ten?" he asked.

"Sure."

"And I should probably head out…"

Her smile faltered, and he felt a surge of regret. "It's not that I don't want to stay, it's just…" He knew how this looked—like she'd put him in his place, and he didn't want to stay if all he'd get was conversation. But it wasn't like that. He was wanting to stay a little bit too much. This was the first time since his wife's death that he was feeling attraction for another woman, and he wasn't ready to feel this, even if it was one-sided.

There was movement in the doorway again and he looked over to see Tilly holding her empty plate. She wore a loose T-shirt now and a pair of shorts. She looked younger than seventeen. Just a kid… Tilly glanced between them skeptically.

"I should head out," he repeated.

"I guess I'll see you in the morning, then," Melanie replied.

Logan smiled. "Yeah." He glanced toward the sullen teenager again. "See you later, Tilly."

Logan needed to get back to the lodge where he could sit by the lake alone and get his head on straight. Because tomorrow, if all went well, he'd be coming face-to-face with his father. He was here for Harry, not for Mel…even if she was the much more pleasant of the two.

CHAPTER SIX

MELANIE SAT ON the deck the next morning watching the mist swirl over the lake. Her laptop was open on a deck chair next to her, and she'd been perusing the design classes that were offered online from a Denver college. She'd have to start at the bottom—and she was beginning to suspect that a few classes weren't going to cut it. She'd probably need to update her diploma in order to make sure she had a solid foundation.

Melanie flicked over to another tab, a different college with a slightly different offering. She reached for her mug of black coffee and hitched her sweater up a little higher over her shoulders. This would be a hot summer day in just a few hours, but right now, with the sparkle of morning light playing across the mist, the air was chilly. Melanie pressed her bare toes against the cool wood of the deck. She'd been texting with her mother last night, after Logan had left, and her mother was of the firm opinion that Tilly needed to be packed off to an actual blood relative ASAP. It made sense…except, Melanie had agreed to let her stay.

Was she a glutton for punishment?

Melanie's parents held a grudge against Adam for having cheated on her and broken her heart, and that was only natural. They'd been Tilly's grandparents, too, until the divorce, though they hadn't seen much of the kids. Adam's side of the family and their late mother's parents had been upper crust, and Sheila and Steve Banks just couldn't compete. They'd felt…unneeded.

And maybe that was Melanie's fault, too, because it had taken a while before she'd found her footing in her new family, and she'd never really insisted on making sure her parents were included with the kids.

Melanie heard a clatter from the kitchen through the open screen door, and she pushed herself to her feet. Had Tilly's cooking improved in the last year? She took another sip of coffee as she headed back inside, pushing aside the stone frog that had been propping open the door so the screen could swing shut behind her.

Tilly had pulled out a bowl and some cereal and was rummaging through the fridge when Melanie came into the kitchen.

"What are you looking for?" Melanie asked.

"My cashew milk."

"I don't buy it for myself, Tilly," Melanie said. "And I forgot when I went to the store yesterday. Can't you just have regular milk?"

There were no allergies—Melanie knew that much.

"I'll have something else, then," Tilly said. "But you need to pick up cashew milk."

"*You* can pick up some cashew milk," Melanie replied. "I won't be drinking it."

Tilly cast her a mildly perplexed look. "Dad can pay you back."

"It's not about the money."

Tilly swallowed, and her lips turned pale. She put a hand over her stomach and hurried toward the hallway.

That was honest-to-goodness nausea, if Melanie had ever seen it. Great…so it looked like Tilly had the stomach flu. She grimaced as she heard the sound of vomiting from the bathroom, and she waited until it stopped, the toilet flushed, the water ran and Tilly came back out.

"You need to go lie down," Melanie said. "You're sick."

"No, I'm not. I'm fine," Tilly muttered. "I'm actually hungry."

"It's only going to come back up!" Melanie said. "Do you want to lie on the couch and watch TV?"

Tears welled in Tilly's eyes, and she shook her head. "Why does no one listen to me?"

"Because you just threw up for the second time!" Melanie said with a low laugh. "Come on, Tilly. Are you so bent on proving me wrong that you won't even go rest?"

"I'm not sick!" Tilly's voice rose. "I'm pregnant!"

Silence descended upon the kitchen and Melanie stared at her in shock.

"What?" she breathed.

"I'm pregnant." Tilly took a step back. "Are you going to tell my dad?"

Melanie shook her head. "Who's the father? Simon?"

"Yeah. Who else?"

Simon…cruel, immature, manipulative Simon… It couldn't be worse.

"When did you find out?" Melanie asked.

"A month ago."

"So you're what…two? Three months along?" Melanie asked hesitantly.

"I don't know," Tilly replied. "Doesn't a doctor tell you that?"

"Haven't you been to a doctor yet?" Melanie asked.

"I only just told Simon!" she snapped. "I haven't had time! I'm busy. I'm…" Tears welled in her eyes again, and Melanie sighed. The girl was scared. Tilly wasn't mature enough to buy her own choice of milk, and she was pregnant…

"Come sit down," Melanie said. "Let's talk."

"There's nothing to talk about," Tilly retorted. "I'm pregnant, and it's my business. Okay?"

"Is this what you and Simon have been fighting about?" Melanie asked.

Tilly didn't answer, which was confirmation. Then she said, "I want to have this baby. It's mine. Simon can do whatever he wants."

"Actually, Simon needs to financially support his child," Melanie replied. "I don't care what he wants, he fathered that baby and he has a responsibility."

"And that is why I didn't say anything!" Tilly said, shaking her head. "That!"

"What?" Melanie demanded. "I'm on your side!"

"What if I don't want to share my baby with him?" Tilly asked, her voice shaking. "What if I just want him to go away, and I'm fine with that?"

"Tilly, he's going to be a father just as much as you're going to be a mother," Melanie said.

"What would you know about that?" Tilly snapped. "You don't have any kids. You aren't even a mom! You have no idea what any of this feels like!"

Melanie felt the words like a punch. She'd never experienced a pregnancy, that was true. But she'd known what it was to worry about, to love three kids more than she loved herself. And she sure knew how much raising those kids cost! It wasn't only a financial hit, either. It was emotional, spiritual… And whether Tilly liked it or not, that baby was going to grow up one day and ask about its father.

"I raised you, Tilly…" Melanie said past the lump in her throat.

"Whatever…" Tilly shook her head. "But you have no idea what it's like to be pregnant, so don't act like you know!"

Tilly headed back down the hallway and her bedroom door slammed. And Melanie stood there, trying to put a cap on the tears rising inside of her.

You aren't even a mom! Those were the words that hurt the most. And maybe Tilly was right... She didn't know what this stage felt like, but she did know what it felt like to be excluded from it. She remembered being asked once by a young pregnant woman in a kids' clothing store if she should be afraid of the delivery, and Melanie had been tired of telling her complicated story. She was tired of the exaggerated sympathy. *That poor little thing. Losing her mommy. Aw.* So Melanie had faked an answer—something about how she'd forget the pain afterward, and how it was all worth it in the end. She'd even reached out and squeezed the young woman's hand, then fled.

Melanie definitely knew what it was to feel like an impostor.

She put her hands flat on the counter and let out a slow shaky breath.

Don't cry. Don't let that girl see you cry...

Melanie looked around the kitchen, then headed to the freezer and pulled out some frozen waffles. Tilly liked these, too. And if she was pregnant, she needed to be eating. Melanie dropped two in the toaster, then pulled out the glass jar of blueberry syrup.

"Tilly?" she called once breakfast was ready, her voice sounding stronger than she felt right now. "I've got some waffles here. You'd better eat."

Because being a mother also meant putting her own complicated emotions aside for the needs of the child in her care. It meant swallowing her own grief and womaning up when she was needed.

Tilly would also need a doctor's appointment and some prenatal vitamins. Melanie might not have been pregnant before, but she knew that much. And she'd need rest, too, and lowered stress in her life. She'd need to be taken care of a little bit.

The bedroom door opened and Tilly came out, her eyes puffy from crying.

"Blueberry syrup," Melanie said, lifting the bottle. "Your favorite."

Mel's favorite, too, for that matter. But Tilly wasn't going to care about that.

"Thanks," Tilly murmured, slipping into the chair. "I'm pretty hungry."

"No problem."

Melanie's phone pinged, and she picked it up to see a text from Angelina.

Would you all be free for an impromptu Second Chance Club dinner tomorrow night?

Melanie smiled sadly. It was good to have some women in her corner—whom she could open up with a little bit. Because standing here with her stepdaughter only reminded her that being a mom of any kind also meant doing the work without a whole lot of thanks or appreciation. Tilly would learn that, too.

LOGAN PULLED INTO Melanie's driveway at ten o'clock on the dot. The glossy wooden box was on the back seat. He'd held that box for a long time last night, listening to the strange rattle of the objects inside. He might never have come to deliver this box if it weren't for Caroline's diaries. But here he was, hoping that doing right by his late mother would count as doing right by Caroline, too.

Logan had been looking forward to seeing Melanie. But would this visit with his dad really be easier with an audience? If she really did think he was charming, she'd definitely lose that misconception right quick. He wasn't charming—he was normally pretty matter-of-fact. Still, she'd always made him feel like he was more than the sum of his parts.

The front door opened just as he came to a stop, and Melanie appeared without missing a beat. She wore a simple sheath dress of pale yellow with a gauzy white scarf thrown around her neck. She wore a pair of leather strappy sandals and a brown leather purse that matched. She looked good—put together, successful. But when she looked up and he saw her blotchy face and puffy eyes, his heart stuttered.

Had she been crying?

He leaned over to give the passenger-side door a push. She hoisted herself up, a waft of fragrance coming into the cab with her.

"You okay?" he asked.

Melanie put on her seat belt. "Fine. How are you?"

"You're a miserable liar," he said, putting the truck into Reverse and backing out of the drive again. "What's going on?"

"Just a tough morning," she said with a wan smile.

"Were you crying?"

"Yeah—" She shook her head. "It's private. For Tilly, I mean. It's her personal business."

"Are you okay?" he asked.

Her eyes misted again and her chin trembled. "Can I trust you with this—trust you to keep this private for her sake?"

"Of course. My lips are sealed. What's going on?" he asked.

"It turns out Tilly isn't sick. She's pregnant."

"She's what?" Logan shot her a surprised look.

"I know," she replied. "I was stunned. So that explains why she's here. She needs help."

"Is it okay that I'm taking you away from her?" Logan asked.

"I didn't say she wanted help," Melanie said. "And she's fine. She has some morning sickness, and I have the cupboards stocked with food if she wants to eat. There's nothing else I can do but stand there and irritate her." Melanie sighed. "The thing is, she says she wants to raise this baby alone, without Simon. And I don't think she gets how complicated this will be."

"You think Simon will want to be in his child's life?" Logan asked.

"I'm not sure about him, but I know his

parents are going to care. This will be their first grandchild. And we're talking about two rather wealthy families. They can both afford the best lawyers."

"You think it would get ugly?" Logan asked.

"It might. It might not. I don't know. But I feel for her."

Logan fell silent for a moment. Caroline had gotten unexpectedly pregnant, too. And he'd stepped up—a baby changed things. But it shouldn't take a baby to make a man. He should have been better before Graham came along…and after, too.

"So what did you tell her?" Logan asked.

"Just that she'll need to see a doctor, get on some vitamins, that sort of thing."

"How come you were crying?" he asked.

Melanie didn't answer, and when he looked over at her, he saw her dabbing at her eyes. He put his attention back on the road, but he could feel her hesitation next to him.

"Come on," he said quietly. "What happened?"

"She pointed out that I've never been pregnant, and I have no idea what any of this feels like," she said quietly.

"And therefore you shouldn't give her

some reasonable advice about taking care of herself in this delicate time?" he asked ruefully.

"Something like that."

"Did you put her in her place?" he asked.

"No, I made her some toaster waffles and got her to eat."

"Like a mom," he said. "When Graham was about sixteen, his mom caught him getting hot and heavy with his girlfriend. She interrupted them and asked Graham to drive the girl home. We had no intention of becoming grandparents too early." He smiled sadly at the memory. "And Graham got home from dropping her off, embarrassed and angry, and he told Caroline he hated her..."

He could still remember the way the words had landed, like they physically sank into his wife's body... Her shoulders had hunched, and she'd taken an involuntary step back.

"What did she do?" Melanie asked softly.

"She let him march past her and go up to his bedroom, and then she cried," he said with a weak shrug. "Just cried."

Caroline's face had crumpled. No one loved that kid like his mom had.

Melanie's eyes misted. "I get it."

"Being a mom hurts, sometimes," he said.

"Graham didn't mean it. Not really. He was just mad and embarrassed and…sixteen."

"So what did *you* do?" she asked.

"I went upstairs and brought him back down. First, I made him apologize to his mother, and then I sat him down with a calculator and a piece of paper and I outlined how much raising a baby cost—whether he was still with the mother, or not. It was a pretty big reality check for him."

"I'll bet…"

"Obviously, if he had gotten his girlfriend pregnant, we would have been in his corner. We would have helped him step up and grow up, and be the man he needed to be for his child. Neither he nor the girl were ready for that kind of responsibility. So we did what we thought was right, and we parented."

"I think you were right, too."

"All the same, Graham didn't forgive his mother for a couple of months. He and the girl ended up breaking up. I think my talk with him about some real-life consequences put a damper on things between them. But you know what? We were right. Caroline was right. And sometimes when you're right, your kid hates you for a little while."

Melanie smiled faintly. "She doesn't think I count."

"She's wrong." He shrugged. "Can't be the first time."

Melanie chuckled, and Logan felt a wave of relief. He reached over and took her hand before he could think better of it. He gave her a squeeze and was about to pull back when her fingers closed around his.

"Thanks," she said. "You have a way of making everything seem simpler."

Logan looked over at her and saw her gaze was turned out the window. Her hand looked good in his—her fingers slim and pale against his tanned skin. It was nice to be someone's comfort again. It had been a while.

"So where are we headed?" she asked, glancing toward him again.

"Spruce Ridge Retirement Home," he said.

"Is that new?"

"Seems to be relatively new. I don't remember it from our day."

"Are you ready to see your father again after all this time?" she asked.

Logan let go of her hand as he slowed down to make a turn. He wished he could reach out and take her hand again, but she'd pulled hers back and it didn't feel right now.

"I don't know..." he admitted. "I learned a lot in raising my son, and I never could make sense of my dad's choices when it came to me. I would have done anything for Graham. But my father saw me as an embarrassment. My mom tried to find common ground between us, but the harder she tried on my behalf, the more resentful his wife got. It was a weird situation."

"Yeah..."

"She used to tell me not to blame myself for someone else's insecure marriage, but when you're young, it's hard not to blame yourself for just about everything."

The address he was looking for was ahead—a flat building that looked distinctly medical. He slowed the vehicle, double-checked the address and then turned into the parking lot. He found a spot and parked, then looked over at Melanie.

"Thanks for being here," he said.

"I could stay in the truck, if you want," she said.

"Don't be silly," he said. "But this is going to be awkward. So maybe you could just agree to forgive me for whatever happens—"

Melanie chuckled. "Harry is Harry. I'm not blaming you for your father's eccentricities, okay?"

"That'll have to do," he agreed.

Spruce Ridge Retirement Home had a central reception area flanked by two wings. Several older people sat outside under shade trees in their wheelchairs, some staff members leading them in what appeared to be watercolor painting. He scanned faces—would he even recognize Harry? He wasn't sure he would. Age could change a lot in a man. Maybe more pertinently, would his father recognize him?

Logan held the wooden box under one arm and opened the front door, letting Melanie go in ahead of him. The reception area felt dim after the bright summer sunlight outside, and it took a moment for his eyes to adjust. He headed over to the reception desk.

"Hi," he said. "I'm here to visit one of your residents. My father, actually. His name is Harold Eugene Wilde."

"You're Harry's son?" the woman asked, narrowing her gaze.

"One of them," he agreed. "You're probably thinking of Junior… Eugene."

"Yes," she said. "We know him well.

What's your name? I'll see if Mr. Wilde is free."

"I'm Logan McTavish."

She jotted it down, then picked up a telephone receiver. "Just a moment."

Logan stepped back while she murmured into the phone, glancing around. This retirement facility looked like a decent place—lots of light, lots of activity and responsive, energetic staff. Junior had done his research on the place, no doubt. As Logan's gaze moved over a table filled with older people playing cards, he saw a nurse approach an older man and bend down to speak to him. She gestured in Logan's direction, and the older man raised his head, his piercing gaze locking with Logan's.

Logan's breath caught in his chest. That was Harry, all right. Age hadn't changed him much, after all. His face was the same, but more lined. One eye drooped, as did one side of his mouth, but the mustache was the same—iron gray and bushy. Harry stared at him hard for a moment, then turned back to the nurse and murmured something.

The nurse looked in his direction, and then picked up a phone.

"Mr. Wilde will come outside to speak

with you," the receptionist said. "Just a moment."

Logan was forty-two years old, yet under his father's stare, he was still just an eager twelve-year-old asking his dad to help him with his paper route. *Please, Dad? I'm going to save up for that Nintendo! And Mom's going show me how to budget my money...* He was the seventeen-year-old asking his dad to help him with college. *I can't do it alone, Dad. I've saved all I can, and I've got some scholarships, but...* He was the eight-year-old, watching his father cuddle his newest infant son—the one he'd named after himself.

Damn it. Logan wanted something from his father, after all. He'd told himself that this was about being a better man, about doing right by his mother, about proving something to Caroline, even if it were too late. This wasn't supposed to be about Harry, but Logan wanted the same thing he'd been after all along—his father's love.

And he wasn't going to get it this time, either, was he?

CHAPTER SEVEN

HARRY WASN'T THE only one Melanie had recognized. She knew the nurse who'd been talking to him. That was Renata Spivovitch—one of the women from Angelina's First Wives Circle. Renata recognized Melanie at the same time, fluttering her fingers in a wave as she wheeled the older man over to them.

"I know the nurse," Melanie said.

"Oh, yeah?" Logan nodded and cleared his throat.

"Do you want me to stay with you while you talk to him, or…" She hesitated. "I'm happy to wait if you want a bit of privacy."

Renata wheeled Harry up, and for a moment, father and son simply looked at each other.

"You're getting gray," Harry said at last.

"Yeah." Logan raked his fingers through his hair. "It happens to the best of us."

"If you want to take over for Renata here,

and wheel me outside, it looks pretty warm out," Harry said.

"It's nice out, actually," Logan agreed. He handed the wooden box to his father, who attempted to accept it with one hand. Logan laid it on Harry's lap instead. "I'll explain that in a minute."

He looked over at Melanie.

"I did drag you all the way out here," he said.

She shook her head, waving him on. "Go on. I'm fine."

Logan gave Renata a nod, then wheeled his father toward the doors. Melanie stood back and smiled at Renata.

"How are you doing?" Renata asked. "You look good, by the way."

"Thanks." She'd put in some effort this morning, not that she was going to admit to that. "Is it okay if I just wait for him?"

"You know what, I was supposed to take my coffee break, anyway," Renata said. "Do you want to chat for a few minutes?"

Melanie smiled. "That would be nice. How are the kids? You've got three, right?"

"They're doing a day camp thing just outside of town," Renata said. "They're the camp's problems right now."

Melanie chuckled. "I've got my stepdaughter with me now. She's seventeen."

"Oh?" Renata's eyebrows went up. "Come on—let's head outside. There's a bench I like, and you can see when your friend is done with his father."

Melanie followed Renata outside into the fresh air, her gaze instinctively moving toward Logan where he was pushing his father slowly down the sidewalk. Logan bent closer, presumably to hear something his father said, then he stopped, angled the chair toward some trees and pushed the wheels into the grass.

Once at the bench, Melanie sat down next to the shorter woman and shot her a smile.

"This is a nice spot," she agreed.

"So how is it going with your stepdaughter?" Renata asked. "I guess she didn't side with her dad in the divorce if she's here."

"I thought she had," Melanie admitted. "But she showed up on my doorstep, and—" She glanced over at Renata. Renata was a nurse, and she'd have a better idea of what Tilly needed right now. "Can I ask you something...professionally? As a nurse?"

"Of course," Renata replied. "What's going on?"

"It stays confidential, right?"

"Absolutely."

"She's pregnant. And she's got nausea and vomiting, and I've never been pregnant. I have no advice. She won't see a doctor yet, and—"

"Saltines," Renata said.

"What?"

"Saltines. The crackers. They work. They absorb the extra stomach acid and it helps keep the nausea at bay."

"Oh..." Melanie nodded. "Thank you."

"She'll need prenatal vitamins and a doctor's checkup, too," Renata added.

"Right. I'm going to pick those up for her today, and as for the doctor's appointment, that might have to wait until she gets back to Denver."

"You're in over your head, huh?" Renata asked.

"Feels that way," Melanie admitted. "She's resented me for a few years now for not being her real mom."

Renata was silent for a moment. "I was going to save this until our next Second Chance dinner, but Ivan wants to come back home."

Melanie stared at her. "Didn't he want to move the mistress into your house?"

"Yeah, and she broke up with him a few months back. I guess having him all to herself wasn't the fun she thought it would be." Renata sighed and leaned back, crossing her arms as she looked out over the lush lawn.

"Are you considering it?" Melanie asked.

"I'd be crazy to." Her voice was low.

"But are you?" Melanie pressed.

Renata turned toward her with tears in her eyes. "The kids want their dad to come home. And they're furious with me right now, because I'm the mean one standing between them and a united family. And Ivan—he's using that. He's buying them gifts, telling them he still loves me—"

"Can you trust him again?" Melanie asked helplessly.

"Never." Renata shook her head. "Of course, I can't. He had a mistress that he hid very successfully with a thousand little lies, and then when I found out, he refused to give her up. I'm supposed to trust that man again? He lies better than a politician!"

"Do the kids know what happened—what their father did?" Melanie asked.

"I tried to hide the details. We both did.

But I'm sure they figured out some of it. Especially the older one. What about you—did the stepkids know what caused your divorce?"

"I told them," she said. "But the youngest was sixteen, and the older two were already in college, so..."

"But he's still their father, right?" Renata said. "And they'll idolize him no matter what he does."

"That's the truth... So, what will you do?" Melanie asked.

"I don't know." Renata reached out and patted Melanie's arm. "But just know that even when you're the biological mother, kids can still choose their dad's side."

"Oh, Renata..." Melanie breathed. "I'm sorry."

"Enough about me," Renata said, forcing a smile. "What's happening with *him*?"

Melanie looked over to where Logan stood next to the wheelchair, both men staring out toward the lake, not even looking at each other. Logan was tall, strong, his weight shifted to one foot. He'd always been a good-looking guy...

"Logan?" she asked.

"Logan," Renata chuckled. "Didn't we see him at dinner the other night?"

"Yeah, and he helped me boost my car," she said. As if that was all that happened. He'd woken her up, reminded her that she was still beautiful and her life wasn't quite over yet. But he'd also tipped all of her expectations. She thought she knew what she was doing back here in Mountain Springs, and he was such a welcome distraction from the hard work of starting over…

"So?" Renata shot her a curious look. "Anything happening there? I mean, you're at his father's nursing home, dressed rather nicely—"

"He's an old friend," Melanie replied. "An old boyfriend, but still. We were young enough that it was a lifetime ago. I'm not even sure it counts anymore."

"And the dress?" Renata raised an eyebrow.

"I'm reminding myself that I'm still a woman and I can still look good," she replied.

"So there's no spark, then?" Renata asked with a small teasing smile. "It's too bad, because he's cute."

Melanie smiled at that. "A spark… What

is that, anyway? Do I think he's cute? Of course. Do we flirt a bit? Why shouldn't we? We're both single. But his wife died a couple of years ago, and I'm still reeling from my divorce. I'm not ready to trust a man again—not after Adam. And I'm not willing to toss everything aside for a man again, either. I've done that once and lived to regret it."

"Bad timing," Renata said.

"Bad timing," she agreed.

"Love—the real kind—is so rare, isn't it?" Renata asked softly. "It's fragile and beautiful, and when you're young, you think you'll stumble across it over and over again, like butterflies in a field. But you don't. Something changes inside of you, and you can't see the butterflies anymore. Or they don't come to you..."

"How old are you?" Melanie asked.

"Thirty-six."

"Not exactly over the hill, Renata," Melanie pointed out.

"I'm a mother now, with three kids, an ex-husband and a mortgage. When it comes to the dating scene, I might as well be eighty."

"Well, you look great for your age, then," Melanie chuckled. "So we don't have our youth anymore. That's short-lived, anyway.

You've got something better—maturity, depth, beauty."

"I also have a hearty dose of cynicism," she said with a short laugh.

"Girl, that's just survival at this point," Melanie quipped. "You've got a lot to offer to someone worthy of it."

"I keep trying to remind myself."

"Was it the real thing with Ivan? I know you married him, but you know what I mean. Did you marry the guy who made you feel butterflies?"

"I know you'll laugh at me for saying that, but once upon a time when we were young and he only had eyes for me, it was real then. I wouldn't have married him if it weren't. And I still can't explain what went wrong..."

"Do you want him back? In some deep part of your heart?"

Renata shook her head slowly. "I want to stop missing him. That's what I want."

To stop the pain, the regret, the constant questioning of why one woman couldn't be enough... "Yeah, I get that," Melanie said softly.

"You're lucky you've got a nice distraction over there," Renata said, nodding in Logan's direction, then she glanced down at her watch. "My break is over."

"Thanks for the chat," Melanie said. "I'll see you tomorrow night for dinner, right?"

"Yes, tomorrow. I'll be there with bells on," Renata said with low laugh. "I'll be in better spirits by then, I promise."

And Melanie could see why these dinners were so important. No matter how mature or confident a woman was on her good days, she'd always have the bad days where she felt like a failure, like she had nothing left to offer. So maybe this dinner circle wasn't such a bad idea, after all. Friends who truly understood what divorce was like and wouldn't judge weren't so common.

Logan crossed his arms and looked down at his father. Harry was sitting rigidly. His veined hand trembled as he held Logan's phone in front of him, his watery gaze locked on the screen.

"He doesn't look like our side, does he? He must take after Caroline," Harry said.

Our side. That was the first time that Harry had actually included Logan in the familial language.

"Actually, a lot of people say he looks like me," Logan replied.

"Maybe he takes after your mother, then," Harry said, and handed the phone back. "You never looked much like me, either."

Logan put his phone back into his pocket, and he felt that old anger and protectiveness well up inside of him.

"What does it matter who he looks like?" Logan demanded. "He's my son. He's your grandson."

"It's what people look at," Harry replied.

"Is that why you hated having me around? What people would say?" Logan asked.

Harry shook his head. "That was a long time ago. And I didn't hate having you around."

"It sure seemed that way."

"I had a family, Logan," Harry said. "You know what that's like now."

"I was your family, too, Dad." Logan felt his throat tighten.

"Of course, of course," Harry said, heaving a sigh. "You know what I mean."

Except he didn't. And at this point, Logan didn't even want to ask.

"Dot and your mother had their differences," Harry went on after a moment of silence. "Elise liked to make her feel dowdy. She could be very cruel."

"Mom wasn't mean," Logan said.

"Your mother should have respected my marriage." Harry lifted his gaze, and there was a self-righteous glimmer in his eyes.

"She did," Logan replied. "She didn't want you back. She just wanted me to have a father."

"She might not have wanted me back, but she wanted me to take notice of her," Harry said. "And that hurt Dot deeply. My family with Dot was a choice."

"And I wasn't," Logan said quietly.

"Well, neither was Graham," Harry chuckled.

Logan bit back a retort and he sucked in a breath, looking for some self-control. "Graham was a surprise, yes, but he's also the best thing that ever happened to me."

"And your wife?" Harry asked primly. "Is she in the top five best things, at least?"

"Dad, shut up!" Logan said. "My wife is dead, and I loved her deeply!"

"You did the right thing by her," his father replied. "I'm not trying to be a jerk here. It isn't worth staying together for the children. You need to go find the woman who's right for you, not try and make something permanent that was never meant to be more than a fling."

"I didn't do that!" Logan snapped. "You never even knew my wife! How would you know?"

"I'm talking about myself and your mother," Harry said. "But if the shoe fits..."

Harry still knew how to push his buttons, and he rubbed his hands over his face.

"What's this, anyway?" Harry asked, tapping the box.

"My mother left it for you in the will," Logan said, and he pulled the envelope from his pocket. "This is the key."

"Hmm." Harry couldn't accept the envelope with his bad hand, and Logan tucked it into his father's front shirt pocket.

"I could help you open it," Logan suggested. "I've been curious about what she left you."

"No."

Logan cleared his throat. "Why?"

"It's private," Harry said simply.

Even this—even this memento from Logan's own mother—was something that Harry would hold away from him?

"I don't know why I came," Logan said quietly.

"Because I'm your father," Harry replied. "Even if you don't like it."

And to prove that he was a better man than his wife had thought. But right now he was filled with cruel words that could effectively crush his old father, words he was biting back.

"For what it's worth," Harry went on, his voice trembling slightly. "I think you've become a good man, over all. You're a lot like me, actually."

"How so?" Logan snapped.

"That." His father waggled a finger at him. "That growl in your voice. That's from me."

"And you think I'm a good guy?" Logan wasn't ready to let that pass quite yet.

"Yeah." Harry nodded slowly. "Yeah. I do. You've worked hard. You married the mother of your child. You built something for yourself. By a lot of people's standards, that would be success."

"And by your standards?" Logan asked.

"I'm the one who messed up with your mother," Harry said quietly. "It wasn't your fault."

And that was as close to approval as Logan

had ever gotten from his father. It was also as close to an apology as he'd ever gotten, either.

Their conversation turned toward Junior and his siblings, and Logan didn't attempt to bring it back around to himself again. This was what rejection felt like—a stubborn insistence that he was overreacting. And at seventy-five, his father wasn't about to change his ways. But when he talked about Junior, Harry's whole face lit up with love.

Later, when Logan and Melanie were back in the truck, Melanie asked tentatively, "How was it?"

"I'm not sure, actually," Logan admitted. "We did some general updating of each other. I gave him a brief history of my life since Graham's birth, and he told me what my siblings have been doing."

"Oh… That sounds formal," she said.

"Yeah," he agreed. "I wasn't sure how I'd feel telling him about Mom's death, but you know, Mom is beyond his reach now. His reaction, or lack thereof, can't hurt her."

"He didn't react?" she asked.

"He said he was sorry to hear it," he replied. "And then he talked about Dot dying. I guess it makes sense. Obviously, his wife's passing was a pretty big loss. He did tell me something interesting, though. Dot felt really badly for how she'd ostracized me. She said so when she was in the hospital."

"Wow..." He heard the tremble in her voice, and Logan glanced over to find her dark gaze locked on him. "That's something."

"I guess so. People get honest when they're facing death."

"Did he say why he hadn't done anything to stop it?" she asked. "I mean, he was the one who let her push you out. You were *his* son."

Except Dot hadn't been all bad. She'd been fighting her own battles against his mom—and now that he'd been married, he could recognize that insecurity. And marriages could be complicated, so he wasn't angry with Dot, either. It was just unfortunate that the adults in his life hadn't been able to sort out their own issues sufficiently to be nurturing to him when he needed it most.

But that was a long time ago. Maybe now what he needed was some respect, or some explanation.

"No, but he did say he thought I'd become a good man," Logan replied. "He's never said that before—he's never said he was proud of me. I should be thankful for that."

"What was in the box?" she asked.

"Don't know. Mom left a key in a sealed envelope, and Harry wouldn't open either the box or the envelope in front of me."

Melanie sighed. "Maybe he was afraid of what he'd find."

"I'm curious, though," he admitted. "I have no idea what she left him. I didn't know she was even thinking of him toward the end. She asked me to buy that box, and I was the one who picked it. I didn't realize it was for him."

"Maybe she missed him," Melanie said.

"It would be a waste of heartbreak," he replied bitterly.

"So, is this over, then?" she asked. "You gave him the box. Your mission is complete. Are you headed back to Denver now?"

He smiled ruefully.

"Not quite yet. I'm going to come by again in a few days. Maybe he'll have opened the box and he can let me know what was in there."

If Harry would even tell him. He sensed more than hesitation in his father. He sensed secrecy. There was a lot his father would rather he not know…and maybe he'd been the same with his other kids.

"I'm glad." Melanie smiled then, and he couldn't help but smile back. "So you're in town for a few more days, at least."

"Yup," he agreed. "I pick up my son from the airport on Sunday—so that's as long as I can hold out here, even if my dad decides to open up."

Logan wasn't ready to go, and it wasn't just because of his father. Melanie had proved to be a strange comfort in difficult times, and he didn't want to leave her behind yet, either.

They were approaching town—the other end of which would lead down to the lake—and Melanie nodded toward an upcoming intersection.

"Do you mind if we stop at the grocery store?" she asked.

"Sure." He signaled the turn and started to slow. "What do you need?"

"Saltines," she replied. "Renata says they help with the morning sickness."

For Tilly. He glanced over at her, feeling a wash of warmth. She always had been sweet. Even after Adam's infidelity and the divorce, even after Tilly had put her through the wringer for years, she was doing her best by the girl. Did Tilly know how good she had it? Because he'd experienced a whole lot less goodwill with his own stepmother.

"What?" she asked, catching his lingering gaze.

"You're a nice person, Mel," he said.

"It hasn't gotten me too far," she said.

"You can look yourself in the mirror," he said. "Not everyone can do that..."

Himself included. He used to think he was a good guy, too—a solid husband, a devoted dad. And then his wife's death had blown that self-image apart. Because Caroline had seen him a whole lot differently... His father had said that he was like him, and that stung, because Logan had worked a lifetime to be nothing like his old man. Was that the part of Logan that had disappointed Caroline so much?

When they got back to the lake house, Logan turned off the engine and he looked over at Melanie.

"You want to come in?" she asked.

He did...which wasn't wise to admit, even to himself, but he really did want to go inside and spend more time with her.

"You sure you don't have something better to do?" he asked.

"Not at all," she replied. "If you're only here for a few more days, I suppose we should make the most of it."

At least this wasn't entirely one-sided. He felt a smile tug at his lips.

"You like having me around," he said.

A blush touched her cheeks. "What do you want me to say here?"

"That you like having me around," he said with a short laugh. And he did. In fact, before he went inside with her, he needed to hear that. He couldn't just be some ghost using up her time. She met his gaze and the lines around her eyes crinkled as she smiled.

"Fine, I like having you here," she said. "And it's nice to—get to know you as an adult, I guess. See you all put together."

"Ditto," he murmured. Because she'd been beautiful as a teenager, but she was a stunning woman. There was something about a woman who'd had time to mature and grow as a person. It deepened her beauty in unforeseen ways. But he'd have to make sure whatever he was feeling stopped there.

They got out of the truck and headed to the front door. When they came inside, he spotted Tilly on the couch covered by a light blanket. She was snoring softly.

Melanie shut the door quietly behind them. "I'll give her the crackers and the vitamins when she wakes up."

Logan glanced around, and Melanie gestured to the deck outside the window.

"Do you want to go outside?" she asked.

"Sure."

Melanie deposited the grocery bag and her purse on the counter, and then tiptoed through the living room to the sliding door. He followed her out onto the deck and she shut the door quietly behind them.

The view was breathtaking. The turquoise water sparkled in the midday sunlight, and the mountains rose rocky and jagged all around them. The air was cooler by the glacier chilled water, and overhead he could see one lone circling eagle.

"Do you ever get used to this view?" he asked.

"Nope," she replied. "Not even after all the years of coming out here."

Logan leaned his forearms against the railing, looking down to the rocky beach and the rickety wooden wharf that stretched out into the water. Across the lake, he could see the lodge—the windows shining with reflected sunlight.

"I didn't want to come back," he admitted quietly.

"Me neither." She shot him a smile. "Funny how life works, isn't it?"

Melanie leaned against the railing next to him, and he moved over a couple of inches so that his arm rested against hers. It felt good to be standing this close to her—to just have her next to him.

"You're a good stepmother," he said, looking down at her.

"I'm not so sure about that," she replied. "When Adam and I separated a year ago, I didn't put a lot of effort into staying connected with the kids. I didn't think I had a right to. And the kids made it pretty clear who they chose—"

"But Tilly's here," he reminded her.

"Which only proves I should have tried harder," she admitted. "Tilly turned to Simon and now she's pregnant. How much of that is my fault for not being there for her?"

"You can't beat yourself up," he said.

"Can't I?" She tipped her head onto his shoulder for a moment, her sun-warmed hair smelling like citrus. He closed his eyes, enjoying the sensation of her leaning against him…

"None of us are perfect," he said quietly.

"You seem to be pretty close," she said.

"My wife didn't think so." He hadn't really meant to say so much, but it had come out before he could think better of it.

"You stayed together, though," she countered. "You were both faithful. Why are so you unsure about that?"

"My wife kept diaries," he said, his voice low. "A few weeks ago, I stumbled across a box of them that I'd put aside. I started to read them, thinking it would be nice to relive some of our memories. I read about how she met me, about her pregnancy with our son, about those early days of mothering...about our life together as the years rolled on. And you know what I found out? I was a jerk."

"I don't believe that," Melanie straightened. "I really don't."

"She wrote it all down—every hurtful thing I said, the times I ignored her feelings, the times I took out my frustration from work on her with some biting comment... She wrote it all down."

"Venting, maybe?" Melanie asked.

"Definitely venting, but there were a few times she wrote something like, *I wonder what life would have been like if I hadn't married him.*" His voice grew thick with emotion, and he swallowed hard. "I remembered a life full of love and growth and adventure together. She remembered me being a jerk—hurting her feelings and messing up. I didn't make her happy, Mel. I tried really hard, but I didn't make her happy."

He turned toward her and Melanie looked up at him. Did she know how pretty she looked right now? He lifted his hand and touched her cheek with the back of a finger, and her skin was so soft under his touch that he lingered there.

"I know the feeling..." she whispered. "I didn't make my husband happy, either. I wasn't enough."

"At least you can be angry with him," Logan said. "He was in the wrong. He was a cheater. Caroline was perfectly faithful. And I can't be upset with my dead wife, can I?"

A lump rose in his throat. He'd said it like a rhetorical question, but he actually wanted an answer to that one. Did it make him a monster to be angry with Caroline? If she'd told him straight how she felt, then he could have fixed something. But she never told him.

"You're a good guy, Logan." She touched his chest through his shirt and lingered there.

"My dad said that. I'm not sure it means anything."

"Your dad is a lot of things," she said quietly. "But he was right about that."

"I meant well," he softly. "But I'm not the guy I thought I was."

"Logan—" She met his gaze, but she didn't finish what she was going to say. He felt his reserve begin to crumble. He'd never said any of this aloud before, and he'd expected to see judgment in her eyes. But it wasn't there…

He stepped closer, looking at her pink lips—the lips he remembered from all those years ago… The lips that used to fill his mind and his plans back when Mountain Springs had been his whole life. And then, before he could think better of it, he leaned closer and let his mouth brush against hers. He wasn't sure what he expected—shock, recoil—but her eyes fluttered shut and he leaned closer still, covering her lips with his own. She felt good in his arms—warm, soft, fragrant. She was a relief, an undeserved comfort.

And then she pulled back, her gaze dropping.

"Sorry…" he whispered.

"It's okay." She licked her lips and glanced

toward the window. There wasn't any movement from inside, but he knew what she was worried about. They weren't as private as they felt out here.

"I didn't mean to do that," he said, and he felt a wave of embarrassment… They were both vulnerable, and they were old enough to know better than to toy with these kinds of feelings.

"Me neither." She smiled faintly.

"I guess we still have that spark," he said softly. "There always was something that drew us together, wasn't there?"

She looked away, stepped back. Was it something he'd said?

"It might be getting complicated, Logan."

"I'll cut it out," he said. But he didn't want to cut things off. "I don't want to mess this up again. I'm perfectly capable of being friends with a woman. I promise."

"We've come a long way, haven't we?" she whispered.

"It seems so…" He met her gaze, and he was suddenly very grateful for having met her again. He wouldn't mess this up. "Come for dinner at the lodge tomorrow. It'll be nice and public. Bring Tilly with you. It'll probably be good for both of you to get out, change the dynamic a bit."

"I can't do dinner," she said. "I have plans with Angelina. How about lunch?"

"I could do lunch." He cast her a smile. "I'm not some passionate teenager anymore, Mel. I really can behave myself."

She laughed and shook her head. "I believe you. I'll see you tomorrow."

That kiss was the wrong move, but he'd make it up tomorrow. He wasn't going to be any good at being more than a friend, and he knew it. For the first time in his life he had some confirmation of why—he was Harry Wilde's son, and it seemed that he fell a little too close to the tree.

CHAPTER EIGHT

MELANIE WATCHED AS Logan's truck pulled out of the drive. Her lips still felt warm, and she sucked in a slow breath. It had been a very long time since she'd had a first kiss. It was a long time since she'd felt a man's embrace *like that*.

It was a long time since she'd been kissed by Logan McTavish, but it was different this time. Was she imagining that? What was it about Logan that he could make her heart ache with just the touch of his lips?

Maybe they were both different now. Older, wiser, a little more battered by life. And his kiss hadn't been the enthusiastic kiss of youth, but a softer, deeper kiss filled with a longing that held no demand. Maybe that was the part that tugged at her heart—he wasn't asking anything of her, and yet he wanted to. She could feel it.

"Is he gone?"

Melanie turned to see Tilly sitting up. She

leaned forward slowly—nauseous still, it would seem, and Melanie felt her face heat. How much had Tilly seen? Hopefully not that kiss…

"I got you some saltines," Melanie said, grabbing the box from the counter. "I asked a nurse, and she says they'll help. Just nibble on a few."

She pulled out a tube of crackers and brought it to the couch. Tilly took it wordlessly, and helped herself to a cracker.

"I also got you some prenatal vitamins."

"Ugh. I can't think about swallowing vitamins," Tilly said, nibbling a saltine. "I saw you kiss him."

Melanie blinked at the sudden change of topic, and she felt her cheeks heat.

"We're just friends. That wasn't supposed to happen," Melanie replied.

"I guess you're single now, you can do whatever you want," Tilly said.

Tilly's primness was irritating.

"I have my own life," Melanie agreed. "Your father is moving on, and I'm going to, too. Eventually."

Later. Much later. But it was better to be honest about these things.

"Whatever…" Tilly took a bite of the

cracker. Her phone blipped and she reached for it, then sighed. "Are you going to sell this place?"

"It's a possibility. I'll have to think about it."

"This lake house is special." Tilly looked up at her. "This meant something to us."

"To our family," Melanie said.

"To me and Michael and Viv."

Right—the siblings.

"But you guys spent half the time here upset that you were forced to come," Melanie countered.

"We still came here every summer," Tilly replied. "So, maybe me and Michael and Viv had some attitude, but it was still our childhood. And we hung out here. We grew up here. Now, you're throwing it away."

"I'm not throwing anything away. I'm trying to figure out how to start over, Tilly. I know you're upset—things didn't turn out the way either of us expected, but you've got to appreciate my situation, too. I thought I'd grow old with your father. I thought I'd help plan your wedding one day. I'm not getting any of that. I *have* to start over. I don't actually have a choice here!"

"You left him," Tilly said woodenly.

"It's more complicated than that," Melanie said. "When someone is cheating, they've made a choice, too. It changes things."

Tilly was silent for a moment. "Yeah. I guess I can see that."

"I'm sorry I couldn't stay, Tilly. One day, when you're older, you'll probably understand that better than you do now. But I'm truly, deeply sorry."

Because the family that Tilly had kicked against had also been the family she'd relied on for stability and support. And Adam and Melanie had torn that apart.

"Do you miss my dad?" Tilly asked quietly.

"Yes." There was no point in lying. "I do. I married him because I loved him, and I do miss him. He's not going to stop being a part of my history. You don't erase fifteen years of marriage. I'm heartbroken. I'm not a wife anymore, and I'm not a mom anymore."

He cheated. He lied. He disrespected her. He thought his money made his behavior acceptable. But she hadn't married him for the financial comfort. She hadn't been willing to raise his kids because he was wealthy. She'd loved them all.

"So like, do you regret not having your own baby? Now, I mean. Looking back on it?"

Yes…with every breath, with every fiber of her being, yes! And she only realized now how much she wanted a baby of her own. She'd spent too many years convincing herself that she didn't. But she couldn't tell Tilly that.

"Tilly, it's over. It doesn't really matter anymore. The thing is, it's possible for a guy to be lovable, to be smart, to have many good qualities and to still be completely wrong for you. You might keep that in mind. There is a quote I saw somewhere—don't cling to a mistake just because you spent a long time making it."

"So my dad was a mistake?" Tilly asked stiffly. Not to be derailed, apparently. Melanie was thinking of Simon now, and hoping Tilly would be smart enough to walk away before she wasted fifteen years on the wrong guy, too.

"I don't know… Your father is a fine man in many ways. He's a great father. He's a brilliant businessman. He's a loyal friend, a handsome guy…" She smiled sadly. "Your father has all sorts of good qualities, but in the end he wasn't good for *me*."

"Because of the other women," Tilly clarified.

"Yes," she said. "I think that blindsided us all."

"Not really," Tilly replied.

Melanie blinked. Tilly's reply had been so quick, so flippant. "What?"

Tilly crunched into another cracker. "We all knew he was doing it. He didn't hide it very well."

"You *knew*?" Melanie felt the air seep out of her lungs.

"Of course," Tilly said. "It was going on for years, from before I understood what was happening. There were a few of them that I even met. His secretary—she was extra nice to me, and I saw them kissing in his office. There was that journalist, too, who did the story on our house and the decor and stuff."

"No..." Melanie shook her head.

"Yeah, her, too. Mind you, it was Michael who pointed that one out. I had no idea for her. There were others."

So the kids had talked about it together—pointed out which women their father was cheating on her with...and no one had let her know! Melanie had sacrificed so much for them, devoted her entire life to raising them, done her very best to give them the love and support they needed, and this was how they'd repaid her?

The truth hit her right in the heart. They hadn't told her because she hadn't been their real mom… Or maybe it was their father's treatment of her that solidified that into their minds. She hadn't been worthy of their father's fidelity, so why should she have been worthy of their love and respect?

"You didn't tell me," she said, her voice choked.

"Dad would have been furious," the girl said with a shrug. "Sorry."

Their father who had seldom punished them for anything, who was lenient to a fault…

It wasn't fear of their father. It was their loyalty to him. The *sorry* didn't sound sincere.

Melanie turned back to the kitchen, her heart hammering. These were the children she'd sacrificed for. This was the tiny little blond toddler who had stolen her heart all those years ago…the little mite who needed a mother.

"Melanie, I'm sorry!" Tilly said. "I was a kid! What was I supposed to do?"

And she was right, she'd been a child, an innocent onlooker. Her father had been in the wrong. So maybe Melanie was more upset with herself for being the last one to notice her own husband's infidelity.

"It wasn't your fault, Tilly," she said. "We were adults, and our marriage was our business. That had nothing to do with you."

Melanie headed for the door and went outside. The tears started to fall before she had even pulled the door shut behind her. There were some apples on the ground underneath the tree, and she thought of the pies she wanted to make, the cobblers, the apple sauce…and she didn't have the heart for it anymore. What did it matter?

She'd chosen to put Adam and his children first—for better or for worse—and she'd thought it was the virtuous thing to do. She'd made a *home* for them…and this was the result.

Melanie centered the heel of her shoe over an apple and crushed it, the tangy scent of broken fruit tickling her nose. Then did the same to another apple and another.

Blast it. The kids had *known*.

CHAPTER NINE

LOGAN HAD NABBED a table by a window overlooking the lake. There were some loons swimming on the smooth water, and the sunlight shimmered. A man and woman kayaked closer to shore, their paddles dipping into the turquoise water. Just a couple enjoying a morning together, making memories. It was so easy to take that stuff for granted. He and Caroline had come to the lake that summer they'd helped his mom move out to Denver. A few months later Caroline would get her first cancer diagnosis. She beat that one, but when the cancer came back the second time, she hadn't been able to.

Last night, he'd sat up with his mother's bracelet in his hands, mulling over the past. Mountain Springs hadn't changed a whole lot. Even the family dynamic around here felt pretty similar. Junior was still strangely protective of their father. Logan was still considered the danger to all things civilized. His father was still distant even when he was trying to connect. They were all the same people with the same issues, the same defense reflexes. And somehow, he was still drawn to Melanie in a powerful way. Was it just this town, that feeling of everything being the same, or was it something deeper?

He turned from the window and noticed Melanie come into the dining room, her stepdaughter just behind her. Melanie wore a pair of tan linen pants and a gauzy white top. Her gaze moved around the room, and when she spotted him, she smiled.

His heart skipped a beat, and he smiled back. He had to stop this—he'd only get his heart mangled in the process.

Melanie and Tilly came up to the table and Logan stood up as they chose their seats.

"Hi," he said, shooting Melanie a smile. "How are you doing?"

"Not too badly." She smiled back, and the fine lines around her eyes crinkled. He liked that—evidence of a thousand smiles.

"I'm glad you came, Tilly," he said, turning to the teenager. "Are you hungry?"

"I guess," Tilly replied, and she eyed him with that distrustful scrutiny of teenagers.

"What's with the formality? The standing, and all that?"

She must have come across a few formal manners in her upbringing within a wealthy family. Logan glanced at Melanie, but she didn't blink.

"It's polite," Logan said. "You are ladies, and I'm showing you some respect."

"People don't do that anymore. We aren't in a black-and-white movie," Tilly replied.

"I do it," he said. "And maybe you should expect a few people to show you some old-fashioned manners."

Like that twit she was dating that Melanie had told him about.

Tilly rolled her eyes. "It's ridiculous. But just don't start dancing and singing, and we should be fine."

Logan chuckled. And maybe to her it was nuts, but looking at that blonde girl who looked so much younger than she seemed to think she was, he wondered what she faced out there on her own. How did people treat this girl? Not half well enough, he'd guess. Money didn't always equal respect.

The waiter came by with menus and glasses of water.

"So, Melanie says that you guys vacationed here a lot?" Logan asked. "I grew up in this town. Like Melanie did."

"Right..." Tilly glanced over at Melanie. "She used to tell us that—about her old friends and stuff. Dad used to say that Mel's life was a constant vacation living in a place like this."

"Not exactly a vacation," Logan said. "She worked hard. She got good grades, made extra money working at a Dairy Queen."

"Beside a lake," Tilly said with a smirk. Yeah, this kid had no concept of what regular people lived like. Had Tilly ever worked?

"I lived in a house in town," Melanie said. "There was no lakeside anything for me. Except when I came to the lake in the summer on a day off. More like an afternoon off, because I was busy saving for college."

"Well, there's a lake now," Tilly retorted.

Melanie didn't answer. This sounded like an old conversation. He cast Melanie a sympathetic look and she shrugged.

"But remember how you used to complain about things?" Tilly said, turning to Melanie. "You were all princess and the pea. Remember that? Dad used to tease you so much!"

"About what?" Logan asked, trying to sound casual, but his hackles were up.

"Like...everything. She hated it when we called her Melanie instead of Mom. And she had this thing about Dad not answering her calls. Like, he'd be in a meeting or driving or whatever, and not pick up, and she'd get all offended. And Dad said it was just a pea, and it was proof that she grew up spoiled rotten."

Tilly laughed and turned back to the menu, scanning the page. Melanie's cheeks had gone pink, and she looked away. So that was how she'd been treated in her marriage. And the kids had joined in on needling her. How many meetings could the guy have possibly been in? And how many of those "meetings" had been something else entirely? He felt his anger rise at the very thought. That had been Melanie's life for the last fifteen years. She'd deserved a whole lot better than that.

"I knew Melanie when she was young, and she was far from spoiled," Logan said. "But one thing I always liked about her was that she knew how she wanted to be treated, and she expected nothing less."

Tilly looked up. "Whatever."

The lazy reply was meant to antagonize him, but he'd raised a teenager of his own, so he wasn't easily put off with these things.

"What do you want to order, Mel?" he asked, turning his attention toward her.

"The burgers look good. But so does the baked onion soup," she said. "What about you?"

"I'm going for the chicken pasta," he said. "I've had it. It's really good."

He dropped his gaze to the menu again.

"Any plans to see your father again?" Melanie asked, and he looked up.

"I was considering getting my brother to come with me," he said, then sighed. "Maybe this isn't about just me and my father anymore. Maybe it's more of a family dynamic."

Melanie raised her eyebrows. "I hadn't thought of that."

"We always did have our quirks," Logan said. "But I tried to connect with Dad, and Junior and I avoided each other. Maybe it's time to just be a family. Dad seems to like talking about him, anyway. Maybe it's time for us to connect, just the guys. With no one to answer to."

"I think it's a good idea," she agreed.

He hoped so. The idea had occurred to him last night, and today, watching Melanie and Tilly together, he was struck by how much of their dynamic had involved the whole family. A marriage might start things off, but kids turned a marriage into a family—with all the connection and warmth, as well as the revealing teasing.

Tilly pulled out her phone and started typing. Melanie's gaze turned toward her stepdaughter, and she pursed her lips.

"Not your business, Melanie," Tilly said without even looking up.

"Do you always talk to her like that?" Logan asked.

Tilly glanced up in Logan's direction. "I'm busy. I'm talking to someone. Okay? Give me a break."

"Melanie deserves more respect than that," Logan said, keeping his voice low. "She doesn't have to open her home to you, but she has because she loves you. She deserves to be spoken to with respect." He paused, unsure of how that was going to land. "And so do you, for the record."

Tilly rolled her eyes and dropped her phone back into her lap. "Sorry, Mel. Jeez. He's got a pea under his chair, too."

Tilly's phone rang and she picked it up again, and suddenly her expression changed. From attitude and insolence, there was suddenly a look that could only be described as "little girl."

"It's my dad," she said, picking up the call. She plugged her other ear and stood up. "I'm going to take this."

Logan watched as Tilly made her way out of the dining room, and he looked back at Melanie. She was watching Tilly go, her eyes filled with unnameable emotion.

"I'm glad he's called her," Melanie said after a moment. "She needs her father, not me."

"I wouldn't be so sure about that," he replied. "I mean, I agree that she needs her dad, but you factor in, too."

"Maybe more than I might like," she agreed. "I had a bit of an epiphany last night."

"Oh?"

"She watched her father cheat on me for years—"

"She knew?" he asked with a frown.

"They all did. I only just found that out. But if she spent her formative years watching her stepmother being cheated on and disrespected, then it explains a lot about how the kids saw me. I was never going to be someone to respect. I wasn't worthy of their father's fidelity, and I wasn't going to get their respect, either."

"Does it explain Tilly's choice in boyfriend?" Logan asked softly. That would have messed up more than just Melanie's relationship with them; it would have done some real damage to the children watching that dysfunction up close.

"It very well might," Melanie replied with tears in her eyes. "I was the woman in the house, and I was the example of how women were treated by their husbands. And Tilly adored her father. She thought the sun rose and set with him. He was her example of what a man was supposed to be. Wouldn't it be heartbreaking if she is putting up with Simon's bad behavior because she watched her father cheating on me?"

IT WASN'T THAT Melanie blamed herself, exactly. She hadn't known that Adam was cheating. As far as she knew, he was moody sometimes. Maybe he was less than doting when he got really busy, but he made up for it other times. He always took her somewhere tropical for their anniversary, and other gifting occasions always came with beautiful jewelry and kind words. No relationship was perfect, was it?

The waiter checked in, then retreated since Tilly was away from the table.

"Is it the boyfriend who she was texting with before?" Logan asked.

"Probably," Melanie replied.

But what was she supposed to do? Tilly was old enough to make some bad choices of her own.

"Is that what it was like in your home?" Logan asked. "The teasing, the disrespect..."

"Not always." She shook her head. "Sure, there were times I felt a little picked on, but everyone got their turn for that. And as for Adam, he wasn't like that all the time. But after that many years together, a couple gets a sort of shorthand. You must know what I mean. You don't necessarily keep up with the sweet-talking."

"I guess so," Logan replied. "I did try to keep up with some basic manners, though."

"Well, you seem special in that," she said with a smile.

"And while you might get more comfortable with each other, the stuff Tilly talked about sounded mean to me."

Melanie nodded. "I know."

"I'm sorry it was like that, Mel. You really did deserve a lot better."

"I guess I have a chance for that now," she said, trying to force a smile.

"So what's the plan?" he asked. "Going forward, I mean."

"Tilly asked if I'm going to sell the lake house, and I think I will," she said. "It has a lot of memories attached."

"I get that," he replied.

"And I'll have to figure out how to be Melanie Banks again."

"Is she different now?" Logan asked.

"Melanie Banks is a completely different person than she used to be," Melanie replied with a short laugh. "I've been married. I've been a stepmom. I've felt what it was like to be wealthy, and what it was like to lose it all. I'm not Adam's wife anymore, and the world won't see me in the same way. Life is easier with a wealthy husband, I can tell you that, but it's also cramped."

"I could see that," he replied.

"What about you?" she asked. "Are you different now that you're widowed?"

If he was going to ask her personal questions, he supposed he should answer a few of hers. He took a moment to consider, then he lifted his shoulders. "Yeah. I am."

"But you'll be okay," she said.

"I've survived," he said with a nod.

"I suppose I will, too."

Logan eyed her for a moment. "If you're planning on selling the lake house, would you move to Denver?"

"I'm not sure," she said.

"It would be a great place to start up a home-decor business," he said. "I could use someone to stage some houses in new subdivisions."

"I'm sure you already have someone to do that," she countered.

"Yeah. I'm not that attached to him, though," he replied with a grin.

"I'm not letting you fire someone to make work for me," she said with a laugh. "Besides, I'm not sure I want Denver again. I'm not sure I want Colorado, even. If I'm starting over, maybe I want something more exotic."

She hadn't actually thought about it until just now, but if she was already starting fresh, it was a great time to make all the changes at once. And while she'd been a Colorado girl her whole life, that didn't mean she had to stay one.

"How exotic are we talking?" he asked.

"I don't know," she admitted. "I'm only thinking of it now. Hawaii? New York? Maybe somewhere in Maine?"

"Wow. That would be far." His eyes saddened.

"Why, would you miss me?" she asked.

"Yeah."

His answer was gut-wrenchingly honest, and she paused, her breath in her throat.

"I mean, you don't owe me anything," he said quickly. "We've only just reconnected. It's not like I even expect you to talk to me again after this trip is over."

Like he'd done to her? Did he think she'd just sweep his memory aside that easily?

"Why wouldn't I talk to you?" she asked.

"I'm just saying, sometimes people run into each other again, and it's great to catch up, but that's all it is." His gaze met hers. "But for me, I hadn't realized how much I missed you until I saw you again. So if you fade off into the distance and have some great exotic life, I'm going to miss you. It's just the truth."

"Oh..." She smiled at that. "So...do you want to stay in touch?"

What would that look like? But the thought of Logan in her life...even somewhat distantly...was comforting.

"Yeah. I really do."

Melanie felt the smile come to her lips. "Me, too."

"So... I have permission to give you a call? Chat? That kind of thing?" His voice deepened, and he met her gaze with a look that made her breath catch. Why did looking at him like this always make her think about going further than just a few phone calls? He'd kissed her out on the deck, and suddenly, the memory of his lips on hers came back in a rush.

She nodded. "Yes. I'd like that, too."

"Okay, then," he said. He leaned back in his chair and shot her a warm smile. "And I *will* call."

She felt her arms tingle with goose bumps at the promise in his voice. He was very easy to fall for, this man. But she wouldn't upend her life for a man again. Whatever they'd be to each other, it wouldn't be romantic.

The waiter came by again, and Melanie looked in the direction Tilly had gone, then shrugged. "I think we'll order. My daughter—" She winced. It was hard to stop referring to her that way. "She'll be back in a while. But I think I'll order her the cheese burger and fries. She always likes that. I'll have the same."

Logan placed his order, too, chicken fettuccini, and the waiter left again.

"Just do me a favor," Logan said once they were alone again.

"Sure."

"Keep Denver on the table," he said. "If you came back, I promise I'd give you something new to associate the city with."

"Would you, now?" she said with a low laugh. "Like what?"

"I don't know. Dinners out. Long walks. Someone to talk to. I'd pass your business card around to everyone in the business."

"In exchange for what?" she asked.

"For nothing at all," he replied. "For being there, in Denver, breathing the same air. That's it. I'd love to have you closer."

And suddenly, despite her resolve, Denver sounded a lot more tempting.

"I have to be honest," Melanie said firmly, "I'm not thinking of Denver."

His smile slipped, then he nodded. "Sure.

I mean, of course. I'm sorry to put you in a weird position there."

Tilly came back into the dining room then, saving Melanie from having to answer. Tilly slid into her chair and dropped her phone on the tabletop next to her.

"I ordered for you," Melanie said.

"What did you get me?" Tilly sounded like the old Tilly again—out for a meal with her stepmom.

"A burger and fries."

"That sounds good."

No argument. That was something.

"So how is your dad?" Melanie asked.

"He's fine. He wanted to check in with me," Tilly said. "He says to say hi."

And in so many ways, this could have been a lunch out two years ago—Tilly bored but accommodating, Adam sending her a message through his daughter... She'd thought she was happy back then. Now, she knew she'd settled. She'd accepted what she could get.

"And I told him I'm pregnant," Tilly added. "So you don't have to worry about that anymore."

Melanie exchanged a glance with Logan. It seemed that Tilly was ready to let her secret out if she was talking this openly in front of Logan.

"How did he take it?" Melanie asked.

Tilly shrugged, but tears welled in her eyes. "He's disappointed."

Melanie reached out and put a hand over Tilly's. "He's just surprised. He's going to be fine."

"He's furious at Simon," Tilly said.

"Oh, sweetie, we all are," Melanie said, and Tilly laughed through her tears.

"I guess so," Tilly said.

"It's going to be fine, okay?" Melanie assured her. "This baby is good news, Tilly. Every baby is good news. I promise you that. This baby is going to be loved."

Tilly nodded, and just then, the waiter came up with the platter carrying their meals. If she and Adam had managed to stay together, this would have been their family situation to deal with as a unit.

But it wasn't. Adam would come pick up his daughter, and he'd finally take over. Melanie looked up and saw Logan's eyes on her. He looked sad, too. Nothing was uncomplicated. Twenty-three years had passed, and everyone's hearts had been entangled with other lives, other loves and the children that had made them families.

CHAPTER TEN

The rest of lunch was taken up with Tilly's plans for having her baby. She needed to talk, it seemed, and if she was opening up, Logan didn't want to get in the way. He'd quietly listened as Tilly talked about her worries that Simon wouldn't care about the baby, that she'd be teased in school when her classmates found out about her pregnancy, and how she worried that even her siblings would see her differently now.

And he listened while Melanie calmly and quietly helped put all those fears to rest. She told Tilly that she couldn't control Simon and her true friends would be supportive. Becoming a mother wasn't something to be ashamed of. It was a beautiful rite of passage that not everyone got to experience. Melanie made this massive upheaval in a teenager's life seem downright manageable.

Maybe it was that Melanie knew Tilly so well, or just that Mel was good on this level—compassionate, a deep thinker. Tilly had definitely come to the right doorstep, he realized. And so had he.

What was it about Melanie that drew him in like this? She had enough problems of her own, and he wanted to help her shoulder a few of those, if she'd let him. But he doubted she would. She was trying to start over, and if he knew her at all, she'd do that on her own two feet.

When the meal was over and Logan had paid, they all stood up to leave. Tilly headed toward the door, leaving them alone for a couple of minutes.

"Thank you," Melanie said quietly. "I'm sorry we took over like that—"

"Don't be," he countered. "This is life, isn't it? Maybe we can talk tomorrow."

"For sure. You said you'd call, right?"

"I did say that." It sounded like she wanted him to.

"See you." She met his gaze briefly, then she followed Tilly toward the door.

He watched as Melanie and Tilly headed out of the dining room, and he sucked in a deep breath. His time here was short, and he needed to at least try to connect with his father again. Maybe he was a bit like his father, but here was where he was determined to differ—he was going to sit down and have another talk with his dad, and this time he wasn't going to let the man push his buttons. He'd try to get to know Harry a little. He'd only regret it if he didn't try. And he still thought it was a good idea to include his brother in this. They were a family, after all—even if an unwilling one.

Logan headed up to his room, found the business card his brother had given him, and dialed the cell-phone number scratched on the back. His suite was neat and tidy after the maid had visited. There was a chocolate on his pillow, and Logan ambled over and unwrapped it as the phone rang in his ear. Logan popped the chocolate in his mouth as Junior picked up.

"Hello?" He sounded wooden, empty. Something was wrong.

"Hi. It's Logan. Is this Junior?" He chewed and swallowed. It was a mint chocolate—a high quality one. "Sorry… Eugene."

"Yeah…" There was a sigh. "I was going to call you, and then realized I didn't have your number."

"Oh." That surprised him. "You got my message, then? I was hoping we could go visit Dad together. It might make you feel better to keep an eye on things."

"Yeah, I don't think we can do that," his brother replied, his voice low. "My dad—" Junior swallowed audibly. "He, um, had another stroke this morning. It was a really big one. They took him to emergency by ambulance, but he didn't make it."

Logan rolled the chocolate foil between his fingers, his pulse hammering in his head. His brother's choice of words hadn't escaped him, even in the shock of the moment. *My dad.*

"Wait…he's dead?" he demanded.

"Yeah. He passed away. I was going to get in touch, but—"

"Right." Logan didn't have the energy or the presence of mind to even bother with how hard his brother had tried…or not. "Just like that?"

"He'd had a few smaller strokes before," Junior reminded him, clearing his throat. Logan thought he could hear some sniffling in the background. "So I guess this was always a possibility, but it's a pretty big shock around here."

"Yeah, I'll bet…" A shock for *them*. What about him?

"I went to see him the other day," Logan said. "He talked about you a lot, actually."

"Yeah?" Junior's voice sounded choked.

"He was really proud of you," Logan said. "You, your family, your success—"

"Did you upset him?" Junior asked.

"What?" Logan shook his head. "Are you asking if I'm to blame for his stroke?"

"No, I'm—" Junior cleared his throat. "I'm sorry. I'm obviously really upset and I'm not thinking straight. Why don't you and I get together and talk—tomorrow, maybe? I'm rescheduling my clients for the week, so I'll have the time to sort things out for the funeral and everything."

"Sure, tomorrow," Logan said. "How about around ten? Do you want me to come to your place, or—?"

"I'll come to you," Junior said quickly. "Where are you staying?"

"Mountain Springs Lodge. Right on the lake."

"Okay, I'll be there at ten." Junior's voice firmed. "That will work for me. Thanks for understanding."

"I'm calling from my cell phone, by the way, if you need to reach me."

"Right." But Junior didn't sound like that

was actually helpful. He likely had no plans to include him in the funeral in an official manner. "We'll talk later."

Junior hung up without a goodbye, and Logan stood there, staring at the phone in his hand. He'd wondered what it would feel like to know that his father was gone when he'd first arrived. He hadn't known how that would feel.

And somehow, he still didn't. None of this felt real. It was a strange wash of shock. Harry Wilde, the father who'd never been quite enough, was dead, and the last conversation he'd had with the man had been Harry talking about Junior's career, his wife, his kids…

They still hadn't managed to get past that wall. And while Junior sounded choked up, and had probably shed some tears already, Logan was dry-eyed.

"My dad is dead." He said it aloud, trying out the words on his tongue. It didn't make them feel any more real.

His chest ached, though—the old ache that he used to carry around with him after Caroline passed, and again after his mother's death. This time, he wasn't sure that he even had a right to it.

Because all these years, Logan had stayed away. He could have visited ages ago. He could have dropped himself on his father's doorstep when Graham was a little kid—introduced the boy to his grandfather. He could have brought Caroline with him. He could have come after she died...

But Logan hadn't. He'd been just as guilty in the breakdown of their relationship as Harry had been. They were both grown men. And just like his father, he'd damaged relationships with the people he loved most. He and Harry were the same—patting themselves on the back for being "family men" while they screwed it up.

"My dad is dead," he whispered again, and this time, his voice caught.

MELANIE WORE A midnight blue dress tonight—one that she'd only worn twice in her lifetime, both to charity events back when she'd been married. It was a silky sleeveless dress with a high neck and a slim fitting waist. The hemline was asymmetrical, cut at her knees in the front and longer in the back. It had been expensive when she'd bought it, but worth it. At least she'd thought so at the time.

She enjoyed some laughter and general updating on each other's lives. Belle had met a nice guy, but she wasn't convinced he was nice enough. Angelina had some ideas about renovating the honeymoon suite at the lodge, and Renata's kids were still upset with her for not taking their father back. Gayle had been a stoic support for the rest of them. Life wasn't always easy, but discussing it over a fine dinner seemed to make it all seem more manageable somehow.

When the evening wound down, Renata was the first to leave. She didn't want to leave her kids alone too long, even though the oldest was a certified babysitter. Belle and Gayle left next, and then it was Angelina's turn to yawn.

"I have to work in the morning," Angelina said, "so I've got to get home."

"It's way past my bedtime, too," Melanie admitted. "Thank you for including me in this."

"Thanks for being included." Her friend shot her a smile.

"Good night, Angelina."

As Melanie gathered up her things, she let Angelina go on ahead, and she made her way out of the dining room. There was one other table of guests who were still enjoying dessert and some drinks, but the staff were cleaning up and obviously getting things ready for breakfast the next morning.

Melanie nodded her thanks to their server, who smiled back.

This had been a lovely evening—almost perfect—and as she came out the dining room door, she spotted Logan on his way back into the lodge. She smiled, but when she saw his face, her own smile slipped.

Logan's face was pale and he looked shaken.

"Hi," she said crossing the foyer toward him.

"Hey." He reached out and touched her cheek—his finger lingering against her skin, and he didn't seem to notice the familiar gesture.

"Are you okay?" she asked, reaching up to take his hand in hers. "Our dinner just ended, and…"

"I, um, went down to a little pub for the evening," he said. "I got some news earlier—my dad died."

Melanie stared in shock for a moment. "He's…gone?"

They'd only seen him a couple of days ago.

"My brother let me know. I called to make

plans to visit Harry together, and… Anyways, it was another stroke, they think," Logan said softly.

"I'm so sorry, Logan," she breathed. "You could have called me."

"Nah, I wanted the time to myself, actually." His hand was still in hers, and he gave her fingers a squeeze but didn't let go. "I wouldn't mind the company now, though."

"Of course."

It was late, and there was a hush in the lodge. The last of the people left the dining room and one couple headed into the sitting room, and the others went up the staircase, their voices low.

"Do you want to go out to the lake?" Logan asked.

They headed for the front door together. The wind was cool, but not cold. Logan's body heat emanated against her. He still had her hand in his, and it felt natural to walk like this together. She leaned against him, and he slipped an arm around her shoulders and tucked her against him.

The night was quiet, a sliver of a moon shining on the smooth lake. They followed the trail that led down to the water, and Melanie could hear the soft ripple of the water lapping against the rocky shore.

"You never know when it's going to be too late, do you?" Logan said quietly.

"I suppose not," she agreed.

"I'm going to see my brother in the morning," Logan said, his voice low. "I guess there are funeral plans and all that. I don't think he wants my help with the funeral, exactly, but..."

"You're family," she said.

"Biologically, maybe."

"You did better by Graham," she said. "That's something, isn't it?"

He nodded slowly, and she leaned her head against his shoulder. She felt his arm tighten around her, and he rested his cheek against the top of her head.

"When you look back on your life, I think you want to see that you behaved well," he said quietly. "I'm a little too much like my father, there. I might have done better by Graham, but I didn't do better by Caroline. Or you."

"I'm okay, Logan," she said.

"You are, but I'm still not proud of the guy I was. And when it came to my father, I'm not proud of how I handled things, either. Sometimes all a man has left is his integrity—if anything, my dad's passing has driven that home for me." Logan looked down at her. "I don't mean to dump my stuff on you. You've got your own challenges right now, and I'm sorry if I—"

"Your father died," she interrupted him. "Don't apologize for something like that."

Melanie leaned her back against his chest, facing the rippling lake and the dark wall of mountain as Logan put his arms around her. She felt safe here, warm and secure. She could feel the grief deep inside of him, and she had no words to fix it.

"Do you ever wonder what might have happened if we'd stayed together?" he asked after a moment.

"We'd be different people," she replied.

He was silent.

"You wouldn't have Graham," she added. "And I don't think you really want to trade in the time you had with Caroline."

"My dad said something when I saw him—he thought I'd only married Caroline because she had my baby. He said something about it not being worth it to stay together for the kids."

"He said that?"

"He said he was talking about himself, but..." He swallowed audibly. "He might have been right. I thought I was happy, but Caroline wasn't. Not according to her diaries. She might have married me for the baby, and I was just stupid enough to think that a faithful guy who paid the bills would be enough to make a woman happy."

"It's not a bad start," she replied.

"It wasn't enough," he said. "What if I hadn't done that—gotten married because of Graham? What if... I'd found you before you married Adam?"

Would that have been better than her marriage to Adam? Would she trade in those years with the wrong guy for another man with different issues? It was hard to say. She was a different person, and the last fifteen years had formed her. Just because a man wasn't the right one didn't make the time with him worthless.

"I was pretty angry with you," she said.

"Because I left."

"That, and because you were so impossible to talk to back then. You opened up when you wanted to, and otherwise, you were like a brick wall. You wouldn't share. You wouldn't say what you were feeling—"

"Hey, I told you how I felt about you," he countered.

"You did. In a romantic moment. But a relationship isn't just about romantic moments, it's about all the ordinary time in between, and that's when you shut down. So, yes, I'd loved you deliriously, but you also made it very hard to maintain a relationship."

He was silent for a few beats, and her heart sped up. His father had just died, and here she was telling him that he was a jerk to date? What was wrong with her? She was about to say something—to take it back—when his deep voice broke the stillness.

"Caroline wrote something pretty similar in her diary," he said.

"Logan—"

"Hey, I'm not feeling sorry for myself," he said, and he straightened, pulling away from her. "I'm just seeing myself differently. Maybe that's a good thing."

Some cool wind picked up, whisking down the mountain and across the glacially chilled water. Goose bumps rose up on Melanie's arms and legs, and they headed back up the gravel path to the lodge. Once inside, Logan led the way up the wide carpeted staircase. Some of the doorknobs had Do Not Disturb signs. She should go home—it was late. But somehow, they'd just fallen into step with each other and it felt good to be with him, to have a strong arm to lean against again... Was this loneliness, or something more?

Logan stopped at his door and fished a key out of his pocket. He opened the door and let her step inside first.

The room was neat, but he had a few personal items out—a suitcase sitting on top of a chest of drawers, a pair of shoes by the door and a few shirts hung in the open closet. The bed was neatly made and the patio door was open, a fresh breeze ruffling the curtains.

Logan shut the door and stood there, looking at her, his eyes so full of sadness that it made her tear up in response.

"I'm sorry about what I said," she whispered.

"You were telling the truth."

"I'm still sorry." Because it had hurt him at his most vulnerable, and even if he could be utterly impossible, she still cared.

He didn't answer, but his dark gaze enveloped her, making her catch her breath.

"I should get home," she whispered. She knew she should leave, though her legs didn't seem to be making that happen.

"If you need to," he said. "But I'm not chasing you off…"

Melanie crossed the few feet between them, stood up on her tiptoes, and wrapped her arms around him. He was solid, warm and musky, and she leaned her cheek against his shoulder.

Logan's arms came around her, and he rested his cheek against the top of her head, exhaling a long sigh. His arms felt good around her, however, she wasn't looking for her own comfort, but for his.

He'd lost his father today, and this was all she could offer.

CHAPTER ELEVEN

LOGAN CLOSED HIS EYES, inhaling the soft scent of the woman in his arms. This was the first time he'd been hugged in…a long time. Having her hold him like this—no demands, no seduction—it softened a part of him that he wanted to keep strong. She held him tight, and he could feel the beat of her heart. She was strong, warm, and he realized belatedly that she was holding him up. A lump rose in his throat and tears stung his eyes.

He swallowed hard. He didn't want to give in to these feelings, though his determination to keep his feelings in check was the very thing the women in his life kept complaining about.

"I'm okay," he said gruffly, straightening and pulling back. Her hands lingered against his sides, and he caught them in his own rough grasp.

"Why don't you tell me about Harry—the real guy," she said. "Not the worst stories and not the idealized ones—the ordinary stories about your dad."

"You said you need to go," he reminded her. "I'm not trying to monopolize you here..."

"Half an hour," she said. "Then I'll head out."

She was offering her friendship, and for that he was deeply grateful. Logan pulled up a chair to face the one he already had sitting by the balcony door.

They sat, and Melanie tucked her legs up underneath her. They were a proper foot and a half apart. He didn't trust himself to be closer to her than that. Even though he had some very good reasons not to cross any lines with her, there was something about a dim hotel room and a beautiful woman that emptied his head of all reason. It was better to keep a physical distance.

"Okay...well...let me think." He leaned back in the chair. "My dad liked to fish. That's something. I used to pretend I liked it, too..."

They talked into the night, the half hour she'd allotted coming and going several times over as the moon moved across the sky. This would have been a miserable evening—

dark and lonesome. But with Mel here, their voices murmuring out the patio door and into the night air, he could feel those complicated emotions untangling deep inside of him.

He'd get her safely to her vehicle soon… Really soon…

He wasn't sure whose eyes drifted shut first, but the next thing he knew, it was morning.

LOGAN'S BACK HAD a crick in it, and he winced as he levered himself up to a fully upright position. Melanie was still asleep, her breath coming slow and deep. He paused to look at her. Her hair was rumpled and her lipstick was long gone. She sighed and her eyes fluttered open.

"Morning," he murmured.

"Hmm…" She blinked a couple of times, then shifted, sitting up straight. "What time is it? *Is* it morning?" Her gaze whipped to the open patio door and the golden light filtering in from outside. "Oh, my goodness!"

Logan reached over to the desk where his phone sat and looked at it.

"It's six," he said.

Melanie jumped up, her cheeks flooding with color. "I didn't mean to fall asleep! It's six in the morning? Tilly's back at my place. I feel terrible."

"Why?" he asked with a shake of his head.

"She's going to ask questions! That's why!"

"She's pregnant! I'm pretty sure she's not quite that naive, Mel," he said, a laugh tinging his tone.

Melanie shot him a sharp look. "I've got to get home."

She wasn't returning his smile, and he felt a wave of regret. He hadn't meant to keep her here or cause her any embarrassment. But still, having stayed out with him couldn't be that awful, could it?

Melanie grabbed her high heels and slipped her feet into them. She paused at the mirror and ran her fingers through her hair, then ran her tongue over her teeth.

"I've got a comb and mouthwash in the bathroom," he offered.

"Thank you…"

Logan waited, listening to the water run. He pulled a piece of gum out of his pocket and popped it into his mouth, chewing as he waited for her to come back out again.

The bathroom door opened, and she came out looking smoother, a little more put together. Melanie headed for the door, and as she swept past him, he reached out and caught her hand. "Mel..."

She let him tug her to a stop and turned back, those soft brown eyes filled with worry, embarrassment, some tenderness. Whatever this had been last night, it was nothing to be ashamed of. She'd been there for him in a way that he hadn't experienced in a really long time, and whatever was growing between them had been a lifesaver last night. It wasn't tawdry, and he wouldn't let her run off like it was.

"I'm not the kind of guy who has a woman spend the night, and then sends her off without a kiss, at least," he said with a small smile.

That cracked the tension and she laughed softly. "It wasn't like that, and you know it."

He tugged her closer, then slipped his arms around her waist. "I still have a few standards about how I treat a woman."

Melanie looked up at him, her eyes sparkling at his humor. "I stayed because I care, Logan."

"And I appreciate that more than you know," he said, sobering. "Seriously."

She sobered, too. Her gaze stayed locked

on his and he leaned closer, then brushed a strand of hair out of her eyes.

"This isn't necessary," she whispered.

"I know. Maybe I just want to."

He hovered there, waiting for her to pull back, to push him away, but she didn't. He bent down and lowered his lips over hers. Her eyes fluttered shut, and for a moment, it was just the feeling of their lips, their breath, and then he broke off the kiss and stepped back.

"I want the credit for not having done that even once last night," he said, a smile tickling at the corners of his lips.

"Do you need credit for it?" she asked.

"I really do. Trust me, it's worth recognizing."

Melanie laughed softly, and without another word, pulled the door open and disappeared into the hallway. He went to the door and looked out just as her dark blue dress flowed behind her as she swept down the staircase.

Logan shut the door softly and pressed his lips together. Whatever this was between them, it was starting to mean something to him, and he needed to be careful. Mel deserved better than him.

He pulled out his cell phone. He'd text Graham and give him the news that his grandfather had died. It wouldn't hit Graham too hard—he'd never met Harry. His formative relationships had been with Logan's mom and with Caroline's parents.

But he deserved to know, all the same.

MELANIE ARRIVED BACK at the house, and she spotted a classic Mercedes convertible in forest green parked next to Tilly's red sports car. Adam liked classic cars, but this wasn't one that she recognized. Unless he'd acquired a new one… Had Adam come back from Japan early? Part of her felt relieved—Tilly needed her dad right now. But seeing him again—her heart gave a squeeze. She hated that man for what he'd done to her, and she missed him, too. She missed the family they used to be and her hopes for the future, now shattered.

She didn't want to be his fallback when he was busy with work and wasn't even in the country. And the thought of seeing Adam again reminded her of exactly why she couldn't be playing with whatever she was feeling for Logan. She'd given up too much for love in the past, and she'd learned her lesson.

Because Logan had left her, too. Sure, he regretted it now. Even Adam regretted losing her. Regardless, she'd given her heart over to both men, without restraint and with full trust. She'd been all in—wasn't that how a successful relationship worked? Well, never again.

And yet, Logan's kiss was fresh in her memory—the way he'd pulled her close, the feeling of his lips against hers, the faint tickle of his stubble against her face… It had been an emotional evening, and having her in his room like that… She didn't know what either of them had been thinking. They weren't naive kids anymore. He had some big issues with his late wife, and she'd been betrayed by her husband of fifteen years. Giving in to whatever she was feeling for Logan again wasn't wise.

Melanie parked her SUV in her regular spot and hopped out. How was this going to look, walking in wearing last night's evening wear? A nagging sense of irrational guilt clung to her as she headed up the walk and let herself into the house.

Tilly stood in the kitchen wearing a pair

of low-cut jeans and a white crop top with a bowl held up in one hand. Her belly was as smooth and tight as it had always been. She cast Melanie an arch look.

"Ah. You're back," Tilly said.

"I'm back," Melanie said.

"Where were you?" Tilly asked, lifting a dribbling bite of cereal to her mouth.

"I was with a friend," Melanie said. "I fell asleep. I didn't mean to be out this long."

"Fell asleep." A smile quirked up the corners of Tilly's lips. "Yeah, I seem to remember telling you that once a couple of years ago, and you grounded me for a month."

Melanie tossed her purse onto the counter. "I'm adult. You were not."

"Yeah, and neither one of us *fell asleep*, did we?" Tilly made air quotes with one hand.

Melanie blinked. "I did."

She looked around—Adam wasn't in the room.

"I'm not sure I believe that, Miss Melanie," Tilly replied. "So who was he—that guy who bought us lunch?"

"Logan—" Melanie stopped. She really didn't owe any explanations here. "Tilly, I'm sorry I didn't call. How are you feeling? Nauseated, still?"

"Fine for now," Tilly said, taking another bite. "But I threw up a few times earlier this morning."

"Well, I'm glad you're eating now. Is your father here?"

There was a backpack on the living room floor, some crumpled bags from a fast-food restaurant and a tablet lying on the couch cushion. This wasn't Adam…

Simon came sauntering into the kitchen. He regarded Melanie with mild surprise.

Simon was about as tall as Tilly was, and he wore slim-fitting jeans and a T-shirt with a band logo Melanie didn't recognize. His hair was shaggy, and he had a bandage on his arm as if he had a new tattoo healing.

"Oh, hey," Simon said, then turned to Tilly. "Are you packed yet?"

Tilly shook her head, and said past a bite of cereal, "I'm eating."

"Well, pack!" Simon rolled his eyes. "What are you eating for again?"

"I threw up," she said.

"So quit eating."

"I'm pregnant, Simon," Tilly retorted. "I'm supposed to eat. It nourishes our child. Read a book."

"You're going to be fat, aren't you?" he

muttered, swiping his bag off the living room floor and shoving a stray shirt inside.

Melanie's anger surged inside of her. *Fat?* The father of Tilly's child was going to go there? Her first instinct was to smack the kid, but instead she glared at Simon who was looking around the living room, picking up everything but the garbage lying on the floor.

"Pregnant women eat, Simon," Melanie said tersely. "And weight gain is healthy. What isn't healthy is whatever relationship you two seem to have." She turned to Tilly. "Packing for *what*?"

"We're leaving," Simon answered for her. "Come on, Tilly. Let's go."

"I'm not packed!" Tilly repeated, raising her voice. "And I'm eating!"

"Going where?" Melanie raised her voice to match Tilly's. "Your father is coming here to get you!"

"Whatever!" Tilly shot back. "So tell him not to bother!"

"Where are you going?" Melanie repeated.

"Away. Somewhere. Anywhere. What does it matter? I'm getting out of your precious lake house."

"I don't need you to leave, Tilly." Melanie

lowered her voice. "And I don't like the way he's talking to you."

"It isn't your business, is it?" Simon asked with a snide smile. He carried his bag toward the door. "Pack up, Tilly. Now. I'm not saying it again. I'm putting my stuff in the car."

"Not saying it again?" Melanie raised her eyebrows and turned to face her stepdaughter.

The front door banged shut after Simon, and Tilly took another bite.

"He's always been like this to you," Melanie said, not waiting for Tilly to answer and taking advantage of his momentary absence. "You're pregnant, and he's going to shame you for eating? He's going to boss you around? He isn't good for you, Tilly. You have a baby to worry about now, and stress and fighting isn't good for you."

"Then stop stressing me out," Tilly said bluntly.

Melanie shut her eyes for a moment, trying to find her calm. "Please, don't go."

"He's my boyfriend," Tilly said. "We've got plans."

"It doesn't sound like you do," Melanie countered. "Where will you be staying? What do I tell your dad?"

"Tell him to call me," Tilly said, lifting her phone. "I don't get why you're all upset. You didn't want me here to begin with, and now I'm going."

"You need someone to take care of you," Melanie said, and in that moment, she saw Tilly as she'd been years ago—a frail little blonde girl with big blue eyes who would cry softly at night, remembering her mommy. Then there was the five-year-old with the impish grin, the ten-year-old with so much attitude, but who still liked going clothes shopping with her stepmother… Tilly—the little girl who'd stolen her heart.

The front door opened and Simon came back in. He left the door open partway and slouched toward the kitchen.

"Are you packed?"

Tilly heaved a sigh, put down her bowl and headed out of the room without answering. Melanie turned to Simon, and the boy eyed her from under that shaggy hair.

"Her father is going to be here in a few days," Melanie said. "And you know Mr. Isaacs. If you do anything to hurt his daughter or that baby—"

"Hurt her?" Simon winced. "I'm not going to hurt her! What is with you people?"

"What about you not wanting her to eat?" Melanie said.

"Whatever—I made a comment. Who cares? She's going to eat, okay? I just don't want her getting all fat like being pregnant is some excuse."

"Being pregnant is an *excellent* excuse!" Melanie snapped. "And her body and the weight she carries is none of your business!"

"Kind of is," Simon said, and he raised his voice. "Tilly, hurry up!"

Melanie pulled a hand through her hair. She wasn't going to be able to stop Tilly from leaving, so she needed to change tack here.

"Simon," she said, softening her tone. "Tilly needs support right now. So if you two are going to leave together, then you need to be the one taking care of her. She's nauseated from the pregnancy, she needs rest and she needs to eat. She should probably see her family doctor soon. And she really doesn't need any added stress right now."

"Yeah, well you didn't come home last night. I would know. I was here," Simon said with a short laugh. "So I don't see where all this worry is coming from. She's fine."

What worried her was Simon's relentless verbal badgering and emotional abuse. She'd seen it for years and tried to talk Tilly out of it for just as long. But it wasn't just Tilly anymore—she was more vulnerable now that she was pregnant. And Simon had gone from being the jerk her stepdaughter dated to the guy who could very well stand between her and any help she might need.

Tilly emerged from the hallway with one large bag over her shoulder, and another one balanced on top of her rolling suitcase.

"If you need me, you call, Tilly," Melanie said. "There's no shame in coming home, okay?"

"Shame?" Simon barked out a laugh. "This from the woman who did the walk of shame this morning! We aren't ashamed of ourselves, Melanie!"

It wasn't exactly what Melanie had said, but obviously Simon's mind was moving in other directions. And maybe he was worried about what his own parents would say.

"*You* take care of her," Melanie said firmly. "I'm warning you."

"Or what?" Simon rolled his eyes, and she sensed the dare in his gaze. He was feeling powerful right now—making adults beg. He was the father of Tilly's child, and he seemed to have some sway over her. No, he was not going to be kind and supportive. He was going to play with his newfound power.

"I'll call your mother," Melanie said curtly. It sounded stupid the minute it came out of her mouth, but two years ago that would have given the kid some pause.

"Then you have no idea how my mother has been talking about you," Simon laughed, taking the two bigger bags from Tilly and carrying them toward the open door. "Come on, Tilly. Let's go."

"Tilly—" Melanie put her hand on the girl's arm "—I'll come get you if you call. Okay?"

Tilly pulled her arm free. "I don't need you to come get me. I'm fine, Melanie. Jeez. You aren't my mother!"

"Maybe you need one!" Melanie shot back. "Maybe you need someone who actually cares, because Simon doesn't!"

"Enjoy the lake house," Tilly said, turning her back.

Simon pulled her big suitcase, and struggled with the bag that kept falling off the top of it. He muttered to himself as he fought with them out the door, Tilly on his heels.

"And she has a father, Simon!" Melanie called after them. "You'll have to face her dad, personally!"

Simon's expression turned a little less certain, but it didn't slow him down. She went to the doorway, watching them haul the luggage down the stairs. He opened the trunk and manhandled the luggage inside, then slammed it shut. Tilly tossed her bag into the back seat of Simon's car, then got into the front. Apparently, she was leaving her own car parked right here.

Tilly didn't wave, but she did meet Melanie's gaze just once before Simon backed his car up.

Tilly…the girl who'd needed a mother so desperately, and who'd rejected Melanie's attempts to be that mom. Well, she was starting down the path to motherhood herself, and right now all Melanie could think was that if Simon hurt her, Melanie would hurt him back.

Legally, maybe. Or physically. Whichever seemed most effective.

She sighed, rubbing her hands over her face, and shut the door. Then she pulled out her phone and typed out a text to Adam.

Tilly just left with Simon. I tried to get her to stay. I'm sorry.

Had Melanie messed this up?

CHAPTER TWELVE

LOGAN HAD A shower and went down to breakfast. His mind was still on Melanie—had he made a mistake in kissing her? It had been an honest kiss, if nothing else. No, he wasn't looking for a relationship, and he had no intention of inflicting himself on another woman, especially one who was so vulnerable right now. But he'd meant that kiss.

And that might make him a jerk.

He'd loved Caroline with everything he had, and he'd still been a jerk in their marriage. He wasn't going to do that again—hand his battered heart over to a woman and expect her to fix it, because a real man didn't play with these things. He had more issues than he'd ever realized, but keeping those lines clear was difficult when it came to Melanie. He had feelings welling up for her, and he wasn't sure how to stop them.

Junior walked past the dining room doorway just as Logan dropped a few bills onto the table to pay for his breakfast. He got up and intercepted his brother in the foyer.

Junior looked older since he'd last seen him—his face paler and more haggard. The gray in his blond hair seemed more pronounced this morning, and he looked more like Harry. In his hands was the wooden box that Elise had left to Harry.

"Hi, Logan," Junior said, coming over in his direction. "How are you doing?"

"I'm okay," Logan said. "How about you?"

"I've been better." Junior nodded a couple of times, then held out the box. "I thought you might want this back."

"Yeah, thanks." Logan accepted it, the box cool to his touch. He was glad to get it back.

"Oh, and this." Junior fished in his pocket and pulled out the sealed envelope containing the key. So his father had never opened it… That thought was a bitter one. Had he resented Elise so much that he couldn't look into the box she'd left him upon her death? But then, his mother had avoided Harry just as bitterly, and this was his family legacy—pain, resentment and emotional walls. Junior's current profession was ironic, considering their family.

Maybe there was some wisdom in not

opening it. At least Harry knew where he stood with Elise. Would Logan have been better off if he'd left his wife's diaries shut? Sometimes ignorance to someone's true feelings was preferable.

"Why don't we go talk in the sitting room," Logan said.

The space was awash in morning sunlight, the fireplace empty, some chairs pulled up to the full-length windows that overlooked the lake. They headed toward an empty cluster of chairs. Logan put the box down at his feet as he sat. He looked at it for a moment, then up at his brother.

"How are your kids taking Harry's passing?" Logan asked.

"Taylor, my son, is probably taking it the hardest," Junior said. "He's eleven this year, and he and my dad were pretty close."

"Oh, yeah?"

"Before he went to the old folks' home, he and Taylor did a lot together. They just... bonded, I guess. And when he had the strokes and needed more care, I took my family to see Dad every week," Junior said. "Taylor would ask me to bring him to see Papa midweek. Taylor just missed him. And Dad missed Taylor. They liked to watch these kid shows together—you know, the middle school shows that drove me nuts but my dad would put up with just to hang out with Taylor more. I think Dad actually liked them, truth be told."

"Papa..."

"What the kids called him."

Graham hadn't called Harry anything—he hadn't known him. But Harry had been capable of bonding with Taylor, it seemed. Logan felt a wave of jealousy at that. Graham was a good kid, and he'd deserved that. But then, so had Logan—eleven-year-old Taylor had had a better relationship with Harry than Logan had ever experienced with his dad.

"Was he like that with you, too?" Logan asked.

"Like what?" Junior leaned back in the chair, his gaze fixed on the water.

"Loving, open, available," Logan said.

"Yeah, of course. He was a great father—" Junior stopped. "If you'd given him a chance—"

"I tried!" Logan closed his eyes and then lowered his voice. "I tried. Constantly."

"From what I heard, you asked for money," Junior said.

"Once." Logan heaved a sigh. "Only once.

For school. But so what?" He turned to his brother. "I was his son. What if I'd wanted a few of the things that you enjoyed?"

Junior was silent, and Logan leaned back, too, his gaze skimming across the blue water toward the other side of the lake where a few houses were scattered along the edge. He knew which one was Melanie's, and he could see the wharf sticking out into the water.

"I think he wanted to be a better father," Junior said after a few beats of silence. "I'm not saying he did right by you, Logan."

That was a first. Logan looked over at his brother in surprise. "I didn't expect you to say that."

"I'm a dad, too," Junior said. "And a therapist. I know what our kids need from us, what you needed from him. I don't know why you were always held off like that—"

"Your mom's jealousy?" If they were going to get honest, they might as well get it all on the table.

"Maybe," Junior said.

"You didn't like me much, either," Logan added.

"I was a kid," Junior said, shaking his head. "I was jealous."

"Of what?" Logan asked.

"You were everything I wasn't yet. You were older, you were better looking, you had this confidence about you… I was scared that you'd take something away from our family, from my parents' marriage. I thought that by not liking you, I was being loyal to our nuclear family." He shrugged weakly. "I'm sorry."

"Me, too," Logan said. "You know, our father messed up a lot of stuff, Junior. I tried so hard to connect with him. Do you know what he gave me for my birthday every year?"

"No." Junior glanced over.

"Twenty bucks."

Junior pressed his lips together. "I got a Nintendo system one year. A bike another year."

"Yeah, I know." Logan had known about the vast discrepancy between their gifts, the attention they received, their father's love.

"Why did you stop trying?" Junior asked. "When you were an adult, I mean. It might have been different, then."

"Because I called him when Graham was born, and he came down on me because Caroline and I weren't married yet," Logan replied. "And I just…saw red. I mean, he saw my son as some sort of failure on my part.

My son! And he hadn't married my mom, so I saw the connection. I was his failure, too. I was the kid born outside of wedlock. So I married Caroline, and I never contacted him again."

"That's awful," Junior said. "I'm sorry."

"It wasn't you."

"Yeah, well, someone should be sorry, anyway," Junior replied. "And I am."

"Is that a therapy trick?" Logan asked.

"Not a trick, but yes, it's something used in therapy," Junior replied. "It helps people to feel heard."

"Well, cut it out," Logan said.

Junior's face colored, and he leaned forward, his elbows resting on his knees. From his position, Logan could see that Junior had missed a small patch when shaving that morning, and the whiskers shone golden.

"Do you have any good memories of our dad?" Junior asked, looking up.

Logan had been ready for a fight just now—proof that he'd been treated unfairly, pushed aside, neglected by their shared father—and he felt the adrenaline drain out of him. Our dad…

"He gave me a pair of boxing gloves one year for Christmas," Logan said, a lump rising in his throat. "Mom said no, but Dad gave them to me, anyway."

"Yeah?" Junior smiled at that. "He never would let me have boxing gloves. He said I wouldn't like being punched, and you couldn't throw a punch without getting it back."

Logan shrugged. "I guess he wasn't so worried about that with me."

"I asked Dad about you quite a few times when I was growing up," Junior said quietly. "And Dad said that you were strong and smart, and that he wasn't worried about you. He also said you had a really good mom raising you..."

"He said that?" Logan rolled the words around in his mind. An excuse for his paltry offerings when it came to being a dad, or a sincere compliment to Elise. Maybe both.

"I knew better than to ask when my mom was there," Junior added.

"Were they happy?" Logan asked.

Junior was silent for a while. "If you'd asked me this a week ago, I would have told you a different story. I'd have insisted that they were devoted and loving, truly meant for each other."

"Not true?" Logan asked.

"Whether they were meant for each other or not, I have no idea." Junior sighed. "Maybe that was why I kept trying to protect the family—their marriage wasn't that strong. Mom was jealous. And Dad had a couple of affairs over the years, and that changed them…changed *her*."

"Oh…" Logan swallowed.

"Yeah." Junior met his gaze for a moment, then looked away. "He wasn't the perfect family man, Logan. But I loved him, anyway."

Tears welled in Junior's eyes, and Logan reached out and awkwardly patted his brother's shoulder. He didn't say anything for a few moments, and they both sat there with the morning sun warming them through the windows.

"I married Caroline because of Dad," Logan said at last.

"That's a good thing, then," Junior replied, his voice thick with emotion.

"I don't know if it was," Logan replied. "But because Dad came down on me for having a child out of wedlock, I bought Caroline a ring and we got married a few months later. After she'd recovered from the delivery. It was my silent jab at dad. I'd married her. He couldn't hold that against us."

"You weren't happy?" Junior asked.

"Are you asking as my brother, or as a shrink?" Logan asked.

"As your brother."

Logan sighed. "I was happy. I was really happy. I loved her, and I loved my son, and I liked being married. I liked the solidity of it. It felt safe and secure—everything I'd lacked growing up. And my mom loved Caroline, too."

"What was the problem?" Junior asked.

"Caroline wasn't quite so happy," Logan replied.

"What made you feel that way?"

There was something in Junior's tone that had shifted, and Logan slowly shook his head.

"Nope, that was the shrink asking," Logan said.

Junior smiled wryly. "Maybe. Sorry. It's hard to shake. My wife hates it when I sound like a shrink with her, too."

"I'll bet…"

Junior sighed. "It's not easy being the husband, the provider, the dad, the font of half the wisdom in the house… It's a lot of pressure."

That was something Logan could finally agree with. "Yeah, it is."

"At the funeral, I was wondering if you wanted to say something," Junior said quietly.

"When is it?" Logan asked.

"We've settled on Saturday. Noon. At the big Anglican church downtown."

"Is that why you came today? To ask me to speak at the funeral?" Logan asked.

Junior shook his head. "No. But I'm asking now. I think you deserve to be a part of it. He was your father, too."

"You trust me to say something nice?" Logan asked.

Junior eyed him for a moment, then laughed bitterly. "I do. You're a father, too. And my kids are going to be there, and whatever he was to us, however he messed up, he was their grandfather, and they adored him. I trust you not to break my kids' hearts."

"I was being facetious," Logan said.

"I figured. Is Graham coming to the funeral?"

"He's in Europe still," Logan said. "So no. And he didn't know Dad."

"I'd like to meet your son one day," Junior said quietly.

"He might like that," Logan said. "But he's an adult now. It's up to him."

They'd waited a little long for this reconciliation, and the kids had all gone about growing up and bonding with the people who would matter to them. Graham had lost his grandmother, and he'd been broken up at her death, the same way Taylor was over Harry's. There was going to be no making up for lost time with this next generation. They'd be too busy looking forward, as young people did. This particular tangle of mistakes and emotion was his generation's to bear.

"Your brother and sister might not like me talking at the funeral," Logan said.

"Leave them to me," Junior said. "And they'll be fine. Trust me."

What could Logan say about the father he'd spent a lifetime striving to either connect with or forget?

Harry had never been father enough, and they would never reconcile now. At least Logan had been able to see him one last time. Funny how every other relationship could mean so much, but still not touch that space.

"What was it like growing up with a dad who loved you like that?" Logan asked at last.

Junior's gaze turned thoughtful, then he shrugged. "It was…a good way to grow up."

Logan nodded. "My son has that. I always made sure he knew how proud I was of him and how much I loved him. I hope he appreciates it."

"My kids have it, too," Junior replied. "And for what it's worth, your son won't appreciate it. Kids never appreciate what they have. It's perfectly healthy and normal for them to take it all for granted. It's the natural reaction of an untraumatized child."

"Professionally speaking?" Logan asked.

"Yeah." Junior met his gaze and shrugged. "Personally speaking, too. My kids take everything I provide for granted."

Logan's phone blipped, and he pulled it out of his pocket to see a text. It was from Melanie. Tilly took off with Simon.

He knew that she was feeling a whole lot more than her words conveyed. So Tilly had done it—gone back to the loser boyfriend. Logan couldn't help but be disappointed. He liked Tilly's spunk, and it was wasted on some kid who wouldn't treat her right. And at the moment, Logan couldn't help but blame Adam. He was the one who'd laid the foundation for his daughter to accept that kind of treatment. He'd treated Melanie badly for all those years. And Tilly was the one to pay for it.

Junior took his phone out at the same time and looked at his.

"I'd better get going," Junior said. "I told Taylor we'd go through some old pictures of Dad together."

"Yeah, you bet," Logan said. "Graham and I did something similar when my mom died. It seemed to help."

He met his brother's gaze, and for the first time in his life, he no longer saw a rival. They were both trying their best to be good fathers, in spite of it all. Just two men trying to do better by their own kids.

"Well, I'll see you at the funeral, then," Junior said. "And you have my number."

"Yeah." Logan stood up and so did Junior. Logan put out a hand to shake and Junior leaned in at the same time. They both laughed awkwardly, then Logan leaned in and they patted each other's backs in a brief hug.

As his brother left, Logan picked up his phone again and typed a reply to Melanie.

I could come over, if you want.

Her reply was almost instant. Please.

Logan couldn't fix any of this—not his relationship with his late father, not his history with his brother and not Melanie's issues with her rebellious stepdaughter. But he could be there for her.

Just being there with someone was a greater privilege than he'd appreciated in times past. Being asked to just be with someone in his or her tough times—it meant something.

And even though he'd only seen Melanie that morning, he missed her.

CHAPTER THIRTEEN

LOGAN HAD A lot to think about as he drove down the familiar roads that led to the lakeshore. The wooden box was on the passenger seat next to him. He wasn't sure why he'd brought it with him, but he didn't want to open it alone. Sometimes hard emotions could be softened in the company of someone a man trusted.

And that was Melanie. He needed someone with him who wouldn't have a personal stake in the contents. He knew that whatever was inside this box had never been meant for his eyes—it had been meant for Harry's. And it might reveal more about Elise's relationship with Harry than he cared to know. He'd made this mistake with his wife's diaries.

But he'd still open it.

As Logan drove, his mind went back to his visit with his brother. He hadn't expected to bond with Junior, and yet his brother wasn't quite the spoiled brat he used to be. Logan hadn't realized that his father's marriage had been that fragile—they'd kept up appearances. Or maybe, he'd just been too young to know what cracks looked like from the outside.

And now he had an obligation to speak at his father's funeral, and the realization sunk into his stomach like a rock. He should have said no, but he'd been included as part of the family at long last, and he hadn't been able to refuse it.

At the age of forty-two, he should have been wiser. Besides, what could he say about the father who'd sidelined him from the start? His feelings were too loaded—too full of sharp edges and resentment to make for a comforting speech. He should just leave the speechifying to Junior and his siblings. They'd give the version of things that made people feel happy and cozy—the loving dad, the adoring husband, the revered grandfather. No one wanted to see the mistakes someone made in their life. *Don't speak ill of the dead.* Wasn't that the old adage? It wasn't a superstition. It was because it offended the living, and that's whom the funeral was for.

As Logan pulled up to Melanie's lake house, he noticed that Tilly's little red Audi was still parked there. Had she come back, or had she left her car behind?

He knocked on the door, box under one arm, and when Melanie pulled it open, she was on the phone. She angled her head, silently inviting him inside.

"…she's seventeen, Adam," she was saying. "One more year, and she's a legal adult. What was I going to do, wrestle her the ground?"

Logan smiled at that and followed her into the bright kitchen. Logan leaned back against the counter, putting the box down next to him.

"I don't like him, either, but unless you toughened up on that relationship in the last year, I don't remember you ever telling her that." Melanie rubbed her free hand over her face. "And yes, he's a real little jerk. He was complaining about her gaining weight with the pregnancy—already!"

Logan could hear Adam's elevated response to that, and Melanie cast Logan a smile.

"Look—she said for you to call her. That's all I can tell you. And her car is still here, so she'll be back." A pause. "Of course, and I told her she could call me if she needed me…

Yeah…yeah… Uh-huh. She's not an idiot, Adam. I think she'll come to her senses, but as long as she's fighting us—" She sighed. "Look, I have someone here, so I should go… Right… Yep… Call her, Adam! She's your daughter."

When Melanie hung up, she shrugged apologetically.

"Sorry about that," she said. "Adam is still in Japan, and he's worried."

"I'll bet," Logan said. "So what happened?"

"When I got home this morning, Simon was here, and they were about to take off together. I asked her to stay, and she wouldn't." She licked her lips. "Simon makes me nervous."

"He was commenting on her weight?" Logan asked with a frown. That was the part that had snagged his attention.

"He doesn't want her getting fat, he says." Melanie's lips curled in distaste. "He's a pig, that kid. I don't like him, and the last thing she needs is her boyfriend making her feel self-conscious about eating."

"Yeah, no kidding." He frowned. "Have you called his parents?"

"No. I'm leaving that up to Adam. I know

she landed here, and… I raised that child, but I never officially adopted the kids. Without their dad, I'm not a part of this. And Simon's parents know it."

"Fair enough." He met her gaze. "Is Tilly okay?"

"She's fine for now," Melanie replied. "This is more of a long-term worry than a short-term one. She's pregnant, and he's going to undermine her sense of self-worth because her body is doing something that—" She pressed her lips together.

"That what?" he asked quietly.

"That not all of us got the chance to do," she said, and her eyes misted. "But this isn't about me, it's about her. That boy is emotionally abusive, and I've had enough friends and family members who've had babies to know that pregnancy is a really delicate time for a woman, emotionally and otherwise."

"I agree wholeheartedly," he said. "And I've got to say, I don't have warm thoughts about this kid's parents, either. Someone should have been teaching him better." Logan's son was a little older than Simon, but Graham had been raised to respect women. He and Caroline had made sure of it.

"His father is busy, his mother volunteers

a lot and Simon was raised by nannies, none of whom he really respected," she replied. "What he needed was someone to kick his butt a whole lot sooner than this."

"Should we go after them?" he asked.

"Go where?" She spread her hands. "No, we wait. Or we let Adam get back from Japan and deal with his daughter. I think he's the one she's been baiting all this time, anyway."

Logan nodded. "I could see that." Silence fell between them, and she seemed to deflate before his eyes. "Tough morning, huh?"

"Yeah." She nodded toward the box on the counter. "You got it back?"

Logan glanced down at the glossy box. "I saw my brother, and he brought it along. He figured I'd want it."

"How's he doing?" Melanie asked. "With your dad's passing, and all."

"He's okay," Logan replied. "We had a really good talk."

Melanie smiled faintly at that. "I'm glad. Did you find some common ground?"

"Yeah, a bit," he admitted. "And he wants me to speak at the funeral."

Melanie's eyebrows went up, and he smiled ruefully. "Yeah, I'm not sure that's a great idea, either, but I guess Junior wants to include me as…a brother."

"It's only fair," she said.

"Even if it's a bit late," he replied, then sighed. "I'll have to find something nice to say, or just pass on the honor, you know?"

Melanie nodded. "You might find that you have more to say than you think."

But if he started talking, what came out might not be palatable to the rest of the family.

"Look, I was wondering if you might want to come to the funeral," he said. "You can say no—I should have started with that. But Junior has his wife and kids, and everyone else is going to have their own memories of my father, and if you came along…"

It might be a comfort for him alone. But he didn't want to say that out loud.

"Sure," she said. "When is it?"

"Saturday at noon. And I have to head back to Denver to pick up my son from the airport Sunday morning, so…it would be a chance to spend some time with you."

"I'm not sure I'm the important relationship here," she said quietly.

He didn't answer that. Maybe his family relationships had been messy and scarring, but this time with her mattered. She quickly was becoming an important relationship in his life, even if he didn't how to put it into words.

"Adam is coming for Tilly on Saturday evening," she said when he hadn't answered. "If she's back… I don't know what he's planning on doing. Anyway, the point is I can make it to the funeral. There is plenty of time."

Logan hesitated. "You sure?"

"Yeah. I can be there."

It made him feel stronger to think of having her there. She was the only one in this town who understood him, it seemed. Whatever they'd had in their youth had sparked up again, and he found himself opening up to her…

Except she'd already told him that he hadn't opened up quite as much as he thought. He ran his hand over the box.

"I…uh… I thought I might open the box here," he said, "and see what my mother put inside."

"With me?" Melanie's expression softened.

"Yeah. You okay with that?"

She nodded, and Logan fished in his

pocket and pulled out the key, then he picked up the box and looked around.

"Come to the living room," Melanie said.

She'd moved things around again—the TV in one corner, a couch opposite it, two single chairs positioned on the other side of the room facing the wide window overlooking the lake. He sank into one of the chairs and put the box down on an ottoman.

"I don't know what she would have sent him," Logan murmured. "She didn't think much of him. She never had anything good to say about him. She hated that he held me at arm's length."

"But kids don't get an inside view of their parents' relationships, either," Melanie countered.

Logan fit the key into the lock. It didn't turn easily, and he had to jiggle the key and put a hand on top of the box to keep it still as the lock finally clicked open. Then he lifted the lid.

There was a mishmash of items inside, but no envelope or letter containing an explanation. Logan picked up a program from his university graduation. He opened it and found his name circled in the list of graduates. There was a picture of him at high school grad—standing there in his blue robe, his mortarboard on his head and squinting into the sunlight. He handed the items over to Melanie as he sorted through them—his birth announcement, a hospital bracelet from when he had his appendix removed as a teenager, a scattering of pictures from his childhood, including one of him and his father standing together. Logan picked up that photo and looked down at it.

Logan was about ten, and he stood there so tall and proud. His father had his hand awkwardly on Logan's shoulder, and he looked less confident in that photo.

"It's a box of…me," Logan said softly.

"She wanted you to deliver it," Melanie said. "Maybe she was hoping you two would have more of a relationship."

"Talking points?" he asked, lifting up a collection of school photos from the first grade to the twelfth.

"Why not?" Melanie took the photos. "I've never seen these. You were adorable."

"Yeah…" He looked down at the familiar photos, then turned back to the box. There were a few more items—a little car he used to play with as a boy. He remembered this specific car. It was a favorite.

"My mother never asked me if I wanted her to connect me with Dad again," he said, flipping through a few pictures he'd drawn as a kid. There was a series of comics he'd made, his age recorded in his mother's neat handwriting on the back of each. There was a step-by-step set of instructions for how to build a Lego spaceship that he'd designed himself—the instructions drawn in the careful imitation of the company's booklets.

"Wow…" Melanie picked up the instructions, flipping through it. "You were a really bright kid, Logan."

"I think most kids try their hand at that, at some point," he said.

"No, they don't," she replied.

Graham hadn't, but then he'd been creative in different ways. He'd been a whiz in the kitchen since he was eight or nine. But the intimate nature of the contents of this box started closing doors inside of him. His mother had crossed a line here.

"I didn't ask for her to try to meddle," he repeated, and Melanie looked up, meeting his gaze.

"She meant well," Melanie said.

"So what did she expect, that he'd open this box, see all he'd missed and change who he was as a human being?" he said, anger burbling up inside of him. "My mother cared about this stuff. She's the one who collected it all, not him. If anything, he'd only feel some moderate guilt, and close me out even further."

Melanie didn't answer.

"I didn't want this," Logan said, his voice shaking with emotion. "I spent my life begging that man for some sort of relationship, and my mother figured she'd lend a hand at the end? I was tired of the begging! I'd given up!"

Logan tossed the papers and photos back into the box. These mementos encapsulated his childhood. These were the moments that he remembered, and maybe he didn't want to share them with the father who'd never cared enough. "You know, if she really wanted my dad and me to connect, she could have done something about it while she was alive."

Like Caroline—she could have said something while there was still time. Like anyone—they only had so many years to work with, and copping out with some instructions in a will was cowardly.

MELANIE HANDED BACK the intricate bundle of Lego instructions. Logan's expression had cooled, and his lips were pressed in a thin line. She knew that look—this was what he was like when he retreated emotionally, normally in delicate situations when opening up mattered most.

"She was proud of you, Logan," Melanie said quietly. "Maybe you were the best thing she ever did. Maybe this wasn't about giving up your personal memories without your permission. It could have been her own personal affirmation—she raised you!"

Logan looked over at her, and for just a split second, emotion swam in his dark eyes, giving her a hint at what he was hiding beneath the surface. "She didn't have to prove herself to him."

"He married someone else and treated you like an outsider. I wonder how he treated her. She might have had a few things of her own to prove."

Logan raised an eyebrow. "I hadn't considered that." Then he scrubbed a hand through his hair. "I'm sorry—you've got your own issues today. I shouldn't have even brought the box with me."

"You know what?" she said, reaching out and grabbing his arm. "I'm glad you did. And he never saw this, did he? So whatever your mom had hoped for didn't happen. Instead, you got to see what your mom treasured from your childhood, and that's beautiful. Unless..." She swallowed. She wasn't his girlfriend anymore, and she'd started to forget that—expecting more from him than she had any right to expect. "Unless you hadn't really wanted me to see all this, either."

Logan's gaze softened, and a smile tickled the corners of his lips. "Nah. It's okay."

There was something so tender in the look that her breath caught, then he leaned forward, his elbows on his knees.

"I was really proud of that Lego instruction manual... I gotta say," he said. "I worked on it every spare minute for weeks."

"It's impressive, Logan."

"I always was an engineer at heart," he said, then he glanced around the room. "I can see your touch around this house, too, you know."

"Can you? I didn't have time to do much. We stayed for a couple of months, and I'd add a piece of furniture here or there, but the kids were so hard on furniture back then..."

They'd destroyed her efforts just by being kids—shoes on silk pillows, fingerprints on upholstered seats, chip fragments ground into a throw rug.

"I remember trying to keep a garden the same year that Graham decided to start building roads for all his toy cars..." Logan smiled to himself, then glanced over at her again. "They wreck everything within reach, but you can't imagine life without them."

"Yeah..." That summed it up rather nicely. "She still seems to be at it."

He smiled sadly, and then he reached out and took her hand. "Why didn't life get easier?"

"I don't know..." She shrugged. "We asked that question twenty-three years ago, didn't we? When you were getting ready to leave for college, and I was going to miss you so much."

And it was like those years between had folded up like a paper fan, and she could have been that teenage girl again, looking at the boy who held her heart and knowing that it wouldn't last...it couldn't. Being with Logan required being right there next to him, reading his nuances. He wasn't going to open up in emails or phone calls...and yet she'd been so determined to try.

"I'd say you were better off without me, but Adam wasn't much of a catch," Logan said.

Melanie laughed softly. "But you have nothing to regret. You met a woman you loved, started a family... You did good, Logan."

"I tried hard," he said.

"I did, too." She felt the emotion simmering close to the surface in spite of her efforts to cap them. "I just wanted to be enough for them..."

She swallowed, not finishing the thought aloud. She'd wanted to be the kind of woman who could love her family so well that the fact that she was the stepmother wouldn't matter. She'd wanted to be the love of her husband's life... Trying hadn't been anywhere near enough—for any of them. It had seemed like either a woman was enough or she wasn't. But it was based on something that she had no control over. Being good, thoughtful, considerate and dedicated wasn't all there was to it. Hard work didn't cut it with Adam, or with Logan.

Logan seemed to see the complicated emotions on her face, because he stood up, and tugged her hand. "Come here."

"What?" She rose with him, and he

wrapped his arms around her, pulling her in close. He tipped his head to rest his cheek on the top of her head—a familiar position now. It had all happened rather quickly, and she stood there, his strong arms enveloping her with such gentleness, and her heart beating so that she could feel it in her stomach. Being next to Logan, close enough to feel his heartbeat, had always made everything feel possible between them. But she'd been a naive girl back then.

"I'm glad I got to see who you grew up to be," he said, his voice reverberating in his chest against her ear.

"Me, too, with you," she said.

She wrapped her arms around his waist, enjoying the feeling of his breath against her hair and his hand moving slowly over her back. She pulled back to look up at him, and she found his dark gaze locked on hers.

"I'm not the same person I used to be," she breathed.

"Me neither."

"I spent fifteen years trying my hardest to be who my family needed—being mom enough, being wife enough, being woman enough—and I'm done trying, Logan. I don't feel like doing that anymore."

"Woman enough?" He reached up and touched her chin with the pad of his thumb. "Mel, you're woman enough. Trust me on that."

She parted her lips to answer, but the words evaporated. All she seemed able to focus on was that dark intense gaze moving over her face. Years ago, she'd known what his kisses felt like, but it was different now. She let her eyes fall shut just before his lips covered hers.

His kiss started out firm, then softened as he pulled her into him. It was the kiss of a man who knew what he wanted, and knew how to get it. But she felt his self-restraint—his hands stopping at her back, the kiss filled with longing, and yet respectful.

Logan pulled back. "You were too good for him, Mel. You're probably too good for the likes of me, too," he said, his voice deep and soft.

She couldn't help but wonder what his kiss would be like if that self-control shattered. Dare she imagine it? Yet, there was something about being in his arms that made her feel more than she had in a decade... His focus on her, his tenderness. She didn't want to think this through, or talk it out, or ruin the moment with any forethought. Instead, she rose onto her tiptoes and brushed her lips against his once more.

That was all it took, and he let out a soft growl, wrapping her in his arms and lowering his mouth over hers once more. This time, he deepened the kiss, his hands sliding around her waist without hesitation and he exhaled a sigh as one hand moved up into her hair. When he pulled back again, she took a step back and tugged out of his arms. She licked her lips, feeling her cheeks heat.

"That one was my fault," she breathed.

Logan met her gaze. "I'm not trying to complicate things for you."

She'd wanted that kiss—she wanted another one, too, but she couldn't play with this. She needed to restart her life, not trip into another man's arms. What she really needed tonight was a distraction—something to keep her from doing that again.

"Ice cream," she said. "I have a whole tub in the freezer—chocolate. You want some?"

Logan blinked, then laughed softly. "Actually, yeah."

She'd read somewhere that chocolate triggered the same response in a brain as being in love. And since romance wasn't a reasonable option, she'd make do with the runner-up.

And ice cream with Logan… It wasn't quite the same as his kisses, but a friendship between them would last longer. This time around, she was a grown woman, and she wouldn't be pining. Not for Adam, not for Logan, not for the life of being a mom that had slipped between her fingers. She was going to create the life she wanted, and live it. And it wasn't going to rely upon something so fickle as a man's feelings.

CHAPTER FOURTEEN

THAT EVENING AFTER Logan left, Melanie sat on her deck, watching the moonlight glimmer on the water. She had the lake house to herself again, and the silence felt deafening. It was strange how she could long for some quiet and privacy, and when she finally got it, it felt almost ominous.

Angelina had called, and she was on speaker, Melanie's phone balanced on the arm of a deck chair while she stared out over the water.

Was it this lake house, filled with too many memories? This house was lonely when it was just her in it, and she couldn't help but remember evenings just like this one when she'd sat on the deck with the kids watching the sunset. Back then, she'd felt so safe and secure—married to Adam, protected by his wealth. But she'd also felt isolated—her time and energy used up with the kids. She'd declined suggestions she get a nanny and free herself up. These kids needed a mother, not a nanny, and if she'd never have a baby of her own, then they were her chance at motherhood.

And now she wondered if that had been a mistake. Maybe she'd been trying to earn her place in this family. Because while her stepkids never had accepted her, even after all she'd done for them, other moms had their families—their place never questioned. It hadn't been about how hard they worked. So who had been foolish, after all?

"You know what I was told when I was a young woman?" Melanie asked, leaning toward the phone. "They said that if you wanted to find a great guy, become the kind of woman a great guy needs. You have to bring something to the table. And I don't argue that—I think you need to be a whole person with something to offer. But even that isn't enough."

"What did you bring to the table?" Angelina asked.

"I was willing to raise Adam's kids and love them as my own," she said. "That was something no other woman had wanted to give him. I was honest, loyal, willing to work hard. I wasn't there to spend his money. And there were a few other women who would have married him for just that."

"Maybe you should have spent a little more," Angelina said ruefully.

"For what?" Melanie sighed. "I decorated our home. I dressed well, too. It isn't that I didn't do anything for myself, but…what I wanted was a life with him. I wanted intimacy, openness. I wanted a marriage."

"Didn't you have that?"

"I thought so. Apparently, I was wrong. Whatever it was that captures hearts—we didn't have it. But I thought that trying hard would make up for it."

"For Ben and me, it was the opposite," Angelina said quietly. "I was enough for Ben when it was just the two of us. We were madly in love, but when his wealthy family came into the mix, I just couldn't compete. I couldn't be cultured enough, or fit in with their friends. To them, I was always that little peasant that Ben married—and in the end, they won. I didn't bring enough to the table for his circle to accept me."

"Did he leave you?" Melanie asked.

"No, I left him," she replied. "Sometimes you get tired of being a disappointment."

"But look at you now," Melanie replied.

"Even all of this wouldn't be enough for them," Angelina replied. "Love has to overcome a lot of hurdles to bring two people together, and love doesn't always clear them all."

Melanie sighed. "That's my point."

"That said, you're only forty," Angelina said. "You have a long life ahead of you still. Why not find a guy you can grow old with?"

"Because if I could dedicate fifteen years of my life to a man and not know that he was cheating…if I could raise his kids and still end up on the sidelines as not mom enough for any of them… Ange, what I bring to the table is my work ethic—my determination, my loyalty. And I found out the hardest way possible that the one thing I have in my favor isn't nearly enough."

Angelina sighed. "That's not all you bring to the table, Mel."

"It was my brightest asset," Melanie replied. "Looks—they don't count for much without character. Without some substance to back you up, it's just a moderately attractive face and figure. What's that worth?"

Melanie's gaze moved over the water, the moonlight rippling with the jump of a fish. "I need more. I've got to put my own life first, not sacrifice for love all the time. Maybe love needs to sacrifice for me."

"What about Logan?" Angelina asked. "Things seem to be heating up between you two."

"He's got a life in Denver—his son, his business—and I'm not going back to Denver. I've got a chance to finally make the life I want, and if I start sacrificing for a guy again, I know I'll regret it."

"I found a career I loved," Angelina said. "I really enjoy running the lodge and planning for the future. A relationship is supposed to bring out the best in you, but you know what? This lodge brings out the best in me, too. I'm more creative, I'm more energized and I'm able to make a difference in the lives of my friends. That's got to count for something. I don't think the be all end all of life is romance anymore. Now, I think the point of life is help others in their hard times."

There was a blip, and Melanie looked at her phone to see an incoming call—this one from Tilly's cell phone.

"Angelina, I've got a call from Tilly," Melanie said. "I've got to go."

"You bet. We'll talk soon. Bye." Angelina hung up and Melanie picked up the call.

"Tilly?" she said.

"Melanie?" there were tears in Tilly's voice. "You said I should call..."

"Yes!" Melanie said. "Where are you? What's going on?"

"We're at a hotel in Brigham—it's some little town up in the mountains."

"I know it—that's about two hours from here," Melanie replied.

"I need you to come get me."

"Of course. Are you okay?"

"I'm fine. I'm just...mad. And you said you'd come, so..."

"I'm on my way. What's the hotel called?"

"Um..." There was a shuffling sound. "Brigham Hotel. Very creative."

"Are you alone? Is Simon there?" she pressed.

"I told Simon I'm done with him, and I wanted to come back. He said fine."

"Is he still there?"

"Yeah, but it's fine. I'm just mad. That's all. I want to come back."

Melanie sighed. "Okay, as long as you're safe. I'm on my way. Call me if you need anything else, but I'll be there in a couple of hours. Just stay where you are, okay? Don't leave with him again."

"You were right, Mel..." There were tears in Tilly's voice. "I need better than him."

She shut her eyes. An "I told you so" wouldn't be right, but she could feel it with every fiber.

"I'm coming. Hold tight, okay?"

"Okay. Bye."

Melanie hung up. Her heart was hammering. Tilly was up in some tiny logging town—not exactly a safe area for a teenager alone. What on earth were they doing up there?

She looked down at her cell phone. How inconsiderate would it be to call a friend to come with her at midnight? She wasn't keen on driving up to Brigham on her own. Angelina was still up—but it wasn't Angelina she wanted to call.

She grimaced, then dialed Logan's number. She'd let it ring three times and then hang up. But he picked up on the first ring.

"That you, Mel?" he said. He sounded groggy.

"It's me," she said. "Sorry to wake you, but would you be willing to come with me on a bit of a road trip tonight? Tilly called—

she's in Brigham, and she needs me to come get her."

"Yeah..." His voice became clearer. "You bet. I'm up. Do you want me to drive? I could pick you up, or—"

"I'm driving," she said. She wanted him to come along and be the muscle to protect her on that narrow highway in the middle of the night. And she wanted him to tell her it would be okay. But she didn't want him to drive. "I'll be there to pick you up in fifteen minutes, okay?"

"You bet. I'll be outside."

And she felt better knowing that she'd be doing this with Logan by her side. He was the kind of guy who made her feel more capable, just with his company. And if she was about to go confront Simon on Tilly's behalf, Simon might respect a male presence.

Melanie grabbed her keys and headed outside to her SUV. It was time to bring Tilly home.

WHEN LOGAN SETTLED into Melanie's passenger seat, he looked over to find her face looking pale and drawn.

"I didn't actually think she'd call," Melanie said. "I thought she'd call Adam, and I'd hear about it later."

Logan put on his seat belt. "It's like when they're two years old and they fling themselves off a high point and just trust that you'll catch them. They keep doing that—just in different ways. Before you know it, you've got a teenager on your hands who lives with this completely ungrateful belief that Dad—or Mom—can fix anything. They launch themselves out there, and you're not there to catch them anymore, so all you can do is hold your breath."

Melanie pulled out of the parking lot and headed down the gravel road that led to the main road. She seemed different tonight—there was a subtle change in her that he couldn't quite put his finger on.

"Is that what this is?" Melanie asked.

"Sure looks like it," he replied. "But she was right—you were here to catch her."

"I'm two hours away," she said with a shake of her head. "And I'm angry."

"Yeah, well…you're still driving out there." He reached over and squeezed her shoulder, then pulled back again. "There's nothing romantic about parenting."

"I'm pretty type A," she said. "When the

kids were younger, it is was easier to keep everything under control."

They pulled onto the highway into the mountains. The highway this far west was narrower, and when a semitruck thundered past them from the oncoming lane, the entire vehicle trembled.

"So...do you ever get tired of always having to be in control? Keeping all the balls in the air?" he asked.

"Sometimes," she said. "But honestly? I like lining things up in my life, making a plan, ticking things off my to-do list. And at my age, I don't want to let go of that. I think it's a good thing to have some control over your life. If not by now, then when?"

"A solid point," he agreed.

"And I'm tired of that being considered a character flaw. Our home ran well because I ran it. And those kids did well as students because I was on top of their projects and homework. My husband could bring clients home for dinner because I could order the best catering at the drop of a hat. Everyone loves the woman who has things under control until it comes to romance, apparently."

Logan chuckled. "Evidently, you choose the wrong guys."

"Agreed."

Melanie's tone was humorless, and he had to wonder if she was including him. Apparently, he wasn't easy to be with, either.

"So what do you want, then?" Logan asked.

"What do you mean?" She glanced over at him, then returned her attention to the road.

"I mean in life, in the future going forward. What do you want?" he asked.

"I was talking to Angelina just before Tilly called, and she was telling me that she loves running her lodge. She's passionate about it. It's exciting, and it brings out the best in her."

"Huh." Logan looked over at Melanie. "I feel that way about my company."

"I want *that*." She met Logan's gaze with a flash of a smile.

"A business?" he asked.

"Exactly. Something where all my hard work pays off. I'm tired of pouring all my energy into relationships. I want to build something concrete. I'm looking into a design diploma to get myself up-to-date, and then I want to start my own company."

Just not in Denver.

"Then do it."

She nodded, but didn't answer.

"So what's the plan with Tilly?" he asked.

"We're taking her back to my place, and her father is picking her up tomorrow night." She winced, and looked over at him. "I forgot about the funeral, Logan. You're going to be exhausted. I'm so sorry."

He had, too. His father was being laid to rest the next day at noon.

"It's fine," he said. "We'll be tired together…if you still want to come along."

"Hey, you're here for me," she said. "I can be at the funeral for you."

"Is this your work ethic?" he asked. Or did she want to be there?

"This is me as a friend," she said, and her smile softened. "My work ethic is just one of the perks you get."

Logan laughed, and he leaned his head back. They had almost two hours of driving ahead of them.

BRIGHAM WAS A small town surrounding a wood mill up in the Colorado Rockies. Logan had driven up here once when he was paid to deliver a car part to the Brigham auto shop. There wasn't much more in this town than the mill, but the mill offered a solid union job with benefits, so it kept the town on the map.

When they arrived at two in the morning, the town was completely silent. A police cruiser pulled up beside them at a stop sign and the officer silently stared at them for a moment, then turned. Melanie's phone gave the directions to the little hotel just on the edge of town. The neon sign in the window that announced Vacancy flickered, and Melanie pulled into a spot next to a vintage green Mercedes.

"Is that Simon's car?" Logan asked.

"That's it. They're still here." Melanie looked down at her phone and typed into it. "I'll text Tilly."

Logan opened the door and got out. He could hear the buzz of insects and the far-off bark of a dog, answered by the howl of a wolf that made his skin crawl. Nature was pretty close in a town this far from the rest of civilization. The hotel's office was lit up, and the windows of the hotel all had drawn curtains and darkness inside. Except for one, where a light glowed behind the curtains. He was willing to bet that was the right room.

The door opened and Tilly appeared backlit in the doorway. She was wearing a white summer dress, and her hair hung limp around her shoulders. Her makeup was smudged around her eyes. She looked like a lost kid.

"There she is..." He could hear the relief in Melanie's voice as she got out of the SUV. "Tilly, are you okay?"

Tilly shrugged, and her gaze moved over to Logan. "Why did you bring him?"

"Because it's the middle of the night and I was a woman traveling alone," Melanie replied.

"Oh...right. I hadn't thought of the safety thing," Tilly said. "I'm sorry I made you drive all the way out here. Simon and I made up..."

"When he found out I was on my way, no doubt," Melanie said. "Come on. I've driven all the way out here. Is the hotel restaurant open this time of night?"

"Yeah, they cater to truckers," Tilly said.

"Let's go talk and get something to eat," Melanie said.

That was a smart move—make no demands. He'd bet that Tilly would side with Simon in a heartbeat, especially if she'd already made up with him.

"I don't know," Tilly said, glancing over her shoulder. For permission? Simon was in the room, apparently.

"Tell you what," Logan said, stepping forward. "You ladies go talk, and I'll have a chat with Simon."

"I don't think he'd like that—" Tilly began.

"I'm a nice guy," Logan said. "It'll be fine. But we have driven an awfully long way. A conversation isn't too much to ask, is it?"

"I could eat a burger," Melanie said. "What about you?"

Tilly smiled faintly. "That sounds good."

Simon appeared behind her in the doorway. He glared at them, but Tilly walked toward the restaurant with Melanie and Logan breathed a sigh of relief. If Melanie was going to talk any sense into that girl, it would have to be away from Simon.

"I'm not talking to you," Simon said, turning to close the door, but Logan stepped forward and planted his palm against the wood.

"What did you think was going to happen here?" Logan asked. "You ran off with the pregnant daughter of a very wealthy man. Did you think her family would just ignore that?"

"Who are you?" Simon demanded.

"A friend of Melanie's. Now, you can talk with me right now, or I can call the cops. Her father is arriving tomorrow. You aren't getting away with this for long."

At the mention of her father, Simon sighed and let go of the door. "Fine. Whatever. But if you try and hit me or anything—"

"Do I look like some hired thug?" Logan chuckled. "I'm Mel's friend. That's it. And I have a kid a bit older than you, so I might have more insight than you think."

Simon didn't answer, and when Logan stepped into the hotel room, he saw clothes scattered about, some food packaging on the floor. Was he used to someone else cleaning up after him?

"So what's your best-case scenario here?" Logan asked, tossing a backpack off the seat of a chair and easing into it.

"What?" Simon squinted at him.

"All of this—taking off with her. What are you hoping to accomplish here?" Logan asked.

"I don't know. I'm the father of that baby—"

"Yeah, which means absolutely nothing until that baby is born," Logan replied. "And even then, you won't have any more rights to Tilly than you do now."

"I'm not forcing her to do anything!"

Simon said. “She wanted to leave. I picked her up. Sort of like what’s happening here. She called you, and you came.”

“I heard about the way you talk to her,” Logan said.

“So? What did you even hear?”

“Complaining about her gaining weight—”

“Melanie?” Simon asked, his lips turning up in a sneer. “She misunderstood. I don’t know what your problem is.”

“So what did you mean by it?” Logan asked.

“I don’t know. I don’t even remember what I said.”

This was going to be a pointless conversation, Logan could already tell. The kid would just deny, deny, deny and then go home to his rich parents and tell them how awful that man had been to him. And Logan had no desire to have a pack of lawyers on his back.

“So you’re going to be a father,” Logan said.

Simon blinked. “I guess. I mean, she’s pregnant, so…”

“How are you going to support her?” Logan asked.

“I don’t know. We have money,” Simon replied. "We don't exactly worry about that kind of thing the way people on your level do."

"I mean, long term," Logan pressed, ignoring the rudeness. "I assume you're planning on going to college after you graduate high school, right? I mean, your dad might insist upon that. By the time you graduate with a degree, you'll be twenty-two, and the baby will be about four. You'll have to be thinking about schools then, too."

Simon didn't answer, but some of the attitude drained from his expression.

"If you're planning on getting married, then you'll have to be thinking ahead. Her dad is pretty protective of her, I hear. And marrying a girl doesn't cut her away from her family. You'll have to think about her relationship with your in-laws starting now. Because all of this—they're going to remember it."

"Her dad isn't even in the country," Simon replied.

"And while he was gone, you hounded her about gaining pregnancy weight," Logan said.

"I didn't do that!"

"But you care, right?" Logan met Simon's gaze. "You don't want her getting fat, right?"

"She doesn't have to," Simon said peevishly.

Yeah, that's what Logan thought, and he had to quash the urge to smack the kid. He wasn't anywhere near ready to be a father and husband, or even a boyfriend.

"So what's your plan?" Logan asked again. "Are you getting married?"

"I don't know. Not yet. She might get an abortion."

"Hmm." He wasn't sure if that was coming from Simon or Tilly. "So…you'd prefer that?"

"Yeah, I'd prefer that! I'm seventeen! I'm not ready for all that responsibility. I'm taking a gap year to travel when I graduate and—"

"Not if you've got a baby, you aren't," Logan said with a short laugh. "What, you're going to reappear after a year and think everything is going to be fine? Look, I'm going to be straight with you, because I don't know you or your family. Right now, this has all been really intense and probably pretty scary. But the next time Tilly calls someone for help, it might not be us, it might be the cops."

"I didn't hit her or anything!" Simon said, his voice rising.

"You're treating her badly," Logan said.

"You're being mean. You're trying to control her, and you're taking out your anger on her. That kind of behavior is generally described as abuse. Now, you're growing up in the age of the internet, so it shouldn't surprise you to know that ten or fifteen years from now, Tilly could be online telling the story of the father of her child—how mean he was, the things he said when he was angry, how he made her feel. And that's going to reflect on you. Professionally, personally…and you're going to look back on this and wish you'd behaved better."

Simon didn't answer, but his gaze flickered toward the window.

"You can't cut her off from her family, and I think you know that. I don't think you even want to do that. And whatever little joyride you thought you were going to have while her dad was out of the country has gotten severely out of hand."

"Yeah…" Simon breathed.

"And whether Tilly has this baby or not, you're going to have to look her father in the face. You *made* a baby, and you're going to have to answer for your behavior. Don't make this worse than it already is."

"I don't know what to do," Simon said, his voice catching.

"First of all, you can encourage Tilly to come home with us," Logan said. "Then you can have a serious conversation with your parents about the future and how you're all going to handle this."

"My dad is going to be furious," Simon said.

"Maybe so. But you can face that," Logan replied. "I think your father being angry is a lot less intimidating than *her* father being angry. Especially if she loses that baby because of the stress you put her through. Then it wouldn't be a choice anymore, it would be your fault. People don't forgive that kind of thing very easily."

"And what else?" Simon asked, the attitude completely gone now. His gaze was pinned on Logan.

"You're going to have to change the way you treat women—all of them," Logan said. "You know about the Me Too movement, I'm sure. Women don't take that kind of garbage anymore, Simon. They get mad, and when you get enough of them supporting each other, they get even."

If Simon wasn't careful, he'd have a whole

tribe of women coming after him for his bad behavior, and he'd have no one to blame but himself. Simon licked his lips. Was he imagining the same thing?

"You're not too old to change your ways, kid," Logan went on. "But until you have, I suggest you keep a respectful distance from Tilly."

Simon nodded. "Yeah… Maybe she should go back with you, then. I didn't mean to upset her like that. I was just… I don't know. It's pretty intense right now."

Logan looked at Simon—young, spoiled, privileged. And somehow he'd gotten the message that he could treat women any way he chose. Would tonight make any difference in this young man?

Maybe it was a blessing to raise a son with less privilege—with a good woman by his side. Graham had learned to respect women. Logan might not have been a perfect husband, but he'd respected his wife, and Graham had seen that. How were the women treated in Simon's house? Was it anything like how it had been for Melanie?

"You can choose who you want to be," Logan said quietly. Simon didn't answer, and Logan stood up and headed for the door, pausing with his hand on the knob. "I know it can be confusing. It seems like you have to act a certain way to get the other guys' respect. But the stories they tell aren't true. They say they order their women about, but they don't. It's an act. Don't buy into it. And don't worry about everyone else. The trick is to behave in a way that you can be proud of when you look back on it when you're my age. The years pass faster than you think."

The night air whisked past his face as he stepped outside and the summer breeze carried the scent of trees and grass—fragrant with hope, in spite of it all.

The trick was to figure out when you were being a jerk soon enough, and figure out why…because that regret would cling.

Logan had never been as bad as Simon, but he'd been selfish. He'd put his own feelings ahead of Melanie's when he left her behind. He'd been more worried about his own heartbreak than hers. And then he'd managed to make his own wife miserable with his thoughtlessness. He hadn't meant to be that guy…

He headed toward the restaurant, his steps slow and tired. The young people thought they could mess up and make up all their lives…but really they had a small window, and they'd just keep repeating it and regretting it if they weren't careful.

CHAPTER FIFTEEN

MELANIE TOOK A jaw-cracking bite of her cheeseburger. There had been a time when she denied herself some of these simple pleasures. She'd always been so focused on staying slim for Adam, on looking great in those evening gowns she wore to different charity events. She had people to impress back then, and postdivorce, she realized she no longer cared.

"So what happened?" Melanie asked past her bite of food.

Tilly swirled a fry in ketchup and popped it into her mouth. "He was just being such a jerk. He was blaming getting pregnant on me, saying it was my responsibility to make sure this didn't happen, and..."

"He's mean to you, Tilly," Melanie said softly. "Love isn't like that."

Tilly picked up her burger and took a bite, chewing thoughtfully for a moment. "That's what guys are like most of the time. If you want one, you've got to put up with something."

"Something?"

"Either they're mean, or they cheat, or they only want you because your family is rich, or…something."

Melanie looked at Tilly thoughtfully. "Not all of them."

"Enough of them."

"Then why put up with any of it?" Melanie asked. "Isn't it better to be alone than to be treated like that?"

"I don't want to be alone." Tears welled in Tilly's eyes.

"And you never will be," Melanie said quietly. "You've got family—that's what they're for!"

"What about you?" Tilly asked.

"You have me, too. Who came out to get you?"

"No, I mean, you're alone. Your parents live far away, and you're just sitting out in some lake house—"

Was this what Tilly thought of her—some pathetic woman alone in a vacation house? It wasn't like she was some Miss Havisham living in the rotting remains of her wedding… Was that how she came across to Tilly now?

"Tilly, I'm okay with being alone," Melanie said gently. "And I have good friends. I'm willing to face life alone rather than be cheated on. I don't mean to speak badly of your dad, but I couldn't go on like that."

"I know." Tilly sighed.

"Do you think you'll be treated like I was?" Melanie asked. "When you get married, I mean. Do you think it's inevitable that your husband will cheat?"

Tilly was silent for a couple of beats, then she said, "My dad's one of the good ones."

Melanie reached out and put a hand on Tilly's arm. "He is one of the good *fathers*, but don't confuse a husband and a dad. Your father would walk through fire for you, and you can trust him always. But that doesn't mean he was good at being a husband, okay? I know that's hard to hear. But you don't have to be treated like I was."

Tilly didn't speak, and she turned her gaze toward her own reflection in the window.

"If my leaving did anything positive at all, let it be to show you that a woman doesn't have to put up with that," Melanie said quietly. "Never. And you can find a good guy who's an excellent father *and* a devoted husband. You can. You just might kiss a few frogs in the process."

"It sounds very nice," Tilly said coldly.

"The thing is, if you accept bad behavior from men, it's all you'll get," Melanie said. "If you want a better life than that, you have to find people who are kind to you."

"Simon's the father of my baby." A tear trickled down her cheek.

"I know." Melanie's eyes misted in sympathy. "That isn't going to go away, even if you take a step back so you can think."

"He'll dump me," Tilly said.

"Sweetie, you aren't going to want to hear this, but good riddance," Melanie said. "He's mean to you, and you don't deserve any of it. He's narrow-minded, rude, self-centered and frankly, bad for you. Are you happy right now?"

"What?"

"In this moment…for the last long while," Melanie said. "Are you happy? Have you been happy with him?"

"I don't know."

"It would be a good thing to figure out," Melanie said. "I'm not trying to break you up. I just want to make sure you can stand up for yourself, okay? Your dad is coming tomorrow night to pick you up, and you two can sit down and decide how you want this to go. But you need to choose what your life will look like, Tilly. Not Simon. *You*."

"I'm so tired," Tilly whispered.

Melanie understood. When she'd found out about Adam's cheating, she'd come to sit in a little diner much like this one. And she'd eaten a piece of cake and had a milkshake to boot, wiping her tears on a napkin as she ate. She'd felt so exhausted, so drained from all the trying and the hard work that hadn't mattered a bit. All she'd wanted to do was curl up in a cocoon and stay that way, but life seldom allowed that kind of luxury. There were no Miss Havishams outside of literature.

"I know, sweetie," Melanie said. "If you come back with me, you can get some rest, and then talk to Simon when you're ready. At least talk to your father face-to-face before you make any big decisions, okay?"

Tilly nodded. "Okay."

"So you'll come back with me?" Melanie asked.

"Yeah. But I need to talk to Simon first."

They finished eating and Melanie paid the check. When they headed back outside, Logan was standing in front of the SUV, leaning against the bumper. He straightened when he saw them come out. Tilly headed back to the hotel room and Logan cast her an inquiring look.

"She needs to talk to him," Melanie said, and she pulled out her keys. "Do you want to drive on the way back?"

"Are we leaving her?"

"I'm honestly not sure," Melanie said. "She said she'd come with us, but she might change her mind. She isn't going to break up with him because I told her to."

They got back into the SUV, and Melanie leaned her head back, closing her eyes for a moment.

"How did it go with Simon?" she asked, her eyes still shut.

"About the same," Logan said quietly. "I gave him some really good reasons to smarten up, but I'm not sure how much of a difference that will make."

When Melanie opened her eyes, she found Logan looking at her, his eyes filled with regret.

"I'm sorry, Mel," he said. "For everything I did back when I was young and stupid. I was thinking about myself, not about you. I thought it would be easier on me if I didn't have to see how I broke your heart."

"You were a jerk," she said.

"No argument," he replied.

"But you aren't anymore."

"Caroline might have disagreed with that."

She paused. "What reasons did you give Simon to change?"

"Namely, that he didn't want to be my age looking back on the way he'd acted as a kid and have regrets," Logan said.

"Did he care about that?"

"No," Logan replied. "I think he was more worried about the Me Too movement, to be honest. With his family's money, who knows? He might want to run for congress or something."

Melanie laughed at that, then sighed. "I wish she'd just dump him."

"What did it take for you to leave Adam?" he asked.

"Honestly?" Melanie sighed, her mind going back to that painful day. "I was sitting in a diner much like the one Tilly and I were just at. I wanted some sort of privacy, as well as greasy food, so..." She smiled wanly. "An older woman passed my booth and she gave me this look as if she'd seen this a million times already, and she said, 'If I was as pretty as you and as young as you, I wouldn't waste another tear on him. You have a lot of life left.'"

"What did you say?" Logan asked.

"Nothing. She kept moving, and I gave it some thought. I knew women who put up with their husband's affairs because they had too much to lose, and I had just as much on the table, you know? Adam and the kids were my world. My social networks, the neighborhood I lived in, the comforts I enjoyed were all because of Adam. But I'd lived with a whole lot less, and I could again. Then I thought of the woman I'd become if I stayed...and I didn't like her. I'd become jealous, bitter, self-centered... So I finished my cake, and I called a divorce attorney."

"I'm glad you left him," Logan said softly.

"Me, too. But it was the hardest thing I ever did," she said. "And it's not going to be any easier on Tilly to leave Simon. So I don't know if what I said will make any difference to her at all, but maybe it will sink in and give her the strength she needs."

"Maybe her father will go intimidate the kid into submission," Logan suggested.

"Yeah, maybe." Melanie chuckled. "It couldn't hurt."

But it wouldn't last. The Simons of the world got older and meaner. Sometimes they hid their behavior better, but ever so slowly, they sucked away a woman's sense of self-respect. They made the world seem harsher, crueler, lonelier. They made her question if she really had what it took to start over again.

The hotel door opened, and Tilly came out with her suitcase in tow, followed by Simon who stopped in the doorway. Tilly paused to kiss him, and Simon turned his face away. Melanie got out.

"Where are your other bags?" she asked.

"In the trunk, still."

Simon got them out, and after Logan got them stowed in the back of the vehicle, Simon headed back toward the hotel room.

"Did you want the front, Tilly?" Melanie asked.

"No, I'd rather have the back." Tilly settled herself in the back seat and Melanie and Logan got back in.

Simon stood in that doorway until they had driven away, and Melanie looked over her shoulder at her stepdaughter.

"What did you say to him?" Melanie asked.

"I just said that I'd called you all the way out here, and I couldn't make you go back without me. You'd tell my father he was a monster and my dad would call the cops on him."

Melanie chuckled. "That's it?"

"I also told him that if he'd been decent to me, I would never have called you. And I need time to think."

"You're going to be okay, Tilly," Melanie said.

"I don't want to talk anymore," Tilly said, her voice shaking.

"Okay..." Melanie picked up her phone and typed in a text to Adam.

Tilly called me, and I picked her up from Brigham, and she'll be waiting for you to come get her tomorrow.

There was no immediate reply—he might even be on a flight back already, she wasn't sure. She tucked her phone away again and she leaned her head back, watching the dark road.

This wouldn't be the last time Tilly faced

this kind of thing. But every time a woman stood up for herself and decided on her own self-worth, it became a little bit easier.

Logan reached over and took her hand. She hesitated, then twined her fingers through his, because while Melanie was perfectly willing to face life alone, for tonight, she'd accept a little comfort.

LOGAN DROVE BACK to the lodge where Melanie took his place behind the wheel. Tilly had fallen asleep in the back seat, and Melanie unrolled the window to say goodbye.

"It's almost morning," Logan said. "In fact—" he looked at his phone "—it is morning. It's five."

"What time is the funeral?" she asked.

"It's at noon, but Mel, you don't have to come with me," he said. "You have your own stuff to take care of."

"How about you give me the address, and I'll do my best without promises," she suggested.

That sounded a lot fairer, so he texted her the address of the church and tucked his phone away again.

"Thank you for coming along tonight,"

Melanie said, her warm gaze meeting his, then she stifled a yawn.

"Not a problem," he said. "Glad I could help."

What he felt was much deeper than that, however. He was glad he could be a part of this, be a support for Melanie. He owed her that much—to make a few of her burdens a little easier to bear. Maybe this was atonement—like delivering the box to his father had been.

Logan tapped the hood of the vehicle in farewell and headed up toward the front door of the lodge. The sun's rays were peeking over the tops of the mountains, and he swallowed a yawn of his own. He'd sleep for a few hours, and then get ready to bury his father.

Maybe it was better to have been out tonight—distraction from deeper feelings seemed to be his MO. He'd be dealing with his father's death for a very long time to come, he was sure. But not at this moment.

THE FUNERAL WAS held at a local church in downtown Mountain Springs, an ornate building with a tall steeple nestled between lilac and rose bushes. The lilacs were in bloom and the roses only had buds, but the fragrance was comforting. A discreet sign had been erected in front saying that the church was reserved for a private event, but that didn't stop a few tourists from stopping to take photos, anyway.

Logan wasn't sure if Melanie would come. She'd be exhausted and he wouldn't blame her if she didn't make it, but a few minutes after he arrived dressed in an appropriately dark charcoal-gray suit, he spotted Melanie coming through the front doors of the church. Her sleeveless black dress was simple, and a pair of pearl earrings were the only jewelry he could spot.

She was gorgeous, her chocolate-brown hair falling in soft waves around her shoulders, and she paused, scanning the crowd until she spotted him. She didn't smile, but she crossed the foyer toward him, pausing to say hello to a few people as she went.

"Hi," Melanie said when she reached him. "I made it."

"You look great," he said quietly.

"I tried." She smiled faintly then. "How are you holding up?"

"I'm—" He licked his lips. He wasn't sure how he felt. This was a strange farewell to a man who'd held himself back for all of Logan's life. "I'm not sure if what I've planned to say is going to go over too well with this crowd."

"Most of these people aren't his children," she replied. "I don't think it matters if they like it or not. Funerals are for the family, aren't they?"

Logan shrugged. "You might have a point. My siblings might not like it, either, though."

She smiled at that. "You always were a bit of a rebel, Logan. I say roll with it."

Logan raised an eyebrow. "Don't say I didn't warn you."

Organ music swelled from inside the sanctuary. People were already taking their seats, murmuring quietly to each other, shaking hands, nodding sadly… At the front, there were two large photos of Harry, one from when he was a young man and the other more recent. There was a wreath of white flowers and a casket, the lid open. Logan's gaze landed on that casket, and he froze.

"Do you want to go pay your respects?" Melanie asked softly.

"I should," he replied.

"I'll go take a seat, and you can meet me there when you're ready," she suggested.

"Sure."

Logan went slowly up to the front. He waited while an older woman looked sadly into the casket, then stepped aside for him. As he looked down at his father's placid face, he thought he looked almost too peaceful. Harry had never been a tranquil man—he'd been active, annoyed, determined. Whatever had made his father who he was had flown. He didn't want to wait for a wave of emotion, so he turned and headed to where Melanie had taken a seat behind Junior's family.

As Logan slid into the pew next to Mel, Junior turned to give him a nod of greeting. His wife turned, too. She was a pleasant enough looking woman—a little reminiscent of Dot, actually.

"Nice to meet you," Logan murmured, shaking her hand, then nodded to the kids who turned to regard him. The youngest son, Taylor, sat next to Junior, and Logan could see just how much he looked like his dad. Harry had been right—those Wilde genes seemed to have skipped him and Graham.

The minister stood up to speak, saving Logan from finding something to say to his nephew. There was a scattering of other people he didn't recognize, and it was just as well. He really wasn't interested in making acquaintance with other relatives.

"We're here to celebrate the life of our friend and loved one, Harry Wilde," the minister began. "Life is so much shorter than any of us are ready for. Harry was a family man, and he spoke often about his children and grandchildren, boasting about their achievements as only a loving father could." There was a ripple of soft laughter. "I think you all know what I'm talking about! He would have wanted to live longer—I know that. Even though his health was failing, he wasn't finished..."

The minister continued speaking, moving into more spiritual grounds for a short sermon, and Logan leaned forward, letting out a slow breath. He wasn't a part of this. Maybe he should have been, and maybe he even had a genetic right to it, but reality was starkly different.

He felt Melanie's touch on his arm and he slid his hand over hers, centering himself with the feeling of her cool, soft fingers.

"And now, we're going to hear from Harry's son—" The minister cleared his throat, looked toward Junior questioningly, then when he received a nod, he continued, "Logan McTavish."

Logan could hear the murmurs behind him. Logan stood up and headed for the podium, and his hands started to sweat. He gave the minister a nod of thanks, and then turned to face the crowd. Most were staring at him wide-eyed, but there was one face that was fixed on him with sympathy. Melanie.

"Hello, everyone," Logan said, his voice sounded strange to him through the microphone. "You were expecting to hear from Junior, no doubt. Sorry—he's a grown man now, and people call him Eugene, or better yet, Dr. Wilde."

There was a trickle of light laughter.

"For those of you who don't know me, my name is Logan McTavish, and I'm Harry's son from a previous relationship, before he met Dot. But I was never really part of the family. I'm just going to say that, because it's easier than dancing around it. Junior has been trying to fix that lately, and I'm grateful, but the way the rest of you remember my dad—I never saw that side of him."

The room fell silent, and Logan looked over at Junior, his son sitting next to him with wide shocked eyes.

"The thing is, none of us are perfect, and neither was my dad," Logan said. "But I can tell by the way you all remember him that he meant a lot to all of you. You saw the kindness in him, and the nobleness. He did right by you. And I'm glad you have that." He nodded at Junior's son. "But for whatever reason, my dad had a harder time connecting with me. Maybe I wasn't like him. I certainly don't have the Wilde looks, do I? I've been thinking about what I could say about Harry, and here is what I'm left with—my father tried hard to live a good life, and I can see the evidence of that around this room. I think that's important—that we all try. Sometimes, we're going to fall short, and for that, we have to hope that people will forgive us."

Logan looked toward the casket, and for a moment, emotion choked off his voice.

"But I forgive him," he said, tears misting his eyes. "I forgive him for messing it up with me, because that's all I can offer him. But he was proud of you, Junior." He turned to see his brother's ashen face. "Really proud. I got to talk to him a couple of days before he passed, and he talked about Eugene most of all. So I'm grateful that you included me today, and but I'm going to let

Eugene take over now and talk about the memories he has about our father. And I'll let you all grieve for the man who loved you."

A lump closed off Logan's throat, and he couldn't have said another word if he'd wanted to. He looked toward Melanie pleadingly, and she stood up, and made her way to the aisle. He joined her, and she slipped her hand into his as they made their escape.

"Uh—thank you to my brother for being willing to speak..." Junior's voice carried behind him, but Logan wasn't staying to listen. Let Harry's family grieve in peace.

As they erupted outside into the sunlight, Logan rubbed his hand over his eyes.

"That was bad..." he muttered.

"No, that was honest," Melanie replied. "You don't have to stop existing to make other people more comfortable, you know."

Logan looked over at her, and managed a shrug. "Ironically, it's what my father would have wanted—me to back off and let them mourn."

Melanie shook her head.

"No, I'm serious," he said. "Whatever my father's limitations when it came to loving me, he could have made up with me anytime over the last twenty years."

"I'm sure he was a more complex man than any of his children realized," she observed. "That's the way of parenthood—our children simplify us to make themselves comfortable, but even you are more complex than Graham knows."

Melanie slipped her arm through his once more and they started down the sidewalk. At the corner, they took a side street down a tree-lined road, away from the tourists and bustle of the town center. She felt good next to him. Too good, but instead of putting some distance between them, he covered her hand with his.

"You loved him," Melanie said quietly.

"What?"

"You did," she said. "You loved your dad, whether he loved you back or not, you did love him."

"Yeah." His voice was tight.

"I'm so sorry for your loss, Logan."

Such a simple thing to say, but it started a crack in his reserve that crept deeper and deeper as the tears welled in his eyes. He hadn't cried for his father yet, and he'd hoped to do this in private, but he couldn't seem to hold back the flood of emotion. Tears trickled down his cheeks, and Melanie wordlessly wrapped her arms around his waist and leaned her face against his shoulder, holding him tight. He pulled her close against him, buried his face in her hair and cried.

She didn't move, or hurry him. She was like a rock there, holding him up, and when he'd finished, he wiped his eyes, feeling somewhat foolish.

"Sorry," he muttered.

"For what?" she asked softly. "For mourning your father at his funeral? Logan, you'll have to forgive yourself, too. You were enough, you know. You really were."

It was a nice sentiment, but not true. He hadn't been enough of a Wilde to fit in with his father's family, and he hadn't been enough for his wife, either. When it came to Caroline and very likely Melanie, too, it wasn't about his intrinsic worth—this was about his own behavior, his defense mechanisms, his knee-jerk reactions. He might not fit in with Harry's family, but Logan was his father's son in more ways than one—he had the same stubborn streak, the same tendency to clam up about his feelings and the same way of pushing away the people he loved. Given enough time, he'd probably do it with Melanie again, too, and that thought tightened his throat. He bent down and pressed a kiss against Mel's forehead.

"I'm glad you're here," he said gruffly.

She didn't answer, but she slipped her arm through his again, and they continued their slow walk down the sidewalk, the tree-dappled shade cooling the summer air.

"I have to leave tomorrow morning," he said.

"I know. Will you come say goodbye this time?"

"Of course," he said. "You can count on it."

Logan missed her already. But they'd both go back to their lives, and that was as it should be. Sure, they could stay in contact, but it wouldn't be the same. Whatever was happening here would stop. And Melanie would be better off with a proper goodbye and moving on.

CHAPTER SIXTEEN

THAT EVENING, MELANIE awoke from a heavy nap, still feeling foggy. Something had woken her up, and she pushed her hand through her tangled hair, trying to pinpoint what it was. Then she heard the sound of the front door opening and voices—Tilly's and Adam's—and she woke up the rest of the way, her heart speeding up in her chest.

So, Adam had come.

Melanie got up and headed out toward the living area. Her ex-husband stood by the door, and for a moment, he didn't see her. He looked older, with a few more lines on his face. But his old way of standing—legs akimbo, hands in his pockets—brought a lump to her throat. When would that feeling stop? Why couldn't she just hate him and be done with it?

When Adam saw her, he smiled hesitantly.

"Hi, Mel," Adam said. "Sorry to wake you."

Such an ordinary thing to say—something he'd said a thousand times over their marriage. Looking at him in this lake house, she thought it could have been any other summer, when Adam worked long hours and came to see them with that easy smile on his face. Now, of course, she knew what else he'd been up to besides working, and it still hurt in a very deep and personal place in her heart.

"It was a late night last night," Melanie said.

"I got your text after I landed," Adam said. "What happened?"

"Simon was being a jerk," Tilly said. "And Mel came to get me."

"Pumpkin," Adam said, holding a hand out to his daughter. She came forward and hugged him. Adam squeezed her tight, shutting his eyes for a moment, then he released her. "We'll figure this out, okay? I'm pretty excited about becoming a grandpa. And I'll talk to Simon's parents, and—"

"I'm not ready for that," Tilly said.

"Leave it to me, Tilly," Adam said, and there was a note of finality in his voice that was a relief to Melanie—another adult was taking over. She could step back now.

"Thank you for all of this, Mel," Adam said. "You always were the one who held us all together."

"I was," Melanie agreed. "But I'm glad you're here. Tilly needs you."

"Why don't you get packed, Tilly," Adam said. "Let me talk to Mel."

Tilly headed out of the kitchen, and Adam came closer to Melanie and bent down to kiss her cheek. She stepped back, avoiding his touch.

"I miss us being a family," Adam said, his voice low.

"You miss me taking care of things," Melanie replied.

"Yeah," Adam replied, then sighed. "I wasn't good to you. I wish I hadn't messed up like that—"

"Adam, this is long finished," Melanie said. "We're divorced."

"I know..." Adam met her gaze. "Is there someone else?"

"You don't get to ask that," she replied with a shake of her head. "After all you put me through, you have no right to ask that question."

Adam smiled faintly. "So there is."

He was so confident, so sure of himself,

and she could see now why she'd been drawn to him and had continued trusting him all those years. There wasn't any visible chink in that armor.

"You should know that Tilly knew you were cheating on me the entire time," Melanie said. "All the kids did."

Adam's easy smile fell. "What?"

"The kids see more than we think," she replied. "And I'm only telling you this because I think it's done a real number on her. She thinks our marriage is the norm, and it's what she has to look forward to."

Adam swallowed. "Look, I made some mistakes, but—"

"Do you want her with a guy who lies to her and cheats on her?" Melanie asked, raising her eyebrows. "She figures that's the trade-off in order to be loved."

"I know my daughter—" Adam started, his gaze snapping, and she could feel the fight rising in him.

"Not as well as you think," Melanie replied tiredly. "And I have no intention of having a fight with you in my kitchen. You two are due for some long honest talks, and I truly hope it helps her, because otherwise, she'll be with Simon or some other guy who treats her the same, and it will be because she saw more than you thought."

Adam pressed his lips together. "I think you can leave *my daughter* to me."

Melanie cocked her head to one side, regarding her ex-husband with new eyes. There it was—the line he always drew, be it ever so subtly. These were his kids, not hers. Of course, he missed her…she'd held his private life together, but he wasn't going to change any more than Simon would.

"For the record?" Melanie said. "I raised Tilly, too, and I love her. Deal with Simon as you see fit."

Would it make any difference? Likely not. The Isaacs family dynamic would go on, and Melanie would be cut out. Tilly came out with her suitcase and Adam stepped forward to take it from her. He headed for the door, leaving Tilly and Melanie momentarily alone.

"Thank you for—" Tilly shrugged "—letting me stay for a bit."

And this was goodbye. Tilly would go off with her dad, and Melanie would likely never see her again. Because that was how divorces worked when the kids had never been yours to begin with.

Tears welled in Melanie's eyes. "Anytime. I mean that. I know I'm not your real mom, Tilly, but I'm the one who raised you. And I'll always be here for you. I'm what you've got."

Tilly nodded. "Okay."

Melanie wrapped her arms around the girl's thin shoulders and pulled her into a hug. It wouldn't change anything, would it? Tilly wouldn't need her again.

"This doesn't have to be goodbye—not forever," Melanie said.

"Yeah..." Tilly's chin trembled.

"Hey, I'm not going anywhere," Melanie said, smiling past her own tears. "And you obviously know how to find me."

"Mel, I've been feeling really bad about what I said before," Tilly said. "About how we knew about Dad cheating and all that, and..."

"Hey—my relationship with your father wasn't your fault, or your business. Don't worry about it."

"I was going to tell you a few times," Tilly said, "when I was younger, but Michael said that if I told you, you'd divorce Dad and leave us, and I didn't want you to go."

Tilly met Melanie's gaze tearily.

"You were afraid I'd leave you?" Melanie breathed.

Tilly nodded. "Because Mrs. Brent left Mr. Brent when she found out he was cheating on her, right? And Mrs. Klein did. And Mr. Cossens divorced Mrs. Cossens when he found out about her yoga instructor, and—"

"I get the idea," Melanie said. "You kids carried around a bigger burden than I ever thought."

"I guess so."

They'd known too much, hidden too much and tried to control what they could in their world. It was sadly touching that Tilly had hidden that information in hopes of keeping her stepmother. Maybe Melanie hadn't been quite so rejected as she'd thought.

"I might have divorced your dad, but I'm not gone," Melanie said. "Okay? I'm still yours, Tilly. And I always will be. I'm the one who tucked you in, and read you stories. I was your Tooth Fairy and your Easter Bunny, and the one who baked for your bake sales every year… No one can change that, Tilly. No one can take back that time that was ours, together."

But even as she said it, she realized that the

time was slipping away. The past wouldn't change, but the future certainly would.

"I wish I'd been better to you," Tilly said softly.

"Oh, sweetie," Melanie said. "You were a kid. I can forgive that. I suggest you do, too. I love you, okay?"

Tilly leaned in to give Melanie one more hug, and the door opened again and Adam came back inside. He spotted Tilly's last two bags and came forward to collect them.

"Let's go, Tilly," Adam said. "I need you to fill me in on Simon."

Adam would be good for that much—Simon would be quaking before Adam was done with him. Melanie grabbed a box of granola bars from the cupboard and pressed them into Tilly's hands. "In case you get hungry."

Tilly smiled, and she followed her father to the door. Melanie stood in the doorway, watching Tilly get into her father's black pickup truck.

"I'll send a guy for Tilly's car," Adam called.

"Sure." Melanie nodded and watched as he got back into the truck. Adam undid the window and met her gaze with a sad smile.

"It was good to see you again," Adam said.

"Yeah..." Melanie took a wavering breath. "Take care of her."

Adam did the window back up, and the vehicle started to pull away.

How many summers had ended this way—the family leaving a few at a time, and Melanie left alone in the lake house to get things cleaned up for the season? How many times had Melanie stood on this step, her heart sad and full and tired and overwhelmed, and knowing that the time was slipping away far too quickly?

She shut the door and looked around the little lake house—the cozy kitchen, the living room that she could finally redecorate if she wanted to, without the fear of it being demolished by a houseful of kids.

And yet...if by some miracle Tilly let her be a grandma to her baby—and at the thought, her heart sped up just a little bit in hopeful anticipation—then she might have little feet in this place again.

If she stayed.

The thought settled around her as she looked around the place. She'd told Tilly that no one could take away their time together, and that was true. No one could erase the fifteen years of her marriage, what it had meant, or where it had failed her. Even if she moved to a new house, those years wouldn't be erased.

She'd thought that Adam was in the cracks of these walls, but after seeing him today, she realized it wasn't him in the cracks, after all—it was *her*. These had been her summers, her relationships, her stepkids, her hopes and her dreams…even her heartbreak. But these walls had absorbed her soul…not Adam's.

And those last fifteen years has been *her* marriage, too. There was no going back, only forward. She wouldn't sell this lake house—she would finally decorate it to her own tastes, and she was going to wake up morning after morning with Blue Lake out her window, a cup of coffee in her hands and a determination to live a life that was true to her own heart. She was going to take those courses and start over.

Melanie pulled out her phone and started a group text to the women of the Second Chance Club.

Do you girls want to come to my place by the lake? We can sit on the deck with a bottle of wine and toast new beginnings. I could use some company.

Her phone started to ping with replies almost immediately.

Renata replied, I can make it. The kids are with their dad for the next two weeks, so I'm completely free.

I need your address and your wine preferences. I'm in. That was Gayle.

You had me at sitting on your deck by the lake. What time? Belle.

There was a pause, and then Angelina's text came last. Of course! I sense an update is coming? Tell me in person. I'll be there.

Tears misted her eyes. She'd wanted a fresh start, and she was getting one—with some good girlfriends she didn't realize she'd needed, and the lake house she hadn't thought she wanted.

LOGAN TOSSED HIS bag into the back of the pickup truck and glanced at his watch. Graham had sent him a text and his flight was coming in early. As quickly as that, his time here in Mountain Springs was done.

He'd promised that he'd say goodbye to Melanie, and he intended to make good on that. Except this was feeling uncomfortably familiar—his instinct was to avoid those tough emotional situations. Saying goodbye to her was going to be harder than he'd anticipated. But it didn't have to be a forever goodbye—Denver was only a few hours away. Yet, somehow, he knew whatever had happened here was ending.

The drive around the lake from Mountain Springs Lodge toward Melanie's lake house was a long one because there wasn't one direct road that made the loop. But when he finally managed to pull onto the drive that led to Melanie's place, he felt a surge of relief.

It didn't make sense. The last time they'd been romantically involved, they'd been teenagers. And now… Was it just that she'd been here for him during his own turbulent time?

He didn't think so. He wasn't so easily swept off his feet. And while he was grateful that she'd been here with him, his feelings for her weren't rooted in something that selfish.

He was supposed to be too old for this attraction. But maybe it was better that he was heading out now, before he did something impetuous that he'd regret. Mel deserved a good guy who wouldn't disappoint her, and if this trip back to Mountain Springs had shown him anything, it was that he wasn't that guy. He still had to figure out how he'd messed up his marriage so badly before he let himself get entangled with another woman's heart. He had to figure out how to stop making his father's mistakes.

He's already broken Caroline's heart, and he couldn't break Mel's…again.

Logan pulled into Melanie's drive and parked between Melanie's SUV and Tilly's little sports car. The kitchen curtain flicked, and then the front door opened. Melanie was wearing a pair of jeans now, and a gauzy pink blouse that brought out the color in her cheeks. She was barefoot, and she stood there, waiting for him. This wasn't going to make saying goodbye any easier.

"Hi," he said as he got to the door.

"I wasn't expecting you." She smiled, though, and she sounded pleased to see him. "If I'd know you were coming, I'd have asked my friends to stop by another evening."

"You're expecting company?" he asked.

"In an hour or so. There's still time." She stepped back. "Come on in."

Logan followed her inside, and he noticed that a few things had changed again since he'd been there last—the table was in a different spot and the couches and chairs in the sitting room had been rearranged, too.

"I was going to see if you felt like buying me breakfast tomorrow morning before you left," she said. "Or… I could buy you breakfast. I'm not overly picky over who pays."

She was so lovely standing there—her warm gaze meeting his expectantly, humor tickling her lips—that he wished he could say yes.

"I'm actually heading back to Denver tonight," Logan said. "Graham's flight comes in early."

Her smile fell. "Already?"

"Yeah…"

He dropped his gaze. Here was where he was supposed to say goodbye, wish her well, head on back out and pretend that those kisses and long hours together hadn't meant anything. Logan stood there for a moment just looking down at her bare feet, at those pink painted toenails, then he said, "Come visit me."

"In Denver?"

No, it was a terrible idea. What was he doing? Except he couldn't quite bring himself to take it back, either. He stepped closer and caught her hand. "Come see me, Mel. I'm going to miss you. I had no intention of starting anything, but I think we did… didn't we?"

"This is a bad idea, Logan," Melanie said.

"I know," he said with a helpless shrug.

"So what are we supposed to do?" she asked, shaking her head. "Date long distance? Again?"

"I'm not a kid anymore," he said, his voice lowering to a growl.

"Neither am I," she said. "I don't think it's smart to play with this. I'm freshly divorced. I'm in no way ready for…for…." She looked around as if she'd find the words in the air. "You left me once, and I'm not willing to sit out here in Mountain Springs and pine for you again."

"Then come to Denver," he said.

"I'm staying here." She shook her head. "This is where my life is. This lake house… sure, it's full of memories, but they're *my* memories! And at this age, I need them—hard as they are. They anchor me. They tell me who I am. I have a plan, and I threw over my own ambitions when I married Adam. I'm not doing that again."

"Then visit me," he said.

"As friends, or something more?" she asked.

They weren't friends—they were most definitely past that line. But he would only mess up a committed romantic relationship. All he could offer was the same battered heart he'd given Caroline. No better, no worse. And if this visit home had taught him anything, it was that he was more like his father than he'd ever dreamed. He was still the same man who'd made his wife wonder what it would be like to be free of him…

"As…whatever we are right now," he said. "This."

"This?" She shook her head. "This is a recipe for heartbreak, at least for me. I'm not ready to trust another man with my future, and you're not ready to give your heart over to another woman. So what are we even doing here?"

"I don't know about you, but I'm feeling something!" Logan retorted. "What am I doing here? I'm following my heart! Is it stupid? Maybe. But I don't want to just walk away, Mel! Give me some credit for that!"

Tears rose in her eyes and she pressed her lips together. "Maybe I'm telling you to walk away. Guilt-free."

"And if I don't want to?" He caught her hand again and pulled her closer. "What if I want to try?"

Melanie didn't answer, and he dipped his head to meet her lips. She let out a soft sigh, leaning into his kiss as he wrapped his arms around her. She felt so good in his arms, the perfect shape to melt into his embrace. And it had been so long since he'd felt this way—filled with longing and excitement. He pulled back and looked down into her glistening eyes.

"You'll rethink this in Denver." Her voice shook as she pulled out of his arms.

"Rethink it? Is this what you think of me, the guy who would forget about you with a change of scenery? Mel, I love you!"

He startled himself when the words came out, but they were true. He'd fallen for her with the same enthusiasm he had the first time, and whether it was good for him or not, there was no going back on it.

"You..." Whatever she was going to say evaporated on her lips.

"I love you," he repeated. "You're incredible. You're beautiful. You're insightful and kind and...and too good for me. It isn't logical, because logic says I should just go home and put the last week behind me. It's crazy. It's fast."

"It's all of those things!" Melanie said, wiping a tear from her cheek. "You *should* go home!"

"Not until I know if I'm alone in this," he pleaded. "If it's just me, then fine. I can accept that. I've made a fool of myself, but maybe you're worth feeling like a fool for. But if you feel something—"

"You should go home," she whispered again.

His heart fell to the pit of his stomach, and he stared at her in mortification. "I'm sorry, Mel. I should have..."

He'd been an idiot to let his emotions get involved. She was probably smart to send him away. He was trouble—no longer on a motorbike, but trouble nonetheless, and at least she could see it.

"Look, in my own defense, I didn't stand a chance of not falling for you," he said softly. "You're truly incredible."

He wondered if it would have been better to just text her and head on out of town, but he'd promised her. He wasn't ghosting her again. He wasn't hiding from his feelings.

He was done with breaking the hearts of the women he loved.

"Call me if you ever want to," Logan said, pulling open the door.

"Oh, Logan..." Tears slipped down her cheeks. "I love you, too..."

Logan froze, the door partway open and the pine-scented air coming in to meet him. "You do?"

"But what use is it?" she asked, shaking her head. "I can't just trust another guy with my life, and I can't fool around with feelings like these. It's too much! I'm not tough enough to roll with it. Maybe it's been too long since I've dated anyone, but I can't." She shook her head. "And what about you?"

"What do you mean?" he asked.

"Can you just launch yourself into a serious relationship?"

He rubbed his hand over his eyes. "I made my wife miserable, and I don't know why. Or how. Or what went wrong. I've got to take this slow."

"And I don't think it's going slowly between us," she said. "It's burning fast, and if we aren't ready to take the next step, it will burn out."

"Do you think we can be something to each other?" he asked.

She shrugged helplessly. "Maybe later. Much later. I can't go through another heartbreak, Logan. I need to get my balance here. And your life is in Denver. I'm not repeating history."

It was impossible—he knew it.

"I still hate saying goodbye," he said miserably.

"Me, too, but at least this time we get one." Her chin trembled. "And I'm grateful for that."

Logan left the door open and crossed the hallway toward her again. He swept her into his arms. This time his kiss was filled with longing for all the things he wished he could be to her, if he were only a little less damaged, a little less of a risk. The soft scent of her filled his head and his heart, and when he finally pulled back, he knew he had to leave now or not at all.

"I'd better go," he said, his voice choked, and he left, putting one foot in front of the other until he got into his truck. He clutched his steering wheel with a death grip, willing his emotions to stay buried beneath his granite mask. He wouldn't put the burden of his heartbreak onto her.

Melanie stood at the open door, her brown eyes filled with tears, but she raised one hand in farewell as he put the truck into Reverse. He unrolled his window before he took his foot off the brake.

"Call me if you want to talk," he said.

Even if it hurt. Even it made it worse, he wouldn't turn her away.

She nodded, but she didn't say anything, and he knew what that meant. She wouldn't call. And neither would he. This was the goodbye they should have had twenty years ago.

He took his foot off the brake and pulled out of her drive. It seemed that the right thing to do could be identified by how much it hurt. Because a proper goodbye had been the thing they'd both needed…but it left him gutted.

He'd go pick up his son and get back to his life. Melanie had never been his to hold on to, anyway.

CHAPTER SEVENTEEN

MELANIE STOOD IN the silence of her house for a moment, the weight of what had just happened sinking down into her chest. It was then that the tears broke free and her shoulders shook as she dropped to sit on the floor.

She loved him. Maybe she'd never fully gotten him out of her heart. He'd been the first one to break her heart, and now he'd done it again, but she couldn't blame him. She'd known better than to toy with these kinds of feelings with Logan McTavish, and he'd tried to stop himself from falling for her, too. Why couldn't they be better at this twenty years later? Why were they still so apt to tumble down that slope together?

But there was something about that man that tugged her in. In some way, he still felt like hers, except he wasn't. He still belonged to his late wife, and he still felt guilty and responsible to her. They'd both been betrayed in their previous relationships, just in different ways. His wife had never opened up to him and let him fix what was going wrong. And Adam had denied her the same thing by cheating on her. He'd never told her why she hadn't been enough, or why he felt like other women were more exciting.

Was it something about her that fizzled in their relationship? Or was it something about Adam that was broken?

Melanie cried until her tears were spent and her legs felt stiff from sitting on the floor. And then she got up and went into the kitchen.

She had to start over—to have something that was hers, without relying on a man. And ironically, with her lake house and her divorce, she had just that. She should see this painful time as the opportunity it was to build a life that would show Tilly what a woman could do on her own.

Because the kids were watching…always watching. She owed her stepdaughter a good example.

The sun had set when her friends arrived. Melanie had lit some candles out on the deck, arranged a few Adirondack chairs and pulled down the wine glasses that hadn't been used in probably a decade. Her heart was heavy, though, and her tears still felt very close to the surface.

When they'd settled outside on the deck with some soft music filtering out the open patio door, Melanie leaned her head back and looked up at the stars. She could pick out a couple of familiar constellations, and she breathed in the pine-scented air.

Renata and Angelina settled into the other two chairs, and Belle sat on the edge of the deck, her legs swinging. Gayle was next to her, a glass of wine in her hand.

"So why are the kids with their dad?" Angelina asked Renata with a frown. "I thought you had them all summer."

"I got tired of it," Renata said. "I felt like I was being pushed and manipulated from all sides. Ivan kept telling the kids that they didn't see him often because we weren't a family anymore, and the kids were blaming me, and it was getting really ugly. So I decided that if they needed more time with their dad, they'd get it."

"Did that make your ex happy?" Melanie asked.

"Far from it," Renata chuckled. "The kids are wonderful, but they're a lot of work, and I always do that work. When we were married, I was the one to make sure they were dressed and clean and fed and polite and… alive."

Melanie chuckled. "Yeah, I know that feeling."

"So Ivan has the kids for two weeks, and he's already called me three times, asking stupid questions, but he'll figure it out. And so will they. I'm not taking the blame for our divorce, and I'm not standing between the kids and their dad." Renata sucked in a deep breath. "And look at me, out after dark three times in one month."

Gayle smiled. "Look at you, indeed."

"I think that's great, Renata," Melanie said.

"I agree," Belle echoed. She took a sip. "It's very mature of you."

"Thank you for noticing," Renata said with a low laugh. "Ivan called me childish and manipulative."

"Nah," Gayle said. "He wanted time with his kids. Now he can choke on it."

Melanie chuckled. "Oh, it's good for all of them."

Dads mattered. Tilly needed Adam right now. Even Logan had spent his life longing for that connection with his father. At the thought of him, tears prickled her eyes.

"I miss the kids already," Renata said, her smile slipping. "I'm not used to all this freedom."

"I know you want sympathy here," Gayle said. "But the freedom will grow on you. Trust me."

Melanie couldn't help but smile past her own raw emotions, and she took a sip of her white wine.

"So what's the update?" Angelina asked Melanie. "You sounded…momentous."

"I'm keeping the lake house," Melanie said. "I really thought that Adam was too much a part of this place, but when he came to pick up Tilly today, I realized that he's not. He was never here…not often. This is mine. All mine."

"That's powerful," Angelina said with a slow smile. "I'm glad. This is a pristine property. Are you starting up your own business, then?"

Melanie nodded. "I am. Tomorrow I'll enroll in a design course, and come September, I'll be a student again."

"You okay?" Renata asked, fixing her with a perceptive look. "You seem…really sad.

Is it just the adjustment? You said you saw Adam today, right?"

"I did, but it isn't that. If anything, seeing Adam helped matters." Melanie swallowed. "I've been spending a lot of time with Logan, and we started feeling more for each other than was wise. We called it off today."

The women fell silent, and for a moment, all that could be heard was the music from inside and the chirp of insects down by the water.

"Feeling more than was wise..." Belle repeated. "Did you fall in love with him?"

"I didn't say that—" She didn't want to admit to it, at least.

"You didn't have to," Angelina said quietly. "You two always did have a spark."

"A spark isn't enough," Melanie replied, and her chin trembled.

"A spark is something quite extraordinary, though," Gayle said. "It's something some of us spent years and years without."

Melanie couldn't deny that. Whatever she and Logan seemed to share was rare and beautiful...just doomed. And her heart couldn't take any more battering. She'd been through too much. The candles flickered in a gust of breeze and Melanie moved one closer, looking down into the flame.

"I just can't do it," Melanie said woodenly. "I'm tired. I need to be on my own."

There was silence for a moment, then Angelina said, "We don't have to be with men to be happy. Realizing that is why we're all here, I think."

"Amen to that," Belle said, lifting her glass.

"A house on a mountain lake, a group of good friends and plans for the future," Renata said. "If we can't find the good in this…"

"It's a good life," Melanie said. "My stepdaughter needs to see me do this—build a life of my own, find joy in the little things, get excited about my own career—because she's going to have to be stronger than she ever thought possible. A baby is coming, and her boyfriend is the kind of man who sucks a woman's soul dry. So this second start is for her, too. Sometimes you have to show the next generation how to fall down and get back up again."

"Yes," Renata said quietly. "Exactly that."

Melanie had gotten over Logan before, and she could do it again, this time with the wisdom of her life experience behind her. But Melanie's heart was still heavy. She was tired of trying, of throwing her back into her relationships. There were times when trying wasn't going to change a thing.

LOGAN PULLED INTO his garage on the cul-de-sac in the west end of Denver where he and his son lived. Logan and Caroline had bought the house together when Graham was all of five.

They'd been catching up on the drive back from the airport, so Graham had already heard all the pertinent details about his grandfather, his uncle and aunt and cousins. It felt good to be able to tell his son about this—some kind of connection to his side of the family.

Logan got out of the truck and heaved his son's suitcase from the truck bed. Graham came over and grabbed it.

"I've got it, Dad. But thanks."

Graham looked more mature—a few weeks abroad had changed him. Funny how life did that. It wasn't in a physical aging process, just an emotional one that could be seen in the slant of his shoulders and the glint in his eye. He'd matured.

"You know, I was thinking," Logan said. "I can take you to see your grandfather's grave, if you want. I wouldn't mind seeing it, myself."

"You think your brother will even talk to you after that speech?" Graham asked.

"I figure he might." Logan smiled ruefully. "It was honest, but not mean. So, what do you think?"

Graham shrugged. "Yeah, maybe."

Graham carried his suitcase into the house and Logan followed. Graham didn't need a trip back to a grave—Logan could tell. His son was being polite, trying to be supportive, but he'd never met his grandfather and hadn't seemed to suffer without him. Logan had made sure of that. He'd never wanted his son to feel a lack of love from his relatives. There was a whole family out there who had never even brushed against Graham's life. But did it have to be that way?

Logan had never made the rest of their family a priority. He had let them slide off the map. But he was feeling badly about having left the funeral the way he had. Melanie had said he didn't need to stop existing to comfort others, and maybe the same could be said for Graham, too. They had a family out there, whether that was comfortable for all involved or not.

Graham got the suitcase inside the house and Logan picked the mail up from the pile on the floor and flicked on lights. It felt strange to be home—not quite good.

"Your uncle Junior wants to meet you," Logan said.

"I'm not really interested," Graham said. "I'm going to be pretty busy moving into my own place and all that."

"Yeah, you are, but they're your family," Logan said.

"They're yours, too." Graham cast him a curious look.

"I've made mistakes," Logan said, and Graham looked back, sobered. "I probably should have gone home to see my father sooner. I didn't have as much time as I thought. I should have sat down with my dad and hashed out some sort of relationship with him, and I should have gotten to know my siblings. I messed up."

"They weren't really worth it—"

"They were family, Graham. And I hope that one day, if you and I have some sort of falling-out, that you'll try. You won't just give up on me like I did with my own father."

"Is that what this is about?" Graham asked. "You and I have a relationship, Dad. It's not the same thing. Your father pretty much cut you out of his family for the crime of being born to the wrong woman."

"I know..." Logan rubbed his hand over his face. "And you're right that it isn't quite the same, but even if they didn't include me in their family, maybe we can start by including them in ours."

Graham headed through to the kitchen. Logan could hear him muttering about there being no food with both of them having been away for the last few weeks, and Logan pulled out his phone, checking for messages.

He knew whose text he was looking for. He was missing Melanie already.

There was none. He hadn't really expected any. They'd said all there was to say earlier, but... He looked up to see Graham eyeing him skeptically.

"So what happened with that woman?" Graham asked. "The ex-girlfriend, or whatever."

"We're friends," Logan said. Sort of. Maybe they'd be friends in the future, at least.

"That's too bad," Graham said. "I was hoping maybe you were dating."

"You want me to start dating?" Logan asked, surprised.

"Yeah, it's been a few years now, Dad. I mean, I want you to be happy. Mom would have wanted that, too—" Graham paused when he saw his father's face. "What? Did she not want you to move on?"

"She did," Logan said. "It's not that."

He'd been thinking about how to tell Graham ever since he'd read the diaries. He'd considered destroying them, but he couldn't bring himself to do it. He'd been in a guilt-ridden limbo. And he hadn't wanted big family secrets to come between them. This was his chance to do things differently with his own son. "We need to talk…"

"What's going on?" Graham asked.

"The thing is, son, your mom…" Logan rubbed his hands over his face. "I loved her. I really did. You know that. And I've grieved for her really hard, but—"

"But?" Graham said.

"You know how I pulled out your mom's diaries? Well, I started reading them a few weeks ago, and I found out that your mom wasn't all that happy with me," he said at last.

"What?" Graham shook his head. "I don't believe that."

"I want you to know that I did do my best, and there wasn't anyone else in my heart. Just her. I adored your mom, but if you end up reading those diaries, you'll see a different version of me…one I didn't realize existed all those years."

"Were you mean? Did you hit her?" Graham asked.

"No! No! My God, Graham. I know how all of this sounds, but it wasn't anything like that. I think it was just a personality thing. Or all the baggage I came with. I mean, I have a really dysfunctional family. I could be hard to talk to, and to deal with sometimes, and…" He hated opening up about this. He wanted to be his son's hero, not some loser who'd made Graham's mother miserable. Still, it was better to address it now than later. "I guess I made mistakes, and I don't even know exactly how. But I obviously did."

Logan looked up at his son and found Graham shaking his head. "I snagged one. To read while I was in Europe."

"So you knew?" Logan asked hesitantly.

"Hold on." Graham headed to his suitcase and rooted through it, then pulled out a journal. He flipped through the pages. "Read that."

Graham passed the journal over and Logan's heart sank. "I don't need to read more of it, Graham—"

"No. Read it. Seriously."

Logan looked down to where his son was pointing.

This hospital bed is hard—so uncomfortable. I can't sleep. The chemo makes me feel like I'm dying, and I'm looking over at Logan. He fell asleep—he's just wiped. But he's been here, day in, day out. He sits here with me for hours, reading me Reader's Digest *jokes and gossip magazine articles to distract me from the pain.*

Tears misted Logan's eyes. He remembered those long hours together—his months' long vigil with his beloved wife.

This is a good man. I don't know that I always appreciated what a good guy he is, but he's one in a million. I think it's easy to take people for granted when all is well and everyone is healthy. You get annoyed at the little things, and you don't see the bedrock of character that you married all those years ago. I see other patients sitting alone, waiting on visitors, but I've got him here every second he's not at work. When he married me, he meant it. I mean, really meant it. And

I don't know what I expected, or feared, but he's wiped all of that away. I know who I can count on. I know who I'll wake up to when I manage to fall asleep.

Logan turned the page, his fingers trembling.

If I could go back in time and choose all over again, pick the guy I'd spend my life with, I'd choose him. Logan was the best choice I ever made, and I love him. Heart and soul, I love him.

It was her very last entry. The rest of the pages were blank. Logan brushed a tear from his cheek, and he closed the diary reverently.

"Dad, you did just fine by Mom," Graham said. "And maybe that other stuff was just her venting, or just taking you for granted a bit. But from what I can see there, you did well by her. I learned a lot by watching you and Mom, and you taught me to how to treat women. I learned from the best."

Logan nodded, blinking back the tears. Had he really done well by Caroline? Did she really die with no regrets about him? At least he'd taught his son well—he was proud of that.

"I'm glad you showed this to me," Logan said, his voice tight with emotion. "Thanks."

"I'm going to head up to bed," Graham said. "It's late."

"Yeah..."

Graham went upstairs, bumping his suitcase up behind him, and Logan sat on that chair, his heart clenched in his chest. He opened the diary and read those words again, and they felt like forgiveness.

He'd done his best...and maybe that was enough.

Maybe Logan did have something to offer Melanie, after all. He'd been afraid of inflicting his dysfunctional self onto another gentle, kind woman, but maybe he wasn't quite so tough to live with as he'd thought. Maybe the whole package was more worthwhile than he'd thought... Logan might have a whole lot of baggage with his own father, but when he loved, he did so with everything inside of him. And maybe twenty years of marriage and devoted love had worn off a few of those rough edges.

"I'm so sorry, Caroline," he whispered roughly. "I wish I learned some of these things earlier, but you've made me a better man... I owe you that."

CHAPTER EIGHTEEN

THE NEXT MORNING, Melanie ordered a mocha from the barista and stood to the side, waiting while it was made. Her heart was heavy. She'd had trouble sleeping, and when she awoke this morning, she felt hollowed out.

Falling in love with Logan again hadn't been a choice, but it was still stupid. She shouldn't have spent the time with him, but then, she was so tired of heartache. She was tired of being angry, or sad, or melancholy… and Logan was such a breath of fresh air after everything she'd been through. He treated her the way a man should treat a woman he cared about, and that had felt so nice.

The line kept moving, everyone in search of their morning caffeine, and she idly glanced around the coffee shop, her gaze landing on a familiar form leaning back in a chair, gray hair done in an elegant updo.

"Gayle?" she said.

Gayle turned and smiled when she saw her.

"Mocha?" the barista said, and Melanie accepted her tall frothy cup with a murmur of thanks, then headed in Gayle's direction.

"Have a seat," Gayle said. "My date isn't due here for another half hour, so..."

"Your date?" Melanie slid into the seat. "You didn't tell us anything about this last night."

"I don't know..." Gayle's cheeks colored. "I was shy about it, I guess. It's been...thirty-seven years since I've dated a man?"

"I know the feeling," Melanie said. "Well, for me it's more like fifteen—but it feels like thirty-seven."

They both chuckled.

"So tell me about him," Melanie said. "Where did you meet him?"

"At the gym," Gayle said. "There was this walking class—really just an excuse to walk around a track with other human beings, and we got to talking. He's my age, he's a retired lawyer and...he likes me."

"How new is this?"

"This is our second official date." Gayle dropped her gaze. "And I feel stupid. I can't tell people, you know? They already think I'm an idiot for having been married to a gay man for thirty-five years without noticing."

"You aren't an idiot," Melanie said. "Life is hard. That's it."

"I don't know if I'm qualified to even comment on this yet," Gayle said, lowering her voice even more, "but I can already tell that it's different."

"Yeah?" Melanie asked.

"And I don't mean that in some naive this-is-the-man-I'll-marry kind of way. I have no idea if we'll last past another week! Who knows? Who cares? But it's different… *He's* different. The way he looks at me, the way he holds my hand and pulls me in, and—" She blushed again. "I grew up in a cautious generation. We saved ourselves for marriage—which is all very good, don't get me wrong—but I wasn't looking at the right things when I looked for a husband. I wanted someone kind, calm, reasonable, handsome, successful…"

"Sounds like a good list to me," Melanie said.

"It's great, but I didn't realize that he needed to be attracted to me, too," she said. "I thought that was a given. I was *told* that was a given, but it wasn't."

"You must have dated your ex-husband, though," Melanie said.

"We did. For two years, and then we got

married. And he was the perfect gentleman. He never crossed any lines, never wanted more than I did. He kissed me discreetly, told me I was a wonderful woman and that he couldn't wait to make me his wife. And I thought that once I was his wife, the passion would begin."

"And it never did, obviously," Melanie murmured.

"It never did." Gayle shrugged. "I mean, we had children. I won't say more than that, but it was more of a chore. But with Matthew, well, there is a spark there that I've never had before...ever." Tears misted Gayle's eyes. "He's...*attracted* to me!"

"Of course, he is!" Melanie said. "You're beautiful!"

"Well, I'm not someone who takes that for granted. I'm no longer young, and I'm also careful. I did my homework on him. He's not a con, he has friends and family, I even sleuthed out his work history. I'm not about to get myself robbed blind in exchange for a man's attention. But it would seem that he's legitimate."

"I'm happy for you," Melanie said.

"Thanks..." Gayle smiled, and her cheeks pinked. "You were saying that a spark isn't that important last night, and I just think it is. When you've been married for thirty-five years without it, you don't take something like mutual attraction for granted."

But a spark with Logan was so much more than mutual attraction. It was mutual respect, mutual interest and a depth of feeling that frankly, frightened Melanie. They'd fallen in love all over again… And she was afraid of risking her heart, because having her heart broken wasn't quite so easy to recover from as she might want her stepdaughter to believe.

"Gayle, can I ask you something?" Melanie asked softly.

"Sure."

"Aren't you scared?"

Gayle paused, took a sip of her coffee, then shrugged. "Yes. But I took the safe, cautious path once, and it burned me. Taking a risk on something as beautiful and irrational as a spark—it's terrifying! But would I rather live out my life with my heart carefully tucked away? Or take a few chances on something that might give me what I've wanted all these years?"

"Yeah, I can see that…"

Gayle looked out the window, and a smile tickled her lips. “He’s early.”

Melanie looked out the window to see an older gentleman walking toward the coffee shop. He had a little bundle of plastic-wrapped flowers in one hand and a certain hop in his step. Gayle was right—he was excited.

“I’m going to slip out,” Melanie said, giving Gayle’s hand a squeeze. “Have fun.”

Melanie took her to-go cup and headed for the door in time for Matthew to open it and step back to let her through. He was polite, too. Gayle had found herself a nice guy, it seemed.

Melanie headed out onto the street and took a savoring sip of her coffee. Gayle had been through more than Melanie had, and she was willing to take a risk, just on the chance of falling in love with a man who could appreciate what she brought to the table.

And Melanie had a man she *was* in love with, who loved her, too. And that elusive spark—they had it…did they ever have it! And what was holding Melanie back? Fear. She didn’t want to get her heart broken again, sacrifice her careful plans on another try at love… But did she want to give up on the real thing?

Melanie's phone pinged and she looked down at an incoming text.

I'm in town. Would you let me buy you breakfast?

Tears misted her eyes. It was Logan. She stood there for a moment, then typed in her response. I missed you.

He typed back almost immediately.

Me, too. Will you see me?

Yes. Should I meet you at the lodge?

Perfect. I'll get us a table. See you soon…

And Melanie's heart skipped a beat. Logan was back…the very next day. What did that mean? Even if she was willing to take a risk on them, it didn't mean he was any longer. If Logan wanted to just continue as pals, she wasn't sure her heart could handle that.

But Logan was back, and the only way to find out why was to meet him.

LOGAN HAD A table by the window overlooking the turquoise blue of the lake, but his gaze kept moving back to the doorway. The entire drive back to Mountain Springs he was going over how he'd explain this to her…and none of it had been right. All he knew was that every mile that brought him closer to her felt like a relief.

A waitress came by with menus and left them, and just as she was leaving the table, Melanie arrived. She was wearing a light blue summer dress cinched in at the waist. When her gaze landed on him, a smile tugged at her lips, and she headed in his direction. She looked tired. She wasn't wearing makeup and her hair was pulled back from her face.

Logan stood up when she got to the table and waited until she was seated before he sat back down again.

"I still like your manners," she said.

"Yeah?" He met her gaze. "I know it was all of one day, but I missed you."

"Me, too." She dropped her gaze. "More than I thought I would."

"Am I a massive jerk to be glad of that?" he asked.

"Yes," she said, but she smiled. "What brought you back?"

"Last night, my son showed me my wife's very last diary entry. He'd kept that journal for himself, and…" Logan swallowed. "It helped to see what Caroline wrote when she was in the hospital. People take each other for granted when they've been together for a while, and I think we both did that. But when we were there together, it cemented things, I guess. She wrote that she was glad she married me, that I was worth it."

"Of course, she would have been grateful for you…" Melanie reached out to touch his hand, and he caught her fingers instead.

"I honestly wasn't sure this delightful mess that I am was worth a lifetime commitment," he admitted. "I wasn't easy to live with. I could be difficult sometimes. I didn't want to launch myself into something new until I knew I'd dealt with my own issues."

"And have you?" she asked, frowning slightly.

"Yeah. I always thought that Junior was more like our father because he looked like him, but it turns out, I'm a whole lot like him, too. I've got the same stubbornness, the same emotional makeup. You've complained about the same things Caroline did—I close off, I run from my feelings. I did my best to do better by my son, and you know what? If my father's funeral showed me anything, my dad had done his best to do better by other people, too. That scared me. I never wanted to be like him… I ran from it. I don't think I got away, though."

Melanie remained silent, her dark gaze locked on his face.

"But Caroline wrote that my standing by her to the very end had meant the world to her. She wrote that she'd marry me all over again for that… I realized that I might be stubborn, but that can be a good thing. Mel, if you let me love you, I'll just keep on loving you. I'll be too stubborn to do anything else. You can count on me to be faithful—I'm not the kind of guy who cheats. And if you tell me when I mess up, I'll fix it. I don't want to look back on these years, right here, and wish I'd done better."

"I've been so scared, Logan. I mean, I was married for a long time, and lied to for almost as long. That's hard to recover from."

"I get it. I know you might not be able to do this with me, but I had to tell you face-to-face what changed for me."

"This kind of love doesn't come along every day," she said quietly. "I know that, and I've had a good friend explain just how rare this is. What we feel—"

Logan lifted her fingers to his lips and kissed them. He didn't trust himself with words just yet.

"I'm terrified," she whispered. "But I think the best things in life have the biggest risk attached. I was married to Adam for fifteen years, and he was cheating most of that time. I didn't notice, either, because I'd lowered my expectations. And seeing you again—it raised the bar."

"Yeah?" He smiled at that. "Do you mean that?"

"Just promise that you'll share your feelings with me—you won't shut me out."

"I can do that," he agreed. He'd been opening up with her these last couple of weeks, and it had come naturally. He wouldn't be perfect. He'd still clam up sometimes, but he was also stubborn enough to keep trying to improve.

"I don't want you to walk away again," she whispered. "I love you…"

Walk away—it would tear his heart out to

do it. Now that he was here with her, looking her in the face and his heart was stretching toward her, there was no way he could just leave.

"Mel, this might be crazy, but I want to marry you," he said.

"This *is* crazy..." she whispered, but a smile tickled her lips.

"I know, but—"

"Where would we live?" she asked.

Wait—was she considering it?

"Wherever you want," he replied. "I can hire a manger for my company and we can live here, or we could split our time between Denver and Mountain Springs. We can figure it out."

"I need to be able to start my own business, too. That's important to me. I need something that's mine."

"Mel, I'd give you the moon, if it would make you happy," he said. "Take a diploma, start a business, do anything that makes you happy. I'm meeting you halfway. I'm not asking you to dump your life and jump into mine. I'm not that kind of guy."

Melanie's breath caught. "That's not all, though..."

"No?"

"I want a baby." She licked her lips. "I know it's late, and you've already raised one son, but…"

A baby…that really would be a fresh start, and the thought was a little bit scary, but imagining Melanie pregnant with his child—it sped up his pulse in a good way.

"A baby? We could try for one, at least. Yeah."

Melanie's eye sparkled as a smile spread over her face, and her fingers tightened around his. "Okay, then."

"Wait—" He paused, the moment slowing down around him. "Just so we're completely clear here—this detail matters to me—you're agreeing to marry me, right?"

She laughed and nodded, and without waiting for another word, he stood up, circled around the table and pulled her up and into his arms. He lowered his lips over hers and the rest of the dining room seemed to melt around them as they sealed this new promise with a kiss. When he finally pulled back, he looked around uncomfortably to see most of the diners staring at them.

"I might have caused a scene," he whispered.

"I don't care!" she whispered back. "Kiss me again."

And when the woman he loved asked to be kissed again, he couldn't exactly turn her down. When they pulled back, he found the waitress at his elbow.

"Sir, I have a feeling that champagne might be in order?" she asked discreetly.

"Yes, thanks," he said with a grin. "She just agreed to marry me."

"Congratulations," the waitress replied, and she pulled a bottle of champagne off a trolley and popped the cork. "This is on the house, courtesy of Ms. Cunningham."

Logan looked over to see Angelina watching them, her arms crossed over her chest and a smile on her face. She winked when Melanie turned.

"If you aren't a hundred percent sure, you might want to back out now," Logan said, grinning down at her as Melanie turned back toward him.

"Nope," she said with a shake of her head. "I'm in."

"Let's skip breakfast," he suggested. "I want to go ring shopping with you."

"Actually, with that champagne, we'd better have some food in our stomachs," Melanie replied with a twinkle in her eye. "And I have a feeling that's a very expensive bottle..."

Logan checked the label. It was.

"Fine. But after breakfast, it's time for a ring," he said with a grin.

Logan ran his fingers over hers as his heart swelled with love. Coming back to Mountain Springs was supposed to be a goodbye to his mother, his father and the life of trying too hard to belong to a father who'd never appreciated him. But instead, he'd discovered the Wilde family that was uncomfortably his and the one woman he couldn't bring himself to let go...

Second chances didn't always look the way a man expected them to. Sometimes, a new start came in the form of forgiveness spread liberally around for the people who'd tried hard, gotten it wrong, but weren't ready to give up. And sometimes it came in the form of an engagement ring bought in a little shop around the corner, two lives taking a left turn into new happiness.

With Mel's fingers entwined with his, Logan McTavish was home.

EPILOGUE

MELANIE AND LOGAN planned an October wedding. It was held in Mountain Springs Lodge beside Blue Lake and beneath those towering peaks and the autumn blaze of changing trees. When she'd sent her stepkids invitations, she hadn't been sure if they'd even reply, but one by one the RSVPs came in—they wanted to be there. Everyone did, it seemed. Melanie's parents and extended family were traveling out for the event and Logan's siblings were coming, too. His son, Graham, would be his best man. For Melanie, her maid of honor was Angelina, who was taking full credit for getting Melanie and Logan back together with a few subtle nudges, and Melanie couldn't help but laugh every time Angelina told the story.

Tilly was five months pregnant by the time of the wedding, and she'd started the twelfth grade. She looked lavish and sweet in a pink satin dress. She came with her siblings, Michael and Viv—without a date—and Melanie was glad to see it. There had been quite a few phone calls after Tilly left with her dad, and Tilly had blossomed, not only in her pregnancy but in her maturity, as well.

Michael and Viv had both started reaching out after they found out about Tilly's pregnancy. Somehow, it brought them all back together again—the old family dynamic, except improved, more mature. They held each other's memories—no one would understand them quite like each other, and as they looked forward to helping Tilly as best they could, Michael and Viv had started calling Melanie on a more regular basis. They were a family again—just a divorced one. It turned out it wasn't so strange, after all.

On her wedding day, Melanie wore a cream lace dress, tea length and fitted all the way down to just past her knees. She wore her hair up, twined with flowers and pearls, and when the ceremony was done and they were posing for the photographer, Melanie's favorite photo from the day would be a candid shot of Logan putting a pearl pin back into her hair, his fingers lingering against her cheek. Her second favorite photo would be one of Tilly alone as she watched Melanie and Logan take their vows. Melanie saw something new in the teenager's eyes—self-confidence and a flicker of determination—and it warmed her heart to see it.

When the reception started, Melanie stood to throw her bouquet, and she looked over her shoulder at her laughing friends pretending to jostle for position. Just to the side, she saw Tilly standing next to her sister, her hand on her belly and a hopeful little smile on her face. Melanie pulled a rose free and then tossed the bouquet over her shoulder. She turned in time to see it fly over the hands of the other women, and straight at Angelina's face. Her hands went up and she caught it.

"Oh, I'm not next!" Angelina laughed.

"I wouldn't be so sure!" Renata said, and the women laughingly made their way back to their seats.

Logan caught Melanie's eye, and they exchanged a smile. He was so handsome in his tux, and the way he looked at her enveloped her in love. He was the right choice—she could feel it all the way down to her toes. Logan tapped his watch and winked, and she felt a blush rise in her cheeks. The honeymoon suite was waiting for them upstairs, and she was looking forward to being alone with her husband.

Her husband. It still gave her a shiver to think of that. They were well and truly married, the vows said in the church in downtown Mountain Springs.

She was now Mrs. Melanie Banks-McTavish, and it felt right. It felt certain.

She was looking forward to the honeymoon, too, but first…

Tilly had gone back to sit down at the table with her siblings and Melanie smiled at Viv and Michael, then slid into the seat next to Tilly.

"I saved this for you," Melanie said, handing her the white rose.

"Oh, you didn't have to do that…" But Tilly took it, anyway. "I wonder if there's luck in catching a bouquet."

"I doubt it," Melanie replied.

"All the same…" Tilly shrugged.

"Do you know what makes for a happy life, Tilly?" Melanie asked. "A choice to face all of it with some dignity and bravery. And you're already doing that. I couldn't be prouder."

"Do you think I'll end up with a guy

like Logan?" Tilly asked. "But, you know, younger. He's cute for an old guy, though."

Old. Yes, it might seem that way to a seventeen-year-old. Melanie looked back to see Logan giving his son a hug, laughing at something, and love welled up inside of her.

"Absolutely," Melanie said. "When the time is right, though. Hold out for a good one. They're out there."

Tilly dropped her gaze and lowered her voice so that their words remained private. "I wanted to ask you something. I don't know if it's weird or not, but…it might be nice for the baby…like, to have a grandma. If you were interested in that. Maybe…do you think I could start calling you Mom again?"

Melanie's chin trembled and she looked into Tilly's beautiful perfectly made-up face, and all she could see was the tiny girl with the big eyes and the rumpled blond curls who had stolen her heart from the beginning.

"Oh, sweetie, I'd really love that." Melanie pulled Tilly into her arms, and her heart filled to overflowing with love for her new husband and the family she'd gathered along the way to her own happily-ever-after.

* * * * *

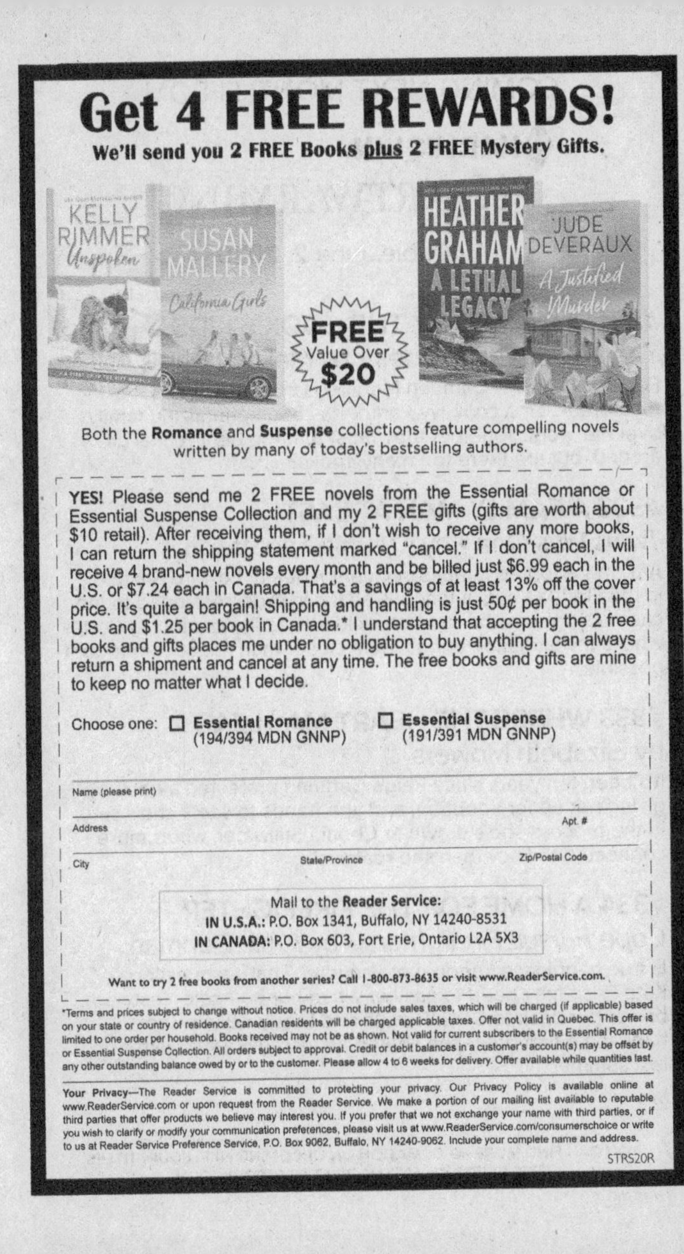
Get 4 FREE REWARDS!
We'll send you 2 FREE Books plus 2 FREE Mystery Gifts.
KELLY RIMMER
Unspoken
SUSAN MALLERY
California Girls
FREE
Value Over
$20
HEATHER GRAHAM
A LETHAL LEGACY
JUDE DEVERAUX
A Justified Murder
Both the Romance and Suspense collections feature compelling novels written by many of today's bestselling authors.
YES! Please send me 2 FREE novels from the Essential Romance or Essential Suspense Collection and my 2 FREE gifts (gifts are worth about $10 retail). After receiving them, if I don't wish to receive any more books, I can return the shipping statement marked "cancel." If I don't cancel, I will receive 4 brand-new novels every month and be billed just $6.99 each in the U.S. or $7.24 each in Canada. That's a savings of at least 13% off the cover price. It's quite a bargain! Shipping and handling is just 50¢ per book in the U.S. and $1.25 per book in Canada.* I understand that accepting the 2 free books and gifts places me under no obligation to buy anything. I can always return a shipment and cancel at any time. The free books and gifts are mine to keep no matter what I decide.
Choose one: ☐ Essential Romance (194/394 MDN GNNP) ☐ Essential Suspense (191/391 MDN GNNP)
Name (please print)
Address
Apt. #
City
State/Province
Zip/Postal Code
Mail to the Reader Service:
IN U.S.A.: P.O. Box 1341, Buffalo, NY 14240-8531
IN CANADA: P.O. Box 603, Fort Erie, Ontario L2A 5X3
Want to try 2 free books from another series? Call 1-800-873-8635 or visit www.ReaderService.com.
*Terms and prices subject to change without notice. Prices do not include sales taxes, which will be charged (if applicable) based on your state or country of residence. Canadian residents will be charged applicable taxes. Offer not valid in Quebec. This offer is limited to one order per household. Books received may not be as shown. Not valid for current subscribers to the Essential Romance or Essential Suspense Collection. All orders subject to approval. Credit or debit balances in a customer's account(s) may be offset by any other outstanding balance owed by or to the customer. Please allow 4 to 6 weeks for delivery. Offer available while quantities last.
Your Privacy—The Reader Service is committed to protecting your privacy. Our Privacy Policy is available online at www.ReaderService.com or upon request from the Reader Service. We make a portion of our mailing list available to reputable third parties that offer products we believe may interest you. If you prefer that we not exchange your name with third parties, or if you wish to clarify or modify your communication preferences, please visit us at www.ReaderService.com/consumerschoice or write to us at Reader Service Preference Service, P.O. Box 9062, Buffalo, NY 14240-9062. Include your complete name and address.
STRS20R

COMING NEXT MONTH FROM

HARLEQUIN

HEARTWARMING

Available June 2, 2020

#331 CHARMED BY THE COOK'S KIDS

The Mountain Monroes • by Melinda Curtis

Perfectionist chef Camden Monroe is burned out and looking for a break. Line cook Ivy Parker has been prioritizing family over her work. Together they must turn the Bent Nickel diner around, but are there too many cooks?

#332 A FAMILY MAN AT LAST

Twins Plus One • by Cynthia Thomason

After his adopted father's accidental death, Edward Smith is in the Florida Keys putting his affairs in order. Assigned to the case is single mother and homicide investigator Monica Cortez, whose investigation brings them closer than they ever thought possible.

#333 WHERE THE HEART MAY LEAD

by Elizabeth Mowers

It's been ten years since Paige Cartman protected a baby by giving her up for adoption, and she needs to see if she's safe. In the process she's drawn to Charlie Stillwater, who's more connected to Lucy than she realizes!

#334 A HOME FOR THE FIREFIGHTER

Cape Pursuit Firefighters • by Amie Denman

Is true happiness freedom or security? That's a question Kate Price may need to answer when her nomadic lifestyle brings her back to Cape Pursuit and Brady Adams, the handsome firefighter she shared an incredible kiss with last summer.